MENDACITY

MENDACITY

Bryan Clark

MENDACITY

BLACK TRIDENT

Published in the United States of America by Black Trident Publishing, LLC
Largo, Florida

This is a work of fiction. Names, characters, places and incidents either are the product of the author's imagination or are used fictitiously. Any resemblance to actual persons, living or dead, events, or locales is entirely coincidental.

Copyright © 2024 Bryan Clark

www.thebryanclark.com

All rights reserved. No part of this book may be distributed, reproduced, adapted or used in any manner without written permission of the copyright owner except for the use of quotations in a book review.

Revised paperback edition May 2024

Book design by Bryan Clark

ISBN: 979-8-9907059-0-6 (paperback)

MENDACITY

DEDICATION

To my brothers in arms,

In the depths we've explored and the darkness we've illuminated, our bonds were forged. This book is dedicated to the valiant hearts and indomitable spirits of the warriors I've had the honor to serve alongside. Though Special Forces Dive teams have a special place in my heart; Rangers, Special Forces, MARSOC, SEALs and units like them, are not just about the courage to plunge into the unknown but about the unyielding fortitude to emerge stronger, together.

A special thanks to the men of SFOD-A 715, who embody strength, willpower, and an unwavering commitment to each other and our missions—your resilience inspires every word penned here. We've faced challenges that demanded every ounce of our strength and found laughter in moments when it seemed impossible. Our camaraderie has been a beacon, guiding us through tempests and calm seas alike.

This dedication is a tribute to you, my brothers, for being the embodiment of true warriors. Your tenacity and spirit have not only shaped this journey but have etched a profound impact on my life. May this book serve as a testament to our shared experiences, our triumphs, our losses, and the unbreakable bond that ties us.

Together, we are more than just dive team members and Special Operators; we are a family forged by adversity, a unit bound by loyalty, and a testament to what true strength and willpower can accomplish.

In deep appreciation and eternal brotherhood,

DOL, RLTW

Bryan

MENDACITY

MENDACITY

ACKNOWLEDGMENTS

At the heart of every endeavor lies the support of those who believe in us, even more than we believe in ourselves. For me, that unwavering support has come from my wife, Elizabeth. This book, much like every chapter of my life enriched by her presence, is a testament to her love, patience, and unwavering belief in my journey.

Elizabeth, your role in the creation of this book has been nothing short of instrumental. From the countless drafts you've read to the meticulous edits you've suggested, your keen eye and insightful feedback have been indispensable. Your ability to see clarity in my thoughts when they were muddled, and to guide my pen when it faltered, has shaped this narrative in ways I alone could never have achieved.

Thank you with love and gratitude,

Bryan

MENDACITY

August 2001

CHAPTER 1

THE SUN WAS ALREADY rising as he moved into his final hide site. At this point, he had been radio silent for the past 12 hours and hoped that with the lack of communication his primary exfiltration point was still a go, even though he didn't care for the means of extraction.

He was alone, and wishing that he had his sniper buddy, but this time he had volunteered to conduct the operation unaccompanied based on mission requirements. He had only completed one other lone sniper operation, and that was during a training exercise in Nevada. At that time his team was conducting a Full Mission Profile, a training event that simulates real world events and conditions to test the men's planning and preparation. The mission was complex and required multiple teams to conduct simultaneous hits in various locations in order to successfully rescue a hostage from a warehouse near area 51. The training area was significant because of the extensive tunnel systems. For the upcoming mission, the team had learned that the rebel group they were targeting had access to unused tunnels that they were now using to smuggle people, weapons and drugs. Conducting the mission as a singleton shooter came with risks, sniper school teaches you to operate in pairs as a team, a shooter and a spotter. This not only helps maintain overall situational awareness while moving, but it also allows the shooter to focus on one thing, taking the shot. His team was selected to rescue the hostage, and during planning they realized that because of the lack of terrain features or concealment areas in the flat desert, the sniper team would have to move through an unused underground rail system in order to get into position. It had been used to move equipment into certain buildings located throughout the compound, probably to avoid the appearance of traffic on the surface of the very secretive plot of land. Though the tunnel could accommodate two individuals without a problem, the movement detection system that was installed in it would not. It would require one sniper with limited gear to move it alone in order to remain undetected, so he volunteered to conduct the mission unaccompanied.

The Remington 700 long action was the weapon of choice for the U.S. Army when it came to sniper operations. The military spec model had a stainless-steel floating barrel, with a two-and-a-half-pound trigger. It was capable of shooting one half minute of angle when used with match grade ammunition. He had a Leupold Mark 4 scope with mildot reticle attached to his rifle, which allowed him to compensate for holds and judge distances out to one statute mile. His rifle was slung on his back. He carried ten rounds of ammunition in the carrier affixed to the buttstock of his rifle. He wore no ghillie suit and abandoned his survival backpack. All he had for personal protection while moving was his 9mm pistol and forty-five rounds, three magazines of 15 bullets each, of paint filled ammunition.

During his movement he wondered if this had been a real-world mission, a single man sniper operation, would he really have volunteered for it?

Training is one thing, but even the best scenarios can't shake out every possibility of your unpredictable enemy. If the mission called for it, and no other course of action was viable, he would like to think so, but the stakes were high, and detection would certainly lead to capture or worse.

His movement was slow and deliberate through the tunnel; he paused to take breaks when he felt rushed, or tired to avoid making a mistake. It took him nearly six hours to make the one-mile movement in total darkness and with no communication. When he emerged from the tunnel, he was five hundred meters away from the warehouse, and in a perfect position to take his shot. The remainder of the team was staged to arrive by helicopter. The hostage takers would attempt to move the detainee once they heard the inbound aircraft and that is when he would be able to take his shot. As the UH-60 Black Hawk helicopters began flying into the target area, the plastic and paper targets began moving out of the warehouse and popping up into windows. He took multiple shots, putting down each target, and lifting his fires before the team made entrance into the building. He took solace in the fact that had it been a real mission, under similar circumstances, he would have made it to his final shooting position without compromise. It gave him the confidence that the training mission was designed to instill.

However, the jungle was a very different environment; in the desert you worried more about heat exhaustion, scorpions and rattlesnakes. The triple canopy seemed to change almost mystically; it would rain from the condensation, and then quickly turn into a sauna as the sun punished the lavish topside vegetation. Birds would squawk and chirp, and in an instant fall silent as predators moved through their areas. Monkeys would give away your position if you upset them in any way so if they found you, it was in your best interest to make them happy. The good thing about this well-balanced ecosystem was the endless number of options it presented for concealment. The vegetation was difficult to move through at times. You could move fairly quickly in some areas, and in others you couldn't move without first swinging a machete to cut a path. This could pose a myriad of problems sometimes, but at least anyone tracking you had to deal with the same issues. You could only move during the day because of the wild life. You didn't want to inadvertently enter into their food chain and be forced to break silence with a weapon. Having a hammock with you wasn't an option, if you didn't, you would only last a few nights on the ground.

Contending with bugs was a never-ending battle, the sooner you conceded to the fact that you must coexist, the better for your sanity. At this moment though he was coping with a group of army ants that he had accidentally laid in. He was attempting to assess whether it was a nest or search party, but his attention was quickly and abruptly averted. His comfort, or lack thereof, would now have to wait because his focus now honed to the Land Rover that had just stopped outside of a suspected drug lab. It was 750 meters away from his position, winds were out of the west at a perceived 5 knots and it was a downward inclination. With this information, he quickly figured out the corrections needed to make a successful shot.

Math was never his strong suit. In sniper school he paid close attention to the portion dealing with wind and distance calculations. Luckily, the Army had years of experience training people from all background and education levels and built all of its systems, no matter how complex, to the education level of an eighth grader; and you were allowed to make a cheat sheet.

Shooting in any type of elevation was a challenge. You had to take many things into consideration. The good thing about training was that you could put yourself into almost any situation and develop a shooting formula for it; it's what snipers call D.O.P.E, or Data on Personal Equipment. If you kept an accurate logbook with these figures, you could easily consult it later and dial in nearly the correct information for the conditions. He had done just that, and was prepared to take his shot.

His target exited the vehicle on the passenger side and walked directly toward the open door of the lab. He was met in route, presumably by the person in charge of the operation. It was finally time to break radio silence after days of unaided movement. The radio switch was on his chest, and even though it wasn't that far away, he moved slow and precise until his fingers touched the knob. With a smooth clock-wise motion he turned it on. He swallowed a few times to clear his throat; now wishing he had stayed more abreast of his hydration, and prepared to whisper.

"Shark 21 this is Hammer 15,"

"Send it Hammer 15,"

"Roger, target acquired,"

"Stand-by,"

"Hammer 15, signal is confirmed, you are cleared to take the shot."

He deliberately moved his hand back to the support position near the bipod of his rifle. With his finger on the trigger, he waited patiently for his target to stand still long enough to send a piece of lead moving 2,694 feet per second through the space between his ears. His breathing was slow and methodical, meticulously controlling every bit of air that passed through his lungs. Time seemed to slow to almost a standstill, everything could be heard; everything could be smelled. It was like being inside the eye of a hurricane, an unnatural still that heightened the senses to levels rarely experienced by individuals un-afflicted by the loss of a sense. As his subject stopped to shake hands, he aligned his mildot reticle for the hold he had calculated, exhaled and pulled the trigger. He quickly chambered another round into his M24 and settled the sight back onto his target.

"Target down, moving to exfil point."

Seemingly without pause, the driver of the Land Rover brought his fully automatic sub-machine gun to the ready as he moved to the rear of the vehicle to peer at the downed subject. He planted himself against the hatch back and began firing in what he thought was the general direction of the shot.

Running in a ghillie suit with a M24 sniper rifle was not easy. Add to that a 3-day assault pack with food, water and ammunition, a 5.56mm carbine rifle, and a M9 pistol and you quickly lose all desire to run very fast or very far; unless people are actively trying to kill you. He was tired and hungry, probably more than slightly dehydrated, and stiff from the lack of significant movement while lying in his hide site. But like prey, he was able to move with vigor and purpose, somehow ignoring the pain of the lactic acid he had stored while laying in the prone position, now being brought to life and pushing around in his muscles as he exerted himself. His knees and ankles cracked and creaked as his feet came down unevenly at times on branches and rocks. He heaved heavily in and out of his mouth, relaxing and contracting his chest muscles while pulling air deeply into his lungs as he exchanged carbon dioxide for oxygen rich fuel. As he built up speed, his senses heightened out of anxiety. His attentiveness allowed his mind to take in and quickly process the pictures his eyes were snapping, and swiftly issue the order to his extremities to rapidly change course to avoid areas that would require timely passage or possibly cause him injury. In a bizarre twist, that no predator ever believes will come to fruition, he knew he was now the hunted.

As he moved to the extraction point, he could hear men yelling back and forth in Spanish very near his position, running in his general direction. *How could this be?* He thought; he had planned that location specifically for its isolation and the fact that locals didn't use that area for anything. No patrols extended out that deep into the jungle, enemy or otherwise and it wouldn't have been possible for gunmen to move to his location from the road that fast. They had to have been there already, but where, how? He took off his pack as he ran down a slight embankment. He had only run three hundred meters but at full sprint with cumbersome equipment it was enough to slow down even the most fit of individuals. He had to lose weight if he wanted to maintain his slight lead. He pulled the pin and released the spoon on the thermite grenade that was rigged in the top of his pack and threw it down just before he jumped into a shallow stream. He had given up the contents of his pack, but at this point, with his life in the balance; it was of little value.

Bark began dancing off of trees near him almost choreographed, as the stereo sounding snap and crackle of gunfire from the ensuing gunmen riddled the areas around him. They were gaining ground. He could hear the helicopter in the distance, moving into position near the extraction point and wondered if he should call it off. A few meters after crossing the stream he quickly turned around and took a knee, bringing his rifle up to the ready and listening for movement to his rear, now front and flanks. He heard movement to the right and peered through his scope in that direction. He hastily placed his reticle on the chest of the man and pulled the trigger. He was hit, but he couldn't wait to assess the effectiveness. As he scanned quickly before continuing movement he noticed a pale-faced male with blonde hair. *An American?* he thought as dirt began kicking up near him. He contemplated holding on him to find out, reasoning to himself that getting his identity might be worth catching a bullet. But mortality got the best of him and he quickly slung his rifle and continued to run.

"Hammer 15 this is Shark 21, you are a go for extraction."

He continued running in the direction of the clearing. He had no idea if it would still be a viable area to posture. He continued to put forth all the energy he could muster in an attempt to put distance between him and his aggressors. He hoped that the helicopter had made it to its staging point before he took his shot. It was only twenty nautical miles away, far enough not to be heard in route, but still close enough to pull him out in an emergency; which is what he now had.

As he ran the remaining fifty meters, he could hear the bird begin to slow down. The sound that the blades of the aircraft made while cutting through the air as it pitched back to slow its forward momentum was distinct. He could see the shadow of his freedom bird begin to crest the trees in the distance; bending vegetation as it submitted to the wind the aircraft generated to maintain altitude.

The aircraft was now playing in full high-fidelity; he could feel but no longer hear the snapping of bullets as they rapidly warmed the air before whizzing past and clipping or burying into nearby foliage. He was now feeling the full effect of the rotor wash from the helicopter as he moved into his primary exfil point, a small opening in the thick jungle canopy. The wait for the rope to be kicked out seemed like a lifetime. At that moment he thought he would almost rather continue running than be gunned down standing under a hovering hunk of metal. Looking up, he watched the aluminum carabineers ballet movements, as they gradually grew larger with each foot they were lowered. Twinkling as they caught light from the sun as they bounced back and forth on their way down. He continued to anxiously divide his attention between the crew chief and the wood line never forgetting for a second that he was being pursued. He stretched his arms upward and retrieved the line, now almost frantic in his need to secure it. He connected the rope that had lowered to his harness and extended his arms outward while looking up at the crew chief; the signal that you were ready to be lifted.

SPIES or Special Purpose Insertion Extraction System was the means in which he was to travel back to the staging area. He had first experienced this system in Survival Evasion, Resistance, Escape or SERE School and didn't much like the exposure of hanging from a rope, dangling under a moving helicopter, but it was part of the price of admission into this elite group. Back then; he was also being chased by aggressors, only this time the bullets being used had the possibility of leaving a soulless carcass and not just bruising.

As he was lifted off of the ground, he noticed that the crew chief was returning fire with the 7.62mm machine gun mounted in the aircraft; they must be close. With his right hand he reached for his pistol that was on his hip, through a cut out on the ghillie suit. Suddenly he felt his stomach rise as if he was on a roller coaster, to sharp a change of direction to have been the bird. As he looked up toward the helicopter wondering why he was not moving in same direction as the aircraft, his back violently made contact with the ground and he could no longer breath. He tried to move but couldn't make his brain connect to his limbs; he raised his head slowly off the ground. The helicopter was still beating the air loudly, though he couldn't feel the wind from the blades anymore, and his ears were ringing slightly. The sun on his face and in his eyes was warm and bright and for a minute he thought he was waking up from an exhilarating dream. The kind with a very bad finale, but in the end are extremely relieving. For when you awake and realize it was all a nasty game being played on you by your brain, the sigh of relief is elating. But the pain was all too real, and when a shadow appeared over him, the looming figure of a man; he knew this horror was reality. *Was his hair really blonde?* At that moment, the moment that he thought he could make out his face, he was struck in the head with the buttstock of a weapon and knocked unconscious.

May 1992

CHAPTER 2

IT WAS 10PM WHEN the phone rang. Brayden sat in front of the television with a TV tray on his lap, the kind you actually have to balance there. He didn't like the freestanding metal TV trays. His father used those to ensure he could eat his dinner while watching the football game instead of eating at the table with the rest of the family. Although Brayden hadn't sunk to the level of mindlessly following his hometown sports team, his nightly routine of eating in front of the tube had transformed into a sort of ritual. One beer from the refrigerator, a plate filled with left overs from the night before and a cheap napkin that will hardly last for two wipes of his chin.

"Hello?" He set down the plastic fork as he chewed the remnants of his last bite while waiting for the voice on the other end of the phone to respond to his challenge.

"Dude, what the heck are you doing? You were supposed to be here an hour ago!"

Brayden struggled to make out each word over the loud but surprisingly clear music.

"Yeah, I know but I have to study for my economics test, my scholarship depends on it…"

He hung up without waiting for a response. Being a popular jock had its privileges and not worrying about whose feelings you hurt when you hung up was one of them. Brayden was scouted out of high school to play for several colleges. He settled for a small school in southern Ohio because the girl to boy ratio was the highest of all the alternative choices. Studying for an exam was the last thing on his mind; he hadn't studied for anything since the 9th grade. He was part way through his third year and like the two before it, he wondered why he stayed. Playing pro football was out of the question and the business degree that he was set to earn was only to please his father and somehow set him up to take over his construction company. Brayden was bored and ready for a change.

He picked up the remote and quickly turned off the television, as the knock at the door was sooner than expected. The TV tray was stashed out of sight under the couch and he piled the plastic ware and dishes into a half full trashcan in the small kitchen. He finished his beer as he swallowed the last bite of food, swapping the can on a picture ledge by the door for a spray bottle of Bianca breath freshener. The door nudged open no sooner than he turned the knob.

"I know I'm early but I didn't want to risk you eating without me again." Said Sara, a member of the student body council and fledgling law student.

"Where are we going tonight?"

"To your favorite place!"

She had no idea why he thought that was her favorite place, favorite food maybe, but not the experience she hoped for. It was take-out Chinese, they ordered at the pay phone by the dorm entrance and it was ready to go by the time they arrived; at least she knew what was in store for the night.

The next morning Brayden awoke to a slamming door. It was intentional, neither note, nor her signature panties left on the floor. It always tickled him that girls would continue to see him for months before realizing that they could not change him. It always started the same way, a smile on game day, a meet at a frat party days later, and then the hook up. The girls thought he was licentious, but not in his mind, he only dated one girl at a time. But even college had a routine, whether you were a nerd, jock, partier or weed head, you had a schedule of events that you set your freshman year and followed to the letter until you graduated. It was the beginning of a lifetime of monotony. Brayden saw his time card life unfolding and wanted desperately to stop it. The will was there, he just hadn't quite figured out the way.

After football practice Brayden usually swam laps to stay loose and keep from being so sore the following day. As he packed up his athletic bag, he noticed a poster on the wall next to the lockers that he hadn't seen before, consciously anyway. *Be All That You Can Be!* was the slogan that was boldly typed across the top of the propaganda. Brayden smiled and thought about a few of his friends that had enlisted in some branch of the military straight out of high school. "Fools" he said under his breath. He zipped up his bag and tossed it on his shoulder. As he walked toward the exit doors he glanced once again at the recruitment poster, *my father would kill me*, he thought.

Brayden arrived at the pool and disrobed down to the swim trunks he had thrown on before leaving the locker room. He slid into the pool with his swim goggles but without his waterproof Walkman that day, not because he didn't want to listen to his workout playlist, but because his thoughts of a life in the military were consuming him. He began his routine with a breaststroke warm up for a lap before transitioning to freestyle. Ironically, he had learned this from reading a Navy Seal training manual while he was still in high school. As he front crawled into his tenth lap, he thought about his grandfather and the fact that he had served during WWII, and went on to be a productive member of society. *Member of society? Like people in the military don't already contribute enough to our society and way of life*, he thought to himself. The truth was, Brayden had no one other than his grandfather and a handful of characters in books and movies to give him any insight into military life. He hadn't kept up with any of the kids he knew that had signed up straight out of high school and his grandfather never spoke a word about it; the only reason he knew he served was from pictures of him in uniform hung around his grandparents' home. For all he knew, once you joined it was like basic training everyday of your life until you decided to get out, if you could even get out without being discharged after a conflict.

Brayden cooled down by treading water in the deep end for five minutes. He hopped out, dried off, and tossed his sweats back on. He was free for the rest of the day, only because his buddy left his personal recorder on a desk in Psychology class for him; he'd have to retrieve it in a few hours. He thought about calling his grandfather to solicit information about military life, but after recalling the circumstances under which he served, he decided against it. The campus had a recruiting office; evident by the guys he sometimes saw walking around in military dress uniforms. They weren't real soldiers, he always thought, they were part of some ROTC program or something like that. As he gathered his things to leave the gym, he was stopped by one of the lifeguards. He had not noticed her before, but she had obviously paid attention to him.

"Aren't you Brayden Smith?" she said while looking back at another female lifeguard, perhaps for encouragement.

"Yes… I don't think I have seen you here before, your name is?"

Instead of verbalizing it she wrote it down on a page from the swim team time sheet book, along with her phone number. Brayden smiled, set the paper on the step of the lifeguard chair and grabbed her by the hand.

"I'm sure your friends can handle the pool for a bit." He said while glancing at her now giggling water safety buddies.

"I was just heading to lunch… can you join me?" Brayden and his new friend left the pool complex; he didn't stop by the recruiting office.

June 1990

CHAPTER 3

BRAYDEN SMITH WAS BORN and raised in Ohio. Up to this point in his life he had only traveled out of the state a hand full of times, mostly for vacations. He's from a middle-class family with two other siblings, Lela and Shale, one and two years younger respectively. Even though he knew without a doubt that this was the family he was born into, he never quite fit in. The family home is in a rural, country area with acres of woods surrounding it. Brayden had explored every inch of them as a kid. He built timber and deadfall forts, ran around with bows and arrows, set make shift traps and fished various ponds and streams. He loved the outdoors and being active, water was like his second home and anything that got the heart racing and adrenaline pumping was right up his alley. Rachel, Brayden's mom; was a swimmer in high school. She taught each of her three children to swim before the age of four. She was outgoing, outspoken and stubborn, and Brayden had inherited it all. Brayden senior however hated the water, and would rather watch anything sporting on the television than possibly injure himself in real life. He was a workaholic though, and instilled a strong work ethic into Brayden junior, the hard way.

Brayden was a free-spirited kid, who didn't like to be told what to do.

Hated following rules that didn't make sense to him, and was always looking for a way out of anything that was time consuming and bore little reward. He hated school, not because it was hard but because he was bored. He caught on very quickly and just as quickly became uninterested. He enjoyed art because it involved so many different mediums to attempt to master, and it changed with every project. His father, however, did not share his enthusiasm and made it difficult for Brayden to follow that path. Brayden at a young age developed a remarkable ability to read people and find out what motivated them. He would then use this to manipulate situations and attempt to get his way, sometimes it worked, most of the time it didn't, but youth allowed him to perfect this skill for future use.

Being talented opened a lot of doors for Brayden. He was never short on friends; although he kept to himself most of the time, and he could just about date any girl that he wanted to. But in high school, there was only one girl he was interested in and her name was Lisa Tippis. Lisa was beautiful to him, not the prettiest, not the most popular, didn't play any sports or belong to any groups or clubs. She was regular, and that's what Brayden loved about her, but she wasn't interested in him. So he began to date her friend Michelle to gain access to what made her tick. He found out what she did for fun, what her favorite foods were, and favorite band, most read book and watched movie. He armed himself with this ill-gotten information and when he was certain he could use it to his advantage, he made his move. It was brilliantly planned and executed. He even manufactured the break-up with Michelle by having one of the guys on the basketball team that he knew she had a crush on, take her out. The plan worked, Brayden and Lisa dated for over two years and Brayden was in love. Lisa was the first girl he had ever truly cared for, the first girl he had ever spent any amount of time or money on, and surprisingly, the only girl to this point he had ever stayed the night with, literally.

Their senior year was coming to a close, colleges were being picked and it was June, Brayden's birthday was days away. He was excited for this one in particular because Lisa had planned it. Her parents were out of town so they could have a responsible party at her house and not have to worry about where to go afterward. It would truly be a day to remember, for more reasons than one.

January 1993

CHAPTER 4

COLLEGE FOOTBALL WAS really no different than high school football to Brayden. The players were bigger, but then so was he, the lights were a bit brighter, and sometimes a TV camera would grace the sidelines. He loved the game and always looked forward to playing it. It was a challenge, both mentally and physically, and for him it was enjoyable whether the team won or lost. "READY, BREAK", the play had been called and Brayden moved back to his position behind the quarterback. The play was easy, especially against this team, their defense was weak on the left side and it was about to be exploited yet again, as it had been all night long. As the ball was snapped Brayden ran right and took a fake hand off from the quarterback before planting with his right foot and running left toward a hole the offensive line had created for him. Once through it, he faked right, planted and ran left toward the sideline. The quarterback looked right, threw a pump fake, then turned left and drew back to fire it right into Brayden's hands. At that moment a large projector screen above the scoreboard showing a Gulf War veteran in full dress uniform caught Brayden's eye. Almost in slow motion he watched, as the stadium appeared to focus all of their attention on this war hero. He only noticed a couple of ribbons on his uniform but he had been to another country, put his feet on foreign soil. He had lived in austere conditions, bonded with other men in a way that books and movies can't even fully portray. He had fought for Brayden's right to be playing on that football field, at that very moment; and at that very moment, Brayden was smacked in the helmet by a football meant to be caught by him. It deflected off the left side of his protective headgear and into the hands of the opposing team. Brayden tripped over a bench, rolled once and bounced to his feet. "Touchdown!", that was all he heard as he attempted to move back onto the field for a view of the event he had just created. Though humiliated, it didn't really matter in Brayden's mind, they were so far ahead that the few points their opponents just achieved only saved them from the embarrassment of leaving the field having scored nothing. Unfortunately, the coach didn't see it that way and he was benched for the rest of the game, there were ten minutes remaining. It was comedy relief when the highlight reels were played later in the locker room.

"It's as if you completely zoned out!" said the head coach of Brayden's inconceivable goof. Brayden gave a light smile as he watched him rewind it over and over, but he couldn't shake the feeling that a uniform with more than a number and college mascot was in his future.

April 1993

CHAPTER 5

"TIME", HE LOOKED up at the analog clock on the wall, the second hand swept past twelve and the minute hand came to rest on the same for the start of another hour. It was three o'clock.

"Set down your pencils and pass your papers forward."

Brayden took a quick scan of his paper and then checked the top left corner to ensure his name was spelled correctly. He always laughed at his grandfather when he said,

"Heck, all you have to do is spell your name correctly!" It actually wasn't that simple, but it couldn't hurt.

The Armed Services Vocational Aptitude Battery or ASVAB is a branch immaterial, multiple-choice test taken by those interested in entering into military service. The test measures your aptitude in multiple areas and is used to narrow down the plethora of jobs available to those that you actually qualify for. It saves the defense department millions of potentially wasted dollars sending someone off to school to learn something they are not capable of comprehending. On the low end, it also determines your qualification for entrance, period. Brayden had just finished taking this test and was actually surprised at the material that it covered. He had not taken the time to study anything as he imagined that it couldn't possibly be that hard. He was actually amazed. Now he had to wait two weeks to find out the results.

Brayden's recruiter was a Sailor. He's not sure why he decided to walk into the Navy office instead of the Marines but he had made a choice and he was determined to see it through. The Navy dress uniform was by far the worst of all the branches. Tradition is one thing, but at some point progress is needed to remain relevant, at least with the youth of today. Never the less, Brayden was interested in the Navy's ability to travel the globe methodically and often. During his research of the branches, the Sailors and Marines appeared the most likely to see distant places, even as soon as their first few years in service. The Army was actually the least likely to put boots on foreign soil unless a war was going on. Brayden was interested in traveling; and doing so on an all-inclusive, large gray yacht didn't seem half bad.

His recruiter's name was Gary Manson; he was six feet tall with dark hair and bronze skin. He looked weathered, perhaps from braving the salty seas or the results of the long tiring work of a boatswain's mate. He was a petty officer first class with over 20 years of service in the Navy, which meant nothing to Brayden; he hadn't taken the time to learn anything about the jobs or ranks found in the branch. It had been two weeks and Brayden was anxious to find out how he scored, and to hear about the possibilities that awaited him. As he walked up to the front door of the recruiting station, he could see Gary moving his way, having seen him through the wall of glass. Brayden opened the door to be greeted by him smiling from ear to ear.

"Brayden, you passed with flying colors," said Gary.

Brayden never really understood this phrase but knew that it was a good thing.

"So where do we go from here?" Brayden replied.

Gary motioned for Brayden to follow him back to his desk. The recruiter office was really just a wide-open space with multiple desks and Sailors sitting in front of them reading, dialing away at a phone or typing up something on a typewriter. The first day that he had walked in, a few kids were sitting in front of the desks discussing options with their respective recruiter. Today it was his turn. As Brayden sat down in the chair in front of Gary's desk, he watched as he pulled pages from a pile until he saw a few with his name on them. One was clearly his ASVAB scores with abbreviations and numbers in multiple boxes; the other was a list of jobs he could choose from.

"Honestly Brayden, you can have just about any career field you want." said Gary as he extended his arm with the papers for Brayden to review.

"Career?" Brayden asked, mostly directed toward himself rather than a question for Gray. Brayden hadn't really thought about whether this was a career choice versus just something to do for the moment.

"Yes, career, that is just what we call it when you pick a particular field. You are not obligated to a career in the Navy at this point." Gary countered.

Brayden took the paper and began studying the contents. Air Traffic

Control Man, nope, Cryptological Technician, nope, Missile Technician on a Nuclear Submarine, nope, Signalman, nope, Hospital Corpsman, hmmm,

"What does a Hospital Corpsman do?" said Brayden.

"They work in the ships hospital alongside the doc's and some have the possibility of becoming field medics for the Marines." Said Gary.

"So, I could actually go on a mission or something with the Marines as a medic?"

"Absolutely!" said Gary.

That was it; Hospital Corpsman seemed like the right fit. He could be on a ship or tagging along with the Marines; Brayden didn't see how it could get better than that.

August 2001

CHAPTER 6

HIS ARMS BEGAN to fall asleep; they were hand cuffed behind his back and he was tied tightly at the elbows with what he believed was a rope. He had never been tied in that manner before, and had no desire to be tied that way again. He was hooded, striped down to his boxers and dripping wet with what he hoped was water. His smell was askew, but he could swear he smelled rust, something clearly metallic, maybe it was his own blood. On his groin and right thigh, he felt a wave of pain that alternated between burning, itching and stinging. He wondered what they could have done to him to achieve this sensation and then remembered laying in the ants just before the causation of his quandary; ironically, he had hoped that was the actual cause of the discomfort. He was barefoot with each ankle tied to a leg at the front of the chair. He could feel a wave of shear exhaustion come over him. The fatigue from the sudden crash as he plummeted off of his adrenaline rush of making the shot, the endorphin release from the fear he experienced during the chase, and the physical thrashing he took during his capture. He was spent, but he intended on keeping his wits.

So far SERE school was still winning as far as suck factor after being captured. The three-week course started with a classroom phase at Camp Mackall, North Carolina, the Special Forces proving grounds. By the time you attended this school in the Special Forces Qualification Course pipeline, you've seen about all you can stand of the pine tree covered area. The classroom portion was one week long and covered wilderness survival, evasion, interrogation tactics and code of conduct explanations, that was just to get the day started. In the evenings you finished up with armed sentry takedowns, knife combative training, hand-to-hand combat techniques, how to correctly stalk and low-vis obstacle course maneuvers.

The second week covered climbing techniques including rappelling from a tower on the camp. This progressed into conducting the techniques from water towers, buildings and varying height walls. Week three was the field phase. Everything that you had learned in the classroom or other controlled environment was now put to use in the expansive forest surrounding the Camp. Everything that you did during this portion of the exercise was conducted with the idea of being covert. You were sent on a recon mission that was to be conducted behind enemy lines. There was actually a unit of infantry men included in this portion that actively attempted to capture you. They would patrol in specific patterns using dogs, night vision devices and vehicles to include helicopters. Your mission was to conduct your recon successfully and return to station. The provisions you started with were meager intentionally. Sometimes you would go a day or two without meals until you were able to catch a rabbit or squirrel in a game snare. In the end, even if you completed the mission successfully, you were taken hostage and moved to the detainment area.

He remembered showing up to the recreation of a WWII prisoner camp after being captured and seeing the only woman in his class. *It can't be all that bad if she is still hanging in there*, he remembered thinking to himself. Once captured, the beatings began. Not to physically hurt you to the point that you needed medical attention, but just enough that you knew you wanted it to stop. The point was to make you realize you had to play the game but always look for weakness in their system that you could later exploit. This would allow you to plan your escape. Only give up information you had to, and do so in increments. Don't volunteer everything at once as that was frowned upon as well, and never give up a fellow detainee.

He wasn't on the run for long, so he hadn't had to search and forage for food up to this point, not that this was an option now anyway, and he'd literally burned up what provisions he had left. And considering the distance and pace of his pursuers, he couldn't have eaten anything even if he had wanted to. Evasion wasn't really an option, as he was knocked unconscious prior to being transported to his current location. Resistance, well, that was yet to be seen as nothing had taken place since he was detained. And his current predicament didn't leave many possibilities for escape, but he would continue to keep his options open.

Obviously, his captors were not new to the hostage taking game. The music was blaring too loud for him to listen for animals, machinery, aircraft or population, and he was placed, it seemed, in the middle of a fairly large room so any sound made echoed, disguising any inferred distance from a wall or ceiling. They even used handcuffs instead of ropes, because he was pretty sure he could get out of the latter. He still didn't understand the rope at the elbows. Right now, the only thing he knew for certain, was that this was not training. He had just watched his targets head explode through his scope and could only imagine what the repercussions would be. As he sobered up to the realness that was about to transpire, he remembered the blond man that he saw just before being struck. *He might be my only hope.* He thought.

His mind began racing and filling with the methods they used to make people give information in war movies. Slowly removing fingers or toes, electrocution and threats of castration. The opening of a metal door interrupted the mentally exhausting guessing game of picking from the never-ending list of possible torture techniques. Through the hood he could see light pour in from the door and disappear as it closed behind whoever entered. He wasn't sure if it was the same day or days later. His sense of time was totally thrown off. He waited in anticipation, not knowing where the person had gone, or if anyone had come in at all. The music was still blaring but he thought he could hear faint footsteps on a metal floor. He tightened his muscles and planted his toes and heels on the floor in an attempt to absorb the inevitable abuse. His hood came off quickly and he noticed, if only for a second, there were three men in the room. He immediately lost focus as his head was battered about, each man took their shots at him, and no one asked any questions. His eyes had almost swollen shut when they shifted their efforts toward his mid-section. The pain was bearable, but he didn't know how much more he could take. The only thing holding him together was the fact that no one had started removing body parts. The punching bag routine ended after what seemed like hours and he was thankful when one of the men bent down to pick up the hood; hopefully signifying it was over for now. He could barely make out the pale-faced blond man through his blood-soaked eyes, but it was definitely him. He had been standing there all along, not saying a word. Had he participated in the one-way pugilist match? What was he doing with the cartels? Was this a mercenary from another country? He had heard about Chechens being used as snipers in Iraq, but in Colombia? He struggled to make out the man's facial features as the hood was lowered to his shoulders. He realized that at some point during the beating the music had been stopped. He was now able to listen to the men walk toward the door, open it and walk through it; and just before the music came back on he heard a man say in perfect English, "Goodnight Brayden."

July 1993

CHAPTER 7

IT HAD BEEN nearly 10 hours since Brayden had eaten anything. He was hot, tired and hungry. As he held himself off the ground, straight as a board, in what was formerly called the push-up position, now called the front leaning rest; listening to the moaning and groaning going on around him by his fellow classmates, he knew he had made the right choice. "ON YOUR FEET!" A voice said loud and forcefully to the recently arrived busload of new recruits. It was the first day of boot camp, day one of the eight-week program that converted you from an ordinary private citizen, to the polished, courteous, Sailor you were to become upon graduation; at least that was the premise.

Brayden had entered what was called the 'Dive Farers' boot camp. It had all the accouterments of the ordinary affair, but threw in a tough pool and physical fitness regimen to prepare you for dive school, Search And Rescue swimmer school (SAR), and of course Basic Underwater Demolition School, or BUDS; the school that produced Navy Seals. Brayden had no intentions of attending any of those schools, not because he didn't want to, but because he didn't even know they existed. His attendance was a snide gift from Gary, but it was exactly the kind of thing he was interested in.

The days were long and your uniform was a bit different, mostly t-shirts and underwater demolition trunks or UDTs. They were made of all cotton with brass d-rings to tighten the draw strap, designed to be worn into a decompression chamber if needed. Brayden enjoyed the specialness of the program. His class of attendees was very small, twelve total, and it allowed them to grow tight as a group. Each morning, they would conduct a two-mile run, followed by a five-hundred-meter swim, using the sidestroke or breaststroke. By the end of week four they were running five miles two times a week and swimming fifteen hundred meters every Friday. And they would still attend the required classes for military customs and courtesies, shipboard firefighting techniques and Naval ship orientations with the regular boot camp that was in progress to ensure they received the required training for graduation.

He learned while in boot camp that he could attend BUDS after his Hospital Corpsman A-school because it was a feeder career field for the Navy Seals. Not all A-schools allowed you to enter this program. BUDS itself was not a course that rated you any particular skill upon graduation. You had to show up with something that could be used after completing the program like, medical skills, communications, engineering, etc. This now became the focus of his drive. Because he didn't have a BUDS contract, he would have to push himself harder to ensure he was at the top of the pack for acceptance into this elite training opportunity. After a physically demanding eight-week program, Brayden had managed to graduate at the top of his class. He had successfully earned himself a shot at BUDS. All he had to do was pass his A-school.

Saving lives was the theme of the Hospital Corpsman's course. Every instructor, during every block of instruction, said this; it seemed, no less than fifty times. The ironic thing about it was, none of the instructors had seen any type of field duty or mishap outside of the occasional scrape and bruise while afloat, ever. In fact, Brayden soon learned that most of the corpsman that were actually experiencing the stories that were told at the schoolhouse, never showed up to teach. One of his instructors even bragged that he was able to avoid the Gulf War by volunteering to be an instructor. *Is this what I signed up for?* Brayden thought, *to be associated with cowards?* Perhaps there was a reason after all that the Navy had the Marines. To do their grungy bidding, and if called upon, to augment ground operations. Brayden was beginning to suspect that everyone in the Navy was simply there to keep the ships afloat, all systems functioning properly and the Marines were the actual muscle keeping the entire operation safe. *At least I'm going to BUDS,* he thought.

The official Navy headgear is called a cover, not a hat and its actual nomenclature is "white hat". You will usually hear it referred to as the Dixie cup, dog bowl or petri dish; the latter was used jokingly in the corpsman schoolhouse environment. Incorrectly verbalizing the appropriate name for the hat was one thing, but improper use of the clothing item was a serious offense.

It was the first time in four months that the students were required to wear their dress uniform. The last time it was worn was for an inspection for proper fit and assembly; that was day two of the course. The normal attire consisted of dungarees, the Navy's version of a collared short sleeve shirt with bell bottom jeans, and a baseball cap. On field days they could wear the Battle Dress Uniform, or BDU, commonly seen on Army personnel. With either of those uniforms, you could neatly stow your headgear on your backside, bill of the hat down and tucked nicely between your belt line and shirt. With the dress uniform however, the white hat had to be held in your hand; therein lied the problem.

There were five days left before graduation and of course the uniform needed to be inspected again to ensure nothing had happen to it since the last time it was worn. There was also a need for rehearsals, and those had to be done in full dress. Brayden along with three of his classmates, were standing near a podium waiting for the formation to be called, in which the inspection would take place. Two of the men, one of them Brayden, were spinning their petri dishes on their index finger while reminiscing about the last field exercise.

"CORPSMAN SMITH, YOU HAVE JUST BOUGHT YOURSELF A 1000 WORD ESSAY ON THE TRADITION OF THE NAVY WHITE HAT AND WHY IT SHOULD NOT BE SPUN ON YOUR FINGER!"

Ah yes, the familiar voice of Hospital Corpsman First Class Mendoza, or HM1 Mendoza. He was newly promoted, short in stature, and teetering on the verge of being overweight, even by very girth generous Navy standards. HM1 Mendoza was the bane of Brayden's existence. For him, Brayden could do nothing right. It was a wonder that he was still in the course. Their initial run in was during the first field portion of the course. Brayden was attempting to insert an I.V. into his patient under low light conditions. The students were limited to using a red-lensed light source to aid them, and were required to start the IV within two sticks in order to receive a passing score. The students were corralled into a spot away from the testing area prior to the exam, and then led away to a separate area once finished. This way you couldn't observe and formulate a game plan, and upon completion you couldn't tell your classmates what to expect.

When Brayden was called up to his patient, he knelt down next to him and went through the correct sequence of assessing responsiveness, sweeping the airway, checking for breathing and confirming circulation. At some point during your checks, you will be told the nature of the problem, and instructed to start fluids, he had just reached that junction. Brayden set his red light to the side and began prepping his equipment. After ensuring a sterile work environment, or as close to it as possible, he prepared to conduct his stick. The then, Hospital Corpsman Second Class or HM2 Mendoza was his grader, and stayed silent the entire time. Brayden thought this was strange because he heard other instructors giving pointers to their students while testing, using the exam to insert some mentoring while being careful not to coach. As he initiated his stick and began advancing the needle, his red lens flashlight went dark. Brayden steadied his partial stick with one hand and began movement with the other toward the light source.

"Don't worry about the light." said HM2 Mendoza,

"Just continue with the exercise."

Brayden paused for a second, thinking of what to say. He looked Mendoza in the face, barely seeing him in the weak illume, and realized he would not be getting an alternate light source. He stabilized the needle, continued advancing his stick, and slid the catheter down the needle and into his patient. After connecting the tubing, taping down the catheter and going through the motions of ensuring he had proper flow, he cleaned his workspace and backed away, signifying completion. HM2 Mendoza turned on his white light and inspected Brayden's work. It was perfect. Proper sequence, attempt at sterilization, one stick, fluids flowing intravenous and not subcutaneous. HM2 Mendoza reluctantly signed off on Brayden's grade sheet and handed it back to him without ever saying a word. Brayden packed away his medical bag and picked up his red-lensed flashlight to secure it back to the side of his aid bag. As he slid it into the pocket he felt the position of the operating switch, it was off. He waited until he was in the holding area, which was far enough into the woods to be concealed from the testing area before attempting to turn on his light. He grabbed the light and let out a long sigh before switching it to the "on" position. Lo and behold, he had light.

August 2001

CHAPTER 8

BRAYDEN SAT IN the middle of what he now called the slaughterhouse, shaking from the coolness that radiated off of the metal structure that he believed he was housed in. He knew that he was still in Colombia, which is very hot at that time of year. However, the crisp early morning air combined with the lack of radiant heat from the sunshine was sufficient to lower the temperature inside the metal room, just enough for him to feel chilled.

His body was in agony from the beatings that he had taken over the past few days. He was losing track of time being isolated in complete darkness with loud music distracting him from the outside world. Each episode he experienced was the same; men entered the room without speaking to him and commenced to beating him until he could no longer sit up straight in the chair. He had only heard the Americans voice once though, which was now beginning to worry him.

He was tired, hungry, scared and confused. No questions had been asked which made him believe that he would never leave his captors custody alive. He had now surmised that the rope at his elbows was there to keep him from falling out of the chair, at the expense of his shoulders. They felt as though they would be ripped from the socket if his body listed to one side or the other too far or too fast. He couldn't have been there for longer than three days as he had not been given water or food. He was beginning to weaken and was quickly deteriorating; this treatment couldn't continue for much longer without him expiring.

As Brayden sat there miserable, trying to keep his mind occupied so that he didn't slip into a state of further desolation, the door opened to his cell. He could feel the cool air rush into the space and hit his mostly naked body. His shivers intensified as the air continued to bounce off of him from varying angles, quickly, suggesting that the room was not as big as he had once thought. As he tried to concentrate and listen for the number of men that had entered the room this time, he was sent into what he imagined shock would feel like. His body stiffened and he struggled to breath and control his extremities as the ice water was slowly poured over him. It likely only took seconds for them to empty the contents of the container onto him, but it felt like forever as he now rocked and shivered uncontrollably trying to warm his now paralyzed frame.

Cold water from the tap was very different from ice-cold water. The average temperature for cold tap water in the United States was between forty-four- and fifty-five-degrees Fahrenheit. There is no cooling mechanism for tap water, it remains cool because of the insulation the ground provided and the fact that the pipes are usually buried deep enough that the earth isolates it from the sun's warmth above. Ice water however is around thirty-four degrees Fahrenheit and that difference in temperature is extreme. Brayden knew from an experiment in middle school science class that ice water stored in a thermal device would cool to a temperature of thirty-two degrees before it reached its equilibrium and could get no colder. He guessed that the water that had been thrown on him had been in an insulated beverage cooler, *it definitely couldn't get any colder*, he thought.

Brayden sat gasping, hoping that he was not going to be beaten while in his current state. The cool air that he felt when the door first opened was now almost insufferable. As he shivered violently, he began to question the men in Spanish, asking why they were doing this to him. Of course he didn't receive a response, and he really wasn't expecting one. He was trying to humanize himself, allowing the men to see that he was just like them, even though he had killed one of them. His tactic didn't appear to be working. The men checked his ties, picked up the container that his bath was delivered in, and departed closing, not slamming, the door behind them.

The intense shivering had triggered a survival mechanism within him and he began feeling the urge to urinate, he was suffering from cold diuresis. He was amazed that he was even able to dribble anything out considering the lack of fluid intake. For a second the core temperature fluid brought a swath of warmth across him, allowing him a brief respite from the bone shattering trembling as his body tried desperately to warm itself. All he could think about was how glorious the warmth of the sun was, and what he would give to be basking in it at that moment.

By all accounts, he shouldn't have even been that cold. It was after all Colombia. *The lowest it could be this time of year was fifty-seven degrees, stop being a pussy!* He thought to himself as he rocked in the chair. His tolerance for cold had been ruined in Ranger School. There were three types of classes at the famed Army school. Really hot, hot into cold and really cold.

Brayden had attended the really cold class. Most thought that it should be the easiest class, all things considered. You received two meals a day instead of one, necessary because the first meal is simply to fuel the shivers. The vegetation was light so movement was quicker, until the first snowfall in mountains. And when the cold air temperature was combined with freezing rain it usually meant you were going back to the camp, but you still had to walk there.

Brayden recalled an incident that happened at the beginning of the evaluated portion of the school at Camp Darby. His patrol had reached the position where the ambush line was to be emplaced. The eight men from his squad that were to form the line, were standing close to the trees that they had been instructed to take up a fighting position near. The cold night air turned to freezing rain within minutes of settling into the location. The entire line stood up and remained standing next to their trees, so as not to lay in the frigid waters gathering quickly at their feet. None of the clothing that the men were allowed to wear repelled water, and no thermal protection was permitted under the thin summer weight uniforms.

As the Ranger Instructor or RI made his way around, looking at the students through his night vision device to ensure they were prepared for the opposition force to begin movement down the road, he noticed the entire ambush line standing near the trees instead of laying down.

"Get the fuck down in the prone position Rangers!" The RI yelled as he moved closer to the infracting students. No one moved and each student looked to his right and left and shook his head west to east at the man next to him signifying that they were going to take a stand.

"Are you fucking kidding me Rangers? I said GET THE FUCK DOWN IN THE PRONE POSITION!" The RI was now yelling at the top of his lungs. Brayden could see through his night vision that their insolence was beginning to perplex the man.

"Ok Rangers, you wanna play games? We'll play some fucking games! Everybody move to the road!" As they began moving the whole twenty meters to the road, two students collapsed and needed to be carried the rest of the way. It wasn't apparent at the moment, but they were suffering from hypothermia. Upon inspection by the medics the two weak body Rangers as the RI called them, were loaded up into troop carriers and driven back to the camp. Everyone else was allowed to warm up on the six-mile walk back to the barracks. They had barely won that battle.

As Brayden sat shaking and rocking in his chair, he wondered how he could mount a revolt in this situation. His inability to warm up angered him and he began yelling at the top of his lungs, pushing just about every ounce of air he could muster out of his chest. He felt like he had cried out for five minutes straight, and as he finished, he noticed that the shivering had stopped. As the echo of his voice ceased bouncing off the metal walls, his shivering returned. *Now that you're finished feeling sorry for yourself, try drinking some of the water from your hood dummy.* He thought to himself. Survival was all about the small victories.

December 1993

CHAPTER 9

HIS REPORT WAS READY; all 1000 words of rhetoric about how cool the Marines were and how utterly weak the Navy was. In hindsight he would realize that he should have just played the game and written about the history of the Navy head covering, but it bugged him that he was clearly singled out for the punishment. He was the only one required by HM1 Mendoza to write an essay about the event, his partner in crime got away scot-free. Not even a warning, nothing. Brayden knew there would be repercussions to his rant, but he was so infuriated by the whole thing that he had abandoned all logic.

It was 0800 and he had just made it through the breakfast line in the mess facilities. The mess was separated into two distinct areas. One side was for the school cadre; the other was for the students. There was no wall or partition, so you simply had to obey the rules or suffer the consequences. Obviously after four months of eating every meal in this facility, Brayden knew exactly where he could and could not sit; but this morning he decided to push the envelope. He sat at a table right over the edge of the instructor, student line. Several cadre members passed him and sat at tables near him without even casting as much as a glance in his direction.

He was almost beginning to feel robbed of his lucidly cavalier attempt at earning some extra physical exercise. Finally, he saw his moment; HM1 Mendoza entered the mess and began making his way through the line. As he passed the beverage refrigerator, the last obstacle before clearly seeing the seating area, Brayden sat up tall and proud in his seat, ready to receive his inevitable and completely instigated tongue-lashing followed promptly by some form of corrective action. Almost right on cue, HM1 Mendoza locked eyes with Brayden and immediately turned flush with anger. He set his tray on the nearest table and bee-lined to his location. Instructors and students alike looked in the direction of the table Brayden was occupying. Everything seemed to stop as HM1 Mendoza's right hand came up to his shoulder, fingers and thumb fully extended and joined, as he then pushed out his arm at full extension into Brayden's face; just inches away from touching him. His head was cocked sideways a bit and from that vantage point, Brayden swore he could count every vein on his head as he opened his mouth to roar.

"I HAVE JUST ABOUT HAD IT WITH YOUR BLATANT DISREGARD FOR RULES AND YOUR SEEMINGLY WILLFUL DISOBEDIENCE OF ORDERS. IF I HAD MY WAY, I WOULD FIND YOU UNFIT FOR MILITARY SERVICE AND DISCHARGE YOU IMMEDIATELY AND WITH EXTREME PREJUDICE!"

The dining facility had fallen completely silent. No one uttered a word, and for the first time in the four months that he had been eating in that room; he could actually hear the wall clock ticking. Brayden refrained from busting out into outright laughter, as he knew that would probably result in a physical altercation, which was not his intent. He had successfully elicited the response that he wanted, right, wrong or indifferent, his goal was accomplished. He reached under his tray and pulled out the essay he was tasked to write the previous day. Set it on the table in front of HM1 Mendoza, pushed his seat back from the table, stood up, picked up his tray, deposited it in the nearest dish collection rack, and departed the building in complete hush.

Brayden went back to his room and mentally re-enacted the events that had just transpired. Anytime he wavered on his actions, or began to second-guess things he had done, he always remembered advice that his grandfather had given him. *Live with no regrets, and apologize to no man.* Though Brayden had not had many experiences up to this point, he always tried to live by those words; and this seemed like a perfect time to apply them. He pulled out his duffle bag and began to pack up the meager contents of his room. He didn't quite know what was going to happen, but he had no doubt that this was his last day at the schoolhouse; secretly he hoped he was wrong. After tidying his room, he grabbed his belongings and headed to the reception area in the main campus building. He wasn't sure which texts books he was allowed to keep so he kept those out in a separate bag to be sifted through when the time came, and that time came quickly. Not even fifteen minutes after he had arrived in the lobby the day runner walked past on his way to find him.

"Oh, corpsman Smith," the runner was obviously shocked to see him.

"I didn't think anyone had sent for you yet."

"They didn't." said Brayden,

"I arrived preemptively."

The runner, a student that was on hold status waiting for enough personnel to arrive in order to begin the next class, did not seem impressed, but it didn't matter to Brayden. He followed the gangly kid up the stairs and into the cadre area. HM1 Mendoza and another instructor were already waiting for him in the hallway. They walked him into the commandant's office where he was required to stand at the position of attention, his two less than friendly escorts stood behind him. The commandant began to speak,

"Seaman Smith."

Being called "Seaman" when you have or are attempting to acquire a specific career field title, like Hospital Corpsman for example; is never a good start. From the beginning of the conversation, which would likely be one way with Brayden in receive mode, he knew graduation was out of the question. The only thing left to disclose was whether or not he could stay in the Navy. The commandant continued,

"Your actions up to this point have been exemplary. Believe it or not, you were in the running for making the commandants list. You had the third highest grade point average in your class, and you have been a first time 'go' at all field events. It's obvious to me that you are a bright and talented young man with a great deal of potential. It's a shame that your disregard for anything authoritative has clouded your judgment, thus affecting the way you will begin life in this organization. Clearly you have a lot of growing up to do, but unfortunately for you, we do not run remedial professionalism classes for those that arrive here delinquent. Seaman Brayden Smith, as of today you're on assignment with the United States Navy as 'needs of the service'. You are not career field qualified, you will not have the opportunity to attend another career producing course in route to your first assignment, and you are no longer eligible to attend the

Basic Under Water Demolition School. Due to the nature of your offense and the undisputable evidence I have before me, your right to appeal has been revoked. You will be placed on two weeks of leave starting today, after which time you will report to your duty station. Immediately upon departing this office, you will report to the administrative section to receive your orders. Seaman Smith, do you have any questions of me?"

Brayden stood there feeling as though he had shrunk two feet. At that moment he felt like he had just made the biggest mistake of his life. Up to that point he had never experienced any feeling close to failure, he really didn't know what it was supposed to feel like emotionally, but he couldn't imagine it was any worse. Losing a chance to attend BUDS was the ultimate slap in the face, he was completely deflated, and he succumbed to defeat. He accepted that it was entirely of his own doing.

"No Sir."

Brayden saluted, executed an about face, and walked out of the office between the two cadre members. As he walked down the hall toward the administrative office, he heard the door close behind him. He remembered his grandfather's words, swallowed hard, stood up tall, and picked up his pace.

May 1994

CHAPTER 10

BRAYDEN HAD ALWAYS enjoyed swimming. As a kid he swam in pools, lakes, ponds and streams. Any body of water that was deep enough to work at staying afloat was his kind of environment. When diving documentaries with Jacques Cousteau were set to air, he would plead with his father to let him watch. He had probably seen every single one ever produced. The ocean and its inhabitants intrigued him, and for the longest time he aspired to be a marine biologist for no other reason than to scuba dive and study marine life. National Geographic episodes with specials on sharks, barracuda, eels, killer whales and other dangerous marine life were his absolute favorite. The fact that this entirely hidden circle of life was happening daily, while land animals lazily went about their business, simply fascinated his young developing mind.

By the age of fourteen he was taking scuba lessons with his uncle who instructed for Scuba Schools International or SSI at the local YMCA. He had his basic, advanced, cavern, wreck, nitrox and intro to cave certifications, all before the age of eighteen. However, none of his civilian diving accomplishments or aquatic interests had prepared him for the rigors of the SAR swimmer's course.

MENDACITY

The school was in sunny Jacksonville Florida; it was only four weeks long, but extremely intense. You learned how to swim moderate distances with fins, mask and snorkel, proper water entry procedures for ship and aviation platforms, how to move to and secure a casualty, standard operating procedures for night operations, and considerations for working in close proximity to large debris. Once complete, you returned to the fleet with the additional duty of rescue swimmer. The only problem was, Brayden would still be a boatswain's mate. He knew the work that his recruiter Gary had done in the Navy was hard, but what he didn't know was that it really wasn't a qualification; it was an on-the-job apprenticeship. A sort of catch all, a job for those that really didn't score well enough to qualify for anything else. Your duty day consisted of polishing any and all brass objects on the boat, oiling hatches, scuttles and manhole hinges, throwing and setting the ships mooring lines, chipping paint and repainting the bare areas you had just created. Every once and a while you were called upon to drive the ship, sounds really cool, but any monkey could do it. Brayden had been in the fleet for almost seven months. The only equable thing about his initial assignment was being stationed in Long Beach California.

He had just completed his first west pack and was still proud and excited about all the countries he had the pleasure of visiting. He was identified early in the deployment to attend SAR school after the fleet returned stateside, because of his almost heroic efforts assisting in the rescue of a young lieutenant. The lieutenant had inadvertently stumbled off the aft end of the ship shortly after anchoring near the coast of Thailand. Thankfully for the young officer's sake the screws were not turning or his fate would have suffered an awful twist. Brayden had been the first in the water after him; he jumped in without any swim equipment, or being properly tethered, as he was standing less than ten feet away from him and couldn't just stand there and watch him flail. Four other sailors stared over the railing watching as the officer struggled to breath. Having just landed on his back he was gasping desperately for air as the wind had violently been knocked from his lungs. Brayden was able to get to him and provide him a semi stable platform from which to catch his breathe. The ships rescue swimmer joined him shortly thereafter and took over. For his actions that day he was awarded a citation.

It was his first award, aside from the obligatory medals earned after completing a lengthy deployment. The ship's captain discovered a short time later after reviewing his service record that he had attended a dive farer boot camp. It surprised him that Seaman Smith would have shown up to the fleet without some type of dive or swimmer additional duty, considering his strong adaptation to an aquatic environment.

The captain later asked Brayden if he would like to attend the SAR course and return as a swimmer for the ship. Brayden accepted and for the first time since leaving boot camp, felt his life might actually be taking a turn for the better; next on his list was finding a real job.

July 1994

CHAPTER 11

BEFORE HEADING TO THE SAR swimmers' course, Brayden had to obtain a medical physical that would clear him as "currently fit for duty". He took this opportunity to upgrade his physical type to a dive physical, which entailed more lab work and an EKG, easy enough to add on and kept his options open, later he was glad that he did.

SAR school was a blast, and after the past four weeks of grueling training, it was time to prove he could do the job under real world conditions. Staring out of the back of a helicopter hovering at sixty feet, Brayden intently watched his dummy that simulated a person in distress. As the aircraft slowly corkscrewed down to 15 feet, he prepared to jump, feet first, into the ocean below. Once in, he would immerse himself below the surface to avoid the spray from the hundred knot winds of the rotor wash. The helicopter made its way back up to fifty feet, and Brayden began swimming to his dummy. Once he reached his victim, he went through his abbreviated medical checklist to determine responsiveness before hooking him up and preparing for the final event. He connected his victim and began the eight-hundred-meter tow that was required to successfully meet the SAR requirements and graduate the course. He finished with time to spare.

Brayden graduated top of his class in SAR school. He technically attended the school in Temporary Duty or TDY status, which meant he was already assigned to a unit and was to attend the school and return. However, he was armed with the admission criteria for dive school, so instead he attempted to broker a deal. The Personnel Specialist or PS at the SAR school was PS3 Brenda Vaughn. Judging by her looks alone, he guessed she was currently single and would likely remain that way for some time, but duty calls and right now he needed orders taking him to Panama City Florida. He was attempting to trick the system. In college you could find a class that you wanted to take and just show up on day one unregistered. If there happened to be seats available, meaning the professor hadn't reached his or her ratio limit, you could begin the class immediately and just wait for the paperwork to catch up. He knew that it worked there, but he was rolling the dice with the Navy.

Brayden asked Brenda out to dinner, and of course because he wasn't stationed there, she would have to pick him up at his temporary enlisted housing unit. Brayden chose the location, a Chinese restaurant, but to his dismay they actually had seating available inside. *My how things change.* he thought. In the midst of the small talk, Brayden made his pitch, by her earlier actions he had already surmised she was game for the evening and wanted to get business out of the way before going any further.

"Brenda, I'm kind of having a problem" he started,

"My captain wanted to send me to scuba school in Panama City right after I graduated SAR, but I don't think the orders are going to show up in time. That's why I have a dive physical instead of the standard one required for SAR. Since you deal with orders all day I was wondering if you had seen anything come across your desk? I'm scheduled to leave here in a day or two and I'm getting a little worried."

Brenda was amazed that he was talking to her about something other than getting her back to a room somewhere. Actually, she couldn't even believe they were sitting down enjoying a meal. In her limited experience with men, it had always been the long, slow, tedious process of personal beautification on her part, in anticipation of a real public outing, only to be driven to the nearest motel and pounded until reaching climax; their climax.

"I haven't seen anything yet Brayden," said Brenda,

"But I will check for you first thing in the morning."

"That would be awesome, I don't want you to go out of your way for me though, getting you in trouble is the last thing I want to do." Said Brayden.

Who was this guy? Brenda thought. He actually cared about what happened to her? She was always treated like crap, and she figured it was because she wasn't the prettiest. She knew deep down that Brayden wanted something, but she actually didn't care. He was being polite, an absolute gentleman. From the start of the evening, she was impressed. She had purposely parked and walked straight to his room with the intent of going inside and getting it over with, after all she had needs too. She entered his small room and stood in the doorway.

"Take a seat." Brayden said.

She figured she knew what was coming next so she took off her shoes and sat on the bed. As Brayden walked past on his way to the closet, she reached out, grabbed his hand and gently pulled him toward her. Brayden tugged her by the hand to her feet, walked her the whole two steps to the door, slipped on his shoes, waited for her to step back into hers and escorted her out of the room.

"Which one is yours?" Brayden asked surveilling the parking area for her car. She was stunned,

"Um, it's over here." She said leading the way to her vehicle.

Once there he walked to her door and opened it for her before hopping in the passenger side. Her mind was racing during the ride, as she didn't know how to behave at this point. *Brayden had her right where he wanted her.*

Brenda took a sip of her beverage and then set her fork on her plate.

"I can generate orders for you to Panama City." She said,

"Once your there it's completely on you, but I'm positive I can get you there."

Brayden smiled and grabbed her hand across the table. She was now flabbergasted; a public show of affection, she just about fainted at the table.

"You know you don't have to do that Brenda" Brayden started,

"If my orders don't show, they don't show, not a big deal, I'm sure he'll send me back. Besides, then I get to see you again."

Brayden removed his hand from hers and reached up to gently touch the side of her face.

Brayden received his orders the following day; though he didn't know if he could even make his flight that same afternoon. He was completely exhausted, Brenda stayed the entire night, and it was apparent that sleep was not in her vocabulary. He vowed if he were in Jacksonville again, he would look her up; she knew that it was a lie, but she honestly didn't care.

Intestinal fortitude is what the Navy Chiefs that ran scuba school said just about every day. Yes, the water is a very unforgiving environment and it does take a special individual to want to work in it day in and day out. You can quickly find yourself outside of your comfort zone. The fact that you even showed up to the school, means that you were willing to set aside any engrained fears, to be one of the handful of divers in the military. Brayden thought it was a joke. It was basically the Navy's version of a PADI course.

The orders Brenda made him worked like a charm, and luckily the course was not full so he was able to occupy a seat. It was four weeks long and covered single and twin eighty diving, the use of sub-slave equipment and lift bags, rigging and tackling from shore, platform and below surface, ships husbandry, and search and rescue techniques. The only thing left to do now, was see if his orders scheme worked back at his unit.

He arrived back at the Long Beach Naval station after eight long weeks of training. Physically he was no worse for wear but the past four weeks had been mentally brutal not knowing what was happening back at the ship. Were they wondering where he was? Was Shore Patrol waiting to put him in handcuffs for being AWOL? Technically he was accounted for; after all he was attending a Navy school, which could be easily tracked. He boarded the ship with confidence, ready to explain himself upon questioning. The officer on watch smiled and welcomed him back aboard,

"Please sign back in at the clerk's office." He said while entering the hourly sounding checks into the watch logbook.

He walked to the office, as it was the middle of the duty day, and handed the clerk his orders and a copy of both his SAR and scuba school certificates.

"How was it?" the young man at the counter asked,

"Very long days, now I need some time to dry out." Brayden said attempting to throw in some humor.

His orders and certificates were placed into his personnel record, he officially signed back in, and he was on his way. So far everything was working in his favor, but he would not be satisfied until he bumped into the ship's captain.

Days later, Brayden was on the fan deck sorting through SAR equipment with the only other swimmer on board. He tried on his BCD and booties to ensure that they fit before being issued. The ship had several sets of scuba gear and because he was now the only diver on board, he set out to inventory his gear and check for serviceability. Brayden noticed the ship's captain climbing down a ladder and tried to make his way into the scuba locker quickly to avoid detection, he wasn't fast enough.

"Seaman Smith." The captain said in a raised tone to ensure he was heard over the noise of pneumatic paint chippers and sanders.

"Good morning, Sir." Brayden said as he rendered a salute.

"I hear you are officially a member of the SAR detachment."

"Yes Sir, I graduated top of my class." Brayden bragged.

"Good job son, we are all proud of you. If I didn't know better, I would think you were trying to find yourself a more challenging job." Said the captain.

Brayden looked at him inquisitively, as certainly the captain knew that SAR was an additional duty and not an actual career field. Brayden shot back,

"What do you mean Sir?"

"Well, you're a diver now, I don't suspect you'll be staying aboard much longer, the junk boats are in short supply nowadays."

Brayden didn't want to stay engaged with the captain any longer than he had to, so he smiled offered his gratitude and disappeared into the dive locker.

"Holy crap, it worked!" Brayden said to himself under his breath.

He was elated, and wondered how, if and when he would be starting his new job. *One thing at a time,* he thought, *there's no way I could actually be getting my dream job.*

July 1995

CHAPTER 12

ONE-YEAR LATER Brayden found himself on orders, assigning him to work on a junk boat tied down a few docks over, keeping him in California. He was actually hoping for something on the east coast, but figured beggars can't be choosers. Working on a junk boat without actually being a salvage diver meant you really never did any substantial work. Most of your dive time was accumulated in the harbor and dock areas, conducting ship bottom searches for possible damage, or scrapping barnacles from the bottom of them. Basically, Brayden had just traded his land based, mouth-breathing job, for a gig sucking down compressed air at depth and doing about the same thing; his dream was incomplete, but at least he was diving.

The salvage-qualified divers were able to do the more rigorous and challenging work. Locking in and out of a diving bell at depth while removing deep sea wreckage, or repairing a screw or sonar dome on a destroyer class ship or larger vessel. He wanted badly to attend this course, but settled for on-the-job training. It would never get him into a suit, but it would keep him busy and in the water.

His goal of attending BUDS was quickly slipping away. His time in the Navy was coming to an end, at least on his first enlistment. He completed and submitted his packet for attendance to BUDS and was put on a waiting list that could last as long as a year. The problem was, he only had six months left in the Navy; ultimately, he made the decision to separate.

September 1996

CHAPTER 13

BRAYDEN DIDN'T ENTER THE Army straight into Special Forces. His initial contract was actually needs of the Army because he had been prior enlisted Navy with close to a two-year break in service. Almost every branch of service gave priority of its jobs to the soon to be newly indoctrinated, or those that transferred branches, instead of allowing their contract to expire. They figured if you removed yourself from military service for that long, you already knew the drill and obviously you desired to serve again under a different organizational structure; or you couldn't find steady work in the civilian market. The one thing he knew for sure was that this time he wanted to jump out of airplanes. He had talked to a few Navy Seals that later ended up as salvage divers and the one thing that excited him the most about the training, was being airborne. His Army recruiter set him up with the Military Operational Specialty or MOS of 25C, Radio Operator and Maintainer with an airborne contract. The Army needed jumping Radio Telephone Operators or RTOs and he fit the bill. Unfortunately, the Army didn't recognize or accept Brayden's Navy boot camp experience as suffice for immediate acceptance into his 25C advanced schooling, he would have to attend the Army's version of boot camp; basic training.

Brayden had not wasted his one-year break in service between the Army and Navy sitting on his hands. He first went back to school and took a few criminal justice classes, but he was not interested in becoming a full-time student again, just in learning a bit of criminal law. While taking his classes, he applied for a job with the National Reconnaissance Office (NRO). He was selected to attend an orientation where you could apply for training after being vetted. After a battery of written, oral, psychological and physical testing, he was accepted into the program. Learning about how the intelligence satellites were used was eye opening. Everything from launch sites, to how to conduct maintenance, to when the birds needed to be replaced entirely was covered. The camera types and zones of operations were of particular interest as the training began to dispel some myths commonly seen in movies and shows. The satellites worked in concert with specially outfitted aircraft to develop a sophisticated picture of a particular area. He also learned about strategic war gaming and ran through myriads of tests that would replicate certain scenarios for them to work through.

His scores were average in most areas, but he excelled with all of the fieldwork.

Two months into his schooling he was academically dropped, but recommended for another pipeline. The Central Intelligence Agency (CIA) had a program that was used as their action arm. It was comprised mostly of former Special Operations Forces or SOF personnel, but no one was discriminated from attending the schooling if selected. Brayden had been recommended for this particular group; it was called the Special Activities Division or SAD. This particular division fell under the National Clandestine Services or NCS and sometimes the Other Government

Agencies or OGA, used to disassociate them from the CIA. Brayden was excited to begin this training, it was more hands on and action oriented. He attended driving schools, shooting schools, learned how to pick locks and install audiovisual listening devices. The academics portion was intense but interesting, which kept him deeply enthralled. This arm of the government was used in high threat areas, where normal operatives would not be assigned. They wouldn't carry anything that would represent them as associated with the U.S. and they understood that the mission required that the U.S. have complete deniability. Tactical SAD units could be used to carry out covert political action while in austere environments, when overt support for a group or faction could damage international relationships. They learned how to use techniques to sway public opinion, such as psychological operations and black propaganda. This could involve financial support for favored political candidates, media guidance, legal expertise and covert poll tampering. He learned how to make influencing leaflets, magazine articles, radio and television spots, all to use for delivering covert messages and propaganda. Even recruiting personnel that worked in the media outlet was practiced, to add further validity to the campaign. Learning how to overthrow a government was very exciting stuff for Brayden, and he excelled at the training, even at its fast pace. When he was weeks away from attending the coveted program at the farm, the source handler's course; he was again dropped from the program.

His assigned mentor had been James Gaul, an older man with a hint of a country accent and a slight limp to his walk. James, at 60 years old, still had a very tenacious demeanor. Having been widowed for the past five years, he was hardened to the cruel tricks that life could play on you. He started his career in the Army as an infantry lieutenant before making his way into Special Forces. As a Green Beret he completed multiple rotations to

Vietnam and eventually worked his way into a position with the Military Assistance Command, Vietnam-Studies and Observations Group or MACV-SOG. This elite organization conducted clandestine unconventional warfare operations to include running black operations involving covert agents, psychological operations and capturing enemy combatants for tactical questioning. After the Vietnam War he returned home and went back to school to get his master's degree in criminal justice. After which he applied for and was accepted into the CIA. He now managed clandestine operations and was the special programs director in charge of developing and managing all emerging requirements; he was a wise and guarded man.

James had seen his share of the world that doesn't exist for the majority of the population; where men and women thwart chaos before it becomes a reality for the masses both home and abroad. People, especially Americans, don't want to know what dangers are lurking, sometimes moments away from ending their way of life. They want to continue their lives in ignorance, trusting that someone is putting themselves in harm's way on their behalf, ensuring their security and lifestyle is able to continue; all of course for free. James knew that freedoms weren't free, personal or otherwise. There was always someone out there sacrificing their life and freedoms for the good of all, and he could see that Brayden was cut from that cloth.

He guided Brayden through most of the course, available for questions and helped him understand each phase of training, giving him tips and hints along the way. Now, with a heavy heart, he was to help him through the relief process. Lots of briefings covering divulgence of classified information. Forms to sign reiterating the disclosure acts to which he was bound, and almost as quickly as he entered into that world, he was out. James had taken a liking to Brayden and hated to see him go. He figured that he was still young, and there were many avenues to eventually lead him back to the organization. He would gain experience, enter a feeder career similar to how James entered the agency, and begin the work he was destined to perform; but for now, because of what he knew, he needed a handler.

CHAPTER 14

ARMY BASIC TRAINING was a joke, and other than shooting, and the fact that he wasn't swimming two miles every morning, it was really no different than the Navy's entry-level program. Customs and courtesies basically remained the same, learning the new rank structure was challenging, but he figured as long as he saluted anything shiny, he would be fine. Draped in a new uniform and now called private instead of seaman, he headed off to his Advanced Individual Training or AIT.

Learning to operate a radio was not terribly difficult. You entered in the frequency of the entity you needed to communicate with, put up an antenna, pressed the push-to-talk button and voila! Now technically, there was a great deal going on. Ensuring you had the correct crypto and truck key installed, antenna theory, frequency range, spectrum analysis, what would the effects of the atmosphere at any given time have on your signal, do you have good line of site, etc. The aforementioned processes, which varied across multiple platform types, is what you were really there to learn and understand, and after months of repetition and practice in just about every condition imaginable, he was finally ready to jump out of an airplane.

Fort Benning Georgia is the home of the Army's airborne school and pretty much nothing else. Columbus Georgia was a hole in the ground compared to the cities that Brayden had lived near up till now; he was glad that he was only there for the school. The course itself was more of the same, some instructors with institutional knowledge that treated students badly because they didn't know as much as them. Jumping out of planes however, was every bit as fun as he had anticipated.

The first jump was the coolest, you really didn't know what to expect. Sitting in the back of the aircraft was no different than any commercial flight, except that the seating was extremely tight and oriented in a more troop friendly manner, and there were no windows to look out of. The aircraft taxied and took off like normal, but that ended the similarities. You flew what was called Nap of the Earth. It's a type of very low altitude flight, flown by military aircraft to avoid enemy detection in high threat areas. This ground hugging technique allowed pilots to use terrain to mask the approaching aircraft and avoid radar contact. Ground to air defense systems could not effectively lock onto aircraft flying in this manner, which made the aircrews feel better. The passengers however, were treated to a g-force filled ride, complete with hard and steep turns and rollercoaster like drops. To the inundated it could be nerve racking at the least. To the weak or faint of heart, it could induce bucket-loading nausea.

Once over the designated drop zone, the crew chief in the back of the aircraft, would let the personnel responsible for ensuring the safety of the jump know, that it was safe to move around and conduct all necessary pre-jump inspections. These individuals were called jumpmasters. Upon completion of all inside cursory inspections of the aircraft and static-line, where the parachutes activating line connected, and its attachment points, it was time to prepare for the actual jump. The doors opened and a jumpmaster stood up and checked out the doors leading edge and outside trailing edge to ensure no one would be snagged or injured while exiting the aircraft. Next, they checked outside the plane to ensure it was flying the correct course to the drop zone, and that no other aircraft were flying in the vicinity that you could hit once in the air. Everyone hooks up when given the command, checks equipment one last time, and stands by to exit. "GO!" walking to the door is surreal, you never expect to see people disappearing from the inside of a plane while it's in mid-flight, especially if nothing is wrong with it. One by one the bodies in front of you are sucked out of a door until it's your turn, and you're turning into the door and looking at a wing above your head, and feeling the propeller blast of a couple of turbo prop engines, and smelling fumes and exhaust as you are swept out of the fuselage and into a medium that cannot sustain the weight of your body. You never really feel like you're falling as you're being pushed horizontally, sometimes staring at the ground sometimes at the sky, until you are jolted to a halt and flung below your now fully inflated canopy. Then it's quiet, you can hear nothing but the low roar of the plane departing now a few hundred feet above you and practically a mile away from you. You continue to look in all directions, being careful not to make contact with any other jumpers in the sky. Until you're low enough that your mind can discern the rate of speed at which you're traveling. You prepare for the impending impact and hope you remember how to properly execute a landing fall. Then it's over, the adrenaline rush has now turned into a wave of exhaustion as you pack up your chute and prepare to do it all again. It's the second jump that scares the hell out of you.

Airborne graduation was a bigger affair than anticipated. Parents of soldiers were filling the bleachers on the parade field, as the newly minted paratroopers prepared to pin on their shiny new set of silver wings. A group of individuals showed up who were not part of the festivities, but were important to the experience all the same. They called themselves Rangers and they were looking for volunteers to attend the Ranger Indoctrination Program or RIP. Brayden had no idea what this entailed, but he knew what Rangers were and decided he wanted to become one. *What's a little more time at Benning?* he thought. What he didn't know was that after completion of this assessment, he would be permanently stationed there in the 3rd Ranger Battalion. At least the weather was warm.

December 1996

CHAPTER 15

BEING A RANGER WAS better than being in the conventional Army. They trained often and hard, but the unit really wasn't for him. Good order and discipline were truly taken to heart. The haircuts you were required to have were ridiculous. Your uniforms had to be immaculate, he had taken to having his Battle Dress Uniform or BDU professionally starched and pressed; as well as having his boots expertly shined. Being yelled at was not really Brayden's cup of tea and it seemed to be a common occurrence while serving there. It was a great place to learn your job though, as your day was filled with classes and training exercises, both in the field and in and around the barracks that you lived in. The one gripe that he had, was not getting to the famed ranger school as quickly as he had hoped; he knew he had to find another home. He wasn't one for following what he thought to be nonsensical orders and he found himself losing patience with those regarded as his leaders. He wanted to leave before repeating his Hospital Corpsman experience.

Brayden didn't have to find Special Forces; they found him. While waiting to conduct a practice airfield seizure, which involved conducting an airborne operation into an airstrip and taking it by force, he observed three large, completely blacked out, SUVs pull up to their air terminal. The vehicle occupants dismounted with beards, longish hair, non-standard clothing, equipment and weapons. Brayden was extremely curious, and wanted to learn more about this group of individuals. After receiving a stern verbal counseling from his platoon sergeant, about what happens to those that betray the regiment, he learned that they were Green Berets. From that night forward it was all Brayden thought about.

Brayden attended the Pathfinder course out of necessity, not his, his squads. They needed someone capable of surveying drop zones in remote locations and Brayden was next in line for a school. While in attendance he met an SF soldier named Steve Landers. To Brayden, Steve was the poster child for special operation. He was tall, built like an athlete and had a tower of power, sometimes referred to as the triple canopy. It consisted of the Special Forces tab, Ranger tab, and Airborne tab all stacked atop the unit affiliation patch.

The Pathfinder course was very math intense, which was not Brayden's strong suit. The school was also predicated on the assumption that you were already a jumpmaster, meaning you would inherently show up with a baseline knowledge of formulas; Brayden was not. Steve volunteered to mentor Brayden through the course and continued to do so when he was selected to attend the Special Forces Qualification Course or SFQC. Brayden had experienced a great deal up to this point in his life; but his true adventure had yet to begin.

February 1998

CHAPTER 16

SPECIAL FORCES ASSESSMENT and Selection or SFAS was a three-week course held at Camp Mackall. Brayden had trained up for months before attending the course. Running, road marching with a fifty-five-pound rucksack and an impressive weight lifting routine that reminded him of his football playing days. All done on his own time, as the Ranger Battalion was not about to give him time during the duty day, to train up to be a traitor. In fact, before he left for the event, his well respected and esteemed battalion senior enlisted leader told him that he hoped he passed selection because if he didn't, he wouldn't be welcome back there. He had to give it everything he had; he gave 100% and then some.

The events were nothing special really, running and road marching with a fifty-five to seventy-pound rucksack, but with a twist. You were given the time you needed to be lined up for the event and in what uniform you should be in to conduct it. They told you the direction in which to start, and that was it. You kept moving following road cones with directional arrows until someone told you to stop. No one talked to you, you weren't permitted to speak to anyone else, and you had no idea how you were doing. You couldn't have a timing device at all, if you were caught with one you were dropped. During the land navigation portion, if you were caught using the roads, or unauthorized trails, you were dropped. During the team week events, there was a forced road march at an absurdly quick pace between each one and if you failed to keep up during one of the movements, you were dropped. After all of that, three weeks' worth of mental and physical punishment, selection wasn't a guarantee; it is called "selection" after all. Brayden started with a class of over 300 and just 35 were selected, one of them being him.

The Special Forces Qualification Course or SFQC was one year long, it featured your military occupational specialty or MOS, and Brayden chose to be a Weapons Specialist or 18B. Having already tried his hand at the medical trade via the Navy, he decided to be the tactical expert this time around. He learned about indirect fire weapons, pistols, rifles, machine guns and the tactics and techniques used to employ them. The small unit tactics phase was more a refresher than training after attending Ranger school. The phase was not very long so the conditions that they attempted to replicate were somehow lost.

Language school was a welcomed break from the fast pace of the physical training portions and a good way to re-acclimate from the Pineland experience. Pineland was the name of the country that you were immersed into during Robin Sage. This phase of training was designed to introduce you to the tedious and often times frustrating process of working with indigenous forces, SFs bread and butter next to Unconventional Warfare. A young and inexperienced SF soldier could find himself working alone with thirty to forty surrogate forces within months of graduating the course. Robin Sage wouldn't prepare you for all circumstances you could find yourself in, but it definitely gave you an excellent base to build on.

Brayden's assigned language was Spanish; he had enjoyed the intense schooling experience and was excited to start conducting missions in the jungles of Central and South America.

August 2001

CHAPTER 17

BRAYDEN COULD FEEL THE temperature changing inside his holding cell. He guessed that it must be mid-day, because it would take all morning for the sun to heat up the structure he was in. His mind was acclimating to the loud music, as he was actually able to get what felt like a few hours of sleep. He wasn't shaking anymore and as long as he kept fairly still, the pain from the punishment he had been taking was almost tolerable.

As he began trying to peer through the hood over his head, something he attempted to do every few hours, the music shut off abruptly. He sat in silence now focusing solely on how heavy and labored his breathing was. He tried to control it so that he could listen for audible clues, but his body was beginning to fail him. His strenuous breathing and the ringing in his ears from the countless hours of blaring music, wasn't enough to drown out the sound of a metal door opening. Multiple sets of footsteps were heard entering the room. He couldn't make out what they were doing but it sounded as though furniture was being dragged around. As one of the men moved closer to him, he heard the sound of a pistol being pulled from its holster. It was a distinct sound that he never paid much attention to until now. Leather, nylon and plastic all make different sounds when the metal sleeping pill dispenser is removed. This particular holster was plastic, which made him wonder for a second if his imprisoners were military. Most civilian holsters were leather or nylon. More importantly at that moment, was what exactly did this individual intend to do with it, now that it was drawn.

As he sat wondering if he would actually feel the bullet entering his head, or just immediately exit the land of the living, he struggled to have his life flash before him. Nothing was coming to him, no visions of his parents and the good times they shared as he was raised, no recap on what he had done in his life up to that point, no snap shots of things he had felt or experienced. *How do scientists even know that your life flashes before you?* He thought. *Everyone that had supposedly experienced it had died after all.* The thought of dying without his own personal blockbuster of epic proportion about his life, was beginning to upset him. Just as he had built up the courage to ask what they were waiting for; his hood was pulled away from his head. His vision slowly came into focus and he could finally make out his holding cell. It was a metal container similar to the ones used to ship goods overseas on container ships. He squinted to make out the ridges in the walls. They looked like large vertical sheets of corrugated metal.

He looked in the direction of the closest individual, the one who had un-holstered his weapon. As he gazed over, he saw the plastic holster clipped onto the man's right side attached to his belt. He also noticed that the barrel of the weapon was not pointed at him, but instead pointed at the ceiling with the magazine well pointed toward him. He again squinted, trying to make out the particular hold that the man had on his pistol. *Now why would he be holding his gun in that manner?* He thought. Obviously, Brayden was suffering from sleep and food deprivation, along with having been beaten into a stupor repeatedly. What was about to happen to him should have been apparent. He watched the man's arm as he raised the weapon from directly in front of him, upward toward the ceiling, then quickly change direction, moving swiftly downward toward his head, it was a very deliberate motion, there was no longer a question of his intent.

May 1999

CHAPTER 18

THE SOURCE HANDLERS course was the only training Brayden had missed during his instruction while in Virginia. James always said that out of all of the training, that was the most rewarding. He now had the opportunity to attend the Special Operations Forces or SOF version of the course. The school was close to five months long and covered a diverse range of surveillance, source handling and tradecraft techniques. It was here that Brayden shined; he enjoyed working with people in that manner. Most of those averse to the program were against it because they felt you were *using* people. This didn't bother Brayden at all; and it was an added thrill to avoid being caught. He learned a valuable lesson while training in one of the cities used for the teaching of the advanced skill.

His task that day, was to recon a route that could be used to get him to a meet site without being trailed, and at least be able to detect his followers if he was. He started out along his daily route driving a rented Chevy Malibu. Leaving the hotel and making his way to the nearby coffee shop to grab a mocha-to-go for the slow drive-in steady traffic to the city. As he made it into the grid, he found a parking spot near the college just on the outskirts and transferred to foot. His foot route was perfect, he had selected turns and stops with all the criteria needed to avoid and or detect any surveillance.

The establishment that he was casing, was very near a financial institution, had he taken this into account he may have had a better outcome. He checked the place to ensure multiple entry and exit points, and outlets to different roads or alleys. As he began taking pictures of the business, he inadvertently snapped a few in the direction of the bank. This particular area is a banking capital for that part of the country, and the manner in which he was taking pictures was viewed as suspicious. Within minutes Brayden was being questioned by the banks security and ultimately handed over to the local police. Because of the understanding that the course had with the authorities, he was later released, but from that moment on Brayden took the remainder of the course and source handling in general very seriously. Brayden wished that he could bring himself to call his old mentor James and tell him of his progression, but unbeknownst to Brayden, he had been keeping tabs on him for quite a while.

It wasn't long after the course that Brayden was required to put his skills to work. He was assigned to the embassy in Bogota, Colombia; this would be his first suit and tie assignment, working out of the defense attaché office. It was a surprisingly large embassy just on the outskirts of the city, planted firmly next to a residential area. A joint force of Colombian Army and U.S. Marines heavily guarded it. On his way to the embassy from the airport he noticed how divided the city was. It was truly the have and the have nots.

As the large SUV with diplomatic plates made its way down the long serine stretches of road into the city, you only needed to look left or right to see poverty that would make ghettos in the United States look like million-dollar condominiums. Openings in walls that were supposed to have windows, building tops lined with laundry drying in the hot sun, and general urban decay; things that Brayden had only seen in a National Geographic magazine up to this point in his life. As they entered into the city it looked like any other metropolitan area. Nice restaurants, malls, hotels, movie theaters; even the cars began to look more like home. As they started down the street that the embassy resided on Brayden noticed a long line of local nationals. Some people by themselves, others clearly couples, and of course entire families. He leaned forward to ask his driver what was going on.

"Why are all these people standing in line out here?"

"They are waiting to fill out a visa application for the United States. Most will be rejected, but this line is here every single day." The driver replied.

Brayden couldn't believe it, and even though he always knew Americans had it easier than most countries, in that moment it hit home.

As he walked through the embassy, he was actually relieved. He had been nervous about the work environment. Anything that involved being dressed up in a suit had to be a rat race, with people running around like idiots kissing the butt of the person above them to ensure their survival. However, this wasn't the case. Everyone had a purpose; analysts were busy with studies of the area and the population, intelligence collectors were reporting findings to decision makers, and non-government agencies were planning projects to help strengthen the country's infrastructure.

Brayden's job was unique; he was a liaison of sorts between the Special Forces (SF), the Defense Intelligence Agency (DIA) and the Defense Attaché Office DAO. He was tasked to find out what routes were being used to move drugs, equipment and money. Brayden thought it ridiculous and redundant as the DEA augmented with CIA had been doing this for years. He was very naïve to the fact that the DoD and State Department don't always willingly share information with each other. Still, Special Operations Command now wanted to build their own independent picture of the routes and means that the cartels were using to move drugs, money and personnel. These lines of communication are called ratlines by the military, and they would use this information to facilitate future Department of Defense operations.

It took a few weeks for Brayden to get used to his new assignment. He had never worked anywhere that required him to live in a five-star hotel; required him! He couldn't live in a low rent safe house on the outskirts of town if he wanted to, due to security risks. On a Special Forces Operational Detachment-Alpha, you could find yourself living in some dicey areas; but while there you lived and worked with the indigenous population you were training with and you inherently came equipped with a lot more firepower.

At the embassy, you had no fighting force at your disposal, and your given weapon was a pistol. Either you worked in a capacity that required you to operate as a singleton when necessary and accepted the risks, or you were shuttled to work day in and day out by an embassy driver. Brayden would be required to operate in both capacities.

Brayden had met the ambassador first thing after arriving to the embassy. Any person filling the position as a military liaison element was required to brief the ambassador on the mission they had been given. Jane Whitehall was prior service Air Force, so she had a soft spot for military personnel. This was not always the case with ambassadors, and Brayden was warned of this before his deployment. He briefed her the plan in a professional manner and didn't hide the possible veracity of the mission. It could be boring, or it could be thrilling, she understood the mission and its requirements and just asked that Brayden keep her informed. This translated into, *properly report to your higher, so that I can receive a report on your actions on my desk*. Brayden knew the drill, and he had no intentions of causing an international incident.

The following day he was set to meet the Chief of Station or CoS. He was a nice, jovial gentleman named Mitchel Ross. Brayden liked the man, but didn't take him at face value, he was the CoS for a reason, and usually it meant you earned your dues; translation, he was likely a master of deceit. The CoS is a senior intelligence representative or field agent that is assigned to a foreign country or post. They are in charge of all collection activities that occur on that soil, regardless of whether it is CIA, DIA or OGA. If you do not work directly for the CoS, he can't necessarily stop you from doing what you are assigned to do, but he can make it extremely difficult, or even aid in your removal from said country if your actions warrant it. This was the case for Brayden as he reported directly to the Colombian Theater Special Operations Command. He didn't work for Mitchel, but he did understand his surroundings and knew it could only benefit him to keep the CoS involved with his operations. Mitchel allowed Brayden to operate freely, with the request that he would cover down on some things for him when he was traveling to certain areas.

One such assignment was the counting of cellular towers in Melgar, a small city to the south of Bogota. This suited him well, as he was traveling there anyway to speak to a local national contractor that worked on the Tolemaida Airbase. Eduardo Manteo was an aircraft engine mechanic that was hired by an American company that contracted overseas. The company, Trenton Industries, was a large and diverse corporation that had contracts ranging from maintenance, to private security. They hired mostly from the population of the country they had contracts in, presumably to cut down on labor costs and increase profit margins. Brayden was scheduled to meet Eduardo in a small restaurant situated on the main highway into the small city. He had previously developed the strategies and methods he needed to put into action, to ensure that the meet was secure and successful. Brayden had already been seated for a while when Eduardo arrived. He insured to watch Eduardo and his surroundings to make sure that he hadn't been followed, he appeared to have arrived clean.

"Eduardo, how are you?" Brayden said offering his hand. Eduardo shook it firmly,

"I am fine thank you." He replied.

This was their initial meet, and Brayden's first time handling an asset. Although he had never worked with him, he felt that he knew a great deal about him. He had been studying his dossier for weeks, along with the packet of routes, locations and pattern of life information that had been built on him. Eduardo had worked as a civilian aircraft mechanic for the Colombian Air force before applying and being hired by Trenton. His access with the military post paid off, as it allowed his past handler's insight to the way information flowed there. At that time, the intent was to find out from whom in that Air force contingent, was information on operations and air insertions being leaked. Eduardo was able to almost single handedly identify the perpetrator.

Brayden had spoken with him on the phone a few times before Eduardo suggested a meet. He had information about a large private runway that he was flown into, to work on a turbo prop engine that was not properly routing exhaust while in flight.

"It struck me as strange", Eduardo started.

"I was flown out to a runway in an unmarked helicopter, owned by the company I work for, and about fifteen minutes into the flight I was asked politely to put on a hood. I complied, even though I thought it odd, and it was removed upon landing on a pristine dirt runway in the jungle. I fixed the engine and requested the aircraft logbook to enter the services provided and affirm its airworthiness. I was instructed that the logbook was actually kept at the Tolemaida airfield, as it was a company plane. I was returned in the same fashion and once back I looked for the logbook and could not find any reference to that aircraft. Maybe it's nothing to worry about, but I just thought it was strange. I didn't want to ask to many questions, so I just let it go."

Eduardo finished speaking, picked up his coke that arrived part way through his story and sipped nervously.

"Do you think you could remember the vicinity of this runway?" Brayden figured it was a long shot but asked anyway.

"No, I wish I had more information but I was hooded and we made lots of turns."

Brayden knew that the chances of finding this particular runway would be almost impossible with so little information. Lots of runways dotted the jungles that were used for both illicit and legal operations. This was beginning to seem like a waste of time. He learned in source handling school that sometimes an agent may have information for you that leads to something fruitful, and other times they just want to feel important, or collect money for their information. Brayden didn't believe Eduardo was motivated by money, but he didn't find anything particularly interesting about his story either. He decided to skip the runway location for now and ask about the company.

"Perhaps if you are invited to be a mobile mechanic again you can take a GPS."

Brayden said almost jokingly, Eduardo didn't smile.

"What about Trenton Industries, have you noticed anything other than this that makes you suspicious?"

Brayden knew that he was stretching, but he wanted to be as productive as possible while he was there. Eduardo looked inquisitive for a second, any and everything could be considered suspicious, this *is* Colombia he thought.

"Not really" he replied,

"Our lead mechanic doesn't know anything about maintenance of aircraft and we keep parts for aircraft that we don't service there, but I'm not privy to the interworking's of the company or what operations the company has around the country."

According to Eduardo's dossier, the accuracy of his information was about a seventy / thirty split, in favor of his information panning out most of the time. Without something to corroborate the information though, there was nothing Brayden could do except report his findings and see if anything came up linking to more material. Nothing he heard sounded like anything nefarious, a little strange, but not outside the norm for Colombia.

Checking into the company couldn't hurt though, so he made a mental note to speak with Mitchel for guidance in the matter.

Before departing the restaurant Brayden gave Eduardo a date, time and location for the next meet. Brayden paid the check for two beverages, one coffee and one coke, said his goodbyes to Eduardo and departed. It was still early in the day so he would be able to map cell towers and return before it was late. As he opened the door to his vehicle, he noticed a car parked at the start of the chain of buildings along the road, with two men seated inside. He had not noticed it before, and probably would have thought nothing of it, except the car was too nice for the area. Brayden had purposely taken an embassy car that was a little older and dated, and absent of diplomatic plates. Even the standard issue bullet resistant SUV wouldn't have stood out in Melgar like the mid-size BMW sedan that these two men were postured in. Brayden turned away naturally and entered his vehicle. He started the car and sat there for a few minutes, wondering what the chances were that they were there for him. He decided he was being paranoid and began to drive away. He hadn't even accelerated up to the speed limit before the men pulled into his lane of travel and began following him.

"Well, there goes my relationship with Mitchel, he only asked me to do one thing, geez." Brayden mumbled to himself.

He decided to drive the speed limit and obey all the traffic laws. This is what he was taught in the surveillance course. You do not want your pursuers to know that *you* know they are following you.

In the course he attended, he had done just that on one of his outings. He never tried to lose them or give them a reason to elevate the aggressiveness of their techniques. On this particular day though, they used him as an example before the transition into some of the more hostile tactics. Part of the way through his route, the surveillance team began speeding up and driving extremely close to his bumper. Brayden continued to drive as he had been taught up to that point. Then the team started to pull alongside and peer at him with malice; again, he kept his cool. Finally, a car that he hadn't even known was in play, slowed in traffic until he was forced to come to a stop allowing the trailing vehicle to pull alongside and extract him from the car. Needless to say, that was the introduction to combating progressively intimidating tactics.

The BMW driver appeared to be taking a page out of that chapter. As Brayden entered a traffic circle, the driver attempted to get along the left side of the car and coax him into turning down a side street, and side streets or alleyways in Colombia are not where you want to get trapped. Plenty of contractors and government workers had been beat, mugged, or kidnapped while traveling in alleyways; they simply don't offer enough options.

Brayden firmly pressed the gas pedal and avoided the suggested deviation. Once oriented back toward Bogota, he continued onto the freeway and headed back in the direction of the embassy. The men followed for a few miles, harassing him by tailing closely and appearing to pull alongside him before dropping back as Brayden accelerated and turned into their advances. After a few miles the men pulled off and Brayden continued the rest of the way clean, to the best he could tell.

He arrived back at the embassy and entered the parking area around the back of the building. He parked his car near the paint booth and walked to the guard stand occupied by Marines. It was after hours, so he requested a local national to drive him to his hotel. While waiting, he filled out an incident report to give to the advanced skills program manager in the morning. It briefly outlined the events validating the reason the vehicle needed to be repainted and relicensed. His driver arrived as he was finishing the paperwork, so he threw the request and pen in his briefcase and glanced inside it at the meager contents.

"Note to self," he said as he entered the vehicle,

"Remember to sign for your pistol in the morning."

On the way back to the hotel, he thought about the men that had clearly been following him. He hadn't really been anywhere out of the ordinary since he arrived in Colombia, and he surely hadn't met with anyone. No one except Mitchel knew that he was meeting with Eduardo, and there would be no reason for him to care. He didn't even know what Eduardo wanted to meet about until they were face to face. As the driver pulled into the pick-up and drop off area of the hotel, Brayden decided to clear his thoughts. Right now, he needed some dinner and a hot shower, he would send up his report in the morning and let Mitchel know what transpired.

June 1999

CHAPTER 19

SEVERAL HOLDING companies owned Trenton Industries. This information alone did not suggest criminal activities, but this was a common tactic used by cartels to own and influence businesses, and airplanes were a hot commodity to drug lords. Brayden sent up his report about the meet and requested any information available about Trenton Industries. He received a great deal of material about the companies dealing with other South American firms, and received evidence outlining the findings of an investigation that had taken place over a year ago, for the alleged aiding in the movement of equipment used to outfit drug labs. Obviously, this equipment by itself is not illegal to purchase or use, but in the quantity that it was being shipped, and to the country it was shipped to, it looked suspicious. The company was cleared and able to continue business as usual, but Brayden wanted more details.

He was able to call in a favor, luckily his connection to James Gaul paid dividends with Mitchel as he and James had attended a few courses together. James dug up the information Brayden was requesting after being approached by a colleague and made aware of Brayden's request. He scrubbed the info for classification and passed it along to Mitchel with a congratulatory theme expressed toward Brayden's accomplishments. Brayden felt ashamed that he had not kept very good communication with James and vowed to give him a call once he was back stateside. For now, he had to chase down what he thought was a lead.

Brayden called Eduardo and without divulging his findings asked if he had access to any of the companies' records. Eduardo thought he might be able to pull something from the shop computer as it was tied into the main office.

"What kind of records are you looking for?" Eduardo asked.

"Anything financial, something showing who they have dealings with on a regular basis; and any aircraft that are maintained on their books that you can't find records on." Brayden said.

Eduardo understood and gave him the code word for the location he would leave the storage device, if he was successful in retrieving anything. Both men hung up their phones and immediately removed the sim-chip to be replaced with another; each already knew which chip to emplace and the associated phone number.

Brayden thanked Mitchel for his help, briefly told him his plans to acquire more information, and returned to his office to study the route for the pick-up location.

The following day Eduardo completed his work as usual and began entering data into the computer located on the shop manager's desk. After entering his required data for the services performed that morning, he began looking for a way to download the company's financial information. He found a portal that required a password and he assumed it would house the material he was looking for. He removed a thumb drive from his pants pocket that he was given from his last source handler. He'd never used it before, but the instruction he was given while being trained was to plug it in if you ever run across a password-protected system. Brayden hadn't brought it up, but Eduardo figured it might be needed for this assignment. He plugged the device into the computer and opened up a folder entitled "key gen". He clicked on the program file inside and watched as it began randomly organizing numbers and letters into what he assumed was every code imaginable. It seemed like forever, and Eduardo didn't have much more time to be alone in the office. Within a few minutes the portal was open and he was presented with several choices, some benign and others with what he was seeking. He opened two different links, one for company finances, and another for property owned. He decided to download both files and was amazed at how long it would take to move a few bytes of information to another location. He glanced at his watch and at the wall clock, not knowing which one was more accurate. He decided to go with his watch since it was running faster, at either rate he didn't have much time. The manager was due back from lunch at any minute and most of the shop would be trickling back in behind him. He had ten percent of the file left to download when he heard the hanger door begin opening; one of the other mechanics was preparing to bring in a Learjet that needed the landing gear serviced. *The manager won't be far behind*, he thought. The file finished and he closed the portal and pulled the memory stick out of the computer without first ejecting it, and walked toward the time card machine to check out for his lunch break. He passed the manager as he had just punched in from lunch, smiled said hello, punched his card and left the hanger. The manager sat down at his desk and noticed a small message in the lower right corner of the desktop window, warning him that a media device was unplugged without first being ejected. He peered at the message with confusion, closed it and continued with his business, reading the Melgar Post.

Eduardo shot a confirmation text to Brayden stating *lunch was still on*, which meant he had achieved his assignment and was heading to the drop off point. He hurried to his car and began his trek into the city. He tried to look for active surveillance, as taught, as he maneuvered his way through the lunch hour traffic. Once in the city grid, he began his planned route used in order to detect anyone following him, before he parked and started the foot portion of his route.

Brayden was in a small café inside of a large mall in the heart of Bogota. He was sitting near a window on the second level, from there he could see a third of the ground floor and would be able to observe Eduardo as he moved along the last leg of his route. He would have visited the café regardless of whether Eduardo had been successful or not, to set a boring pattern for anyone that may happen to be keeping tabs on his whereabouts. Hopefully, from this vantage point, he would be able to tell if Eduardo was clean of surveillance, this had not been a location he had built himself.

Eduardo made his way to a parking garage after slowly weaving his way through several blocks. He wanted it to appear as if he had been looking for a spot on the street, before entering the garage. He backed into a parking space and waited for several minutes to observe what cars would pass him, no other cars appeared. He exited his car and began the remainder of his movement on foot. Once out of the garage, he walked toward the intersection he had just turned in from. There was a convenience store across the street, he made his way there and purchased a newspaper. While standing in line, he glanced out of the front windows of the store to look for any static locations that could be used to follow him into the drop, he appeared to be clean.

Eduardo walked into the mall from a side door and moved directly to a bench seat next to a large merry go-round. The mall was filled with happy children and their parents. The build-a-bear store, that was famous for bringing smiles to kids' faces and emptying parents' wallets and purses back in the United States, was conducting its grand opening, the first one in Colombia. Most were enjoying the festivities from afar, as the prices for this luxury service exceeded the financial capabilities of most Colombians. The TGI Friday's that had been put in the year before, was a favorite hangout for embassy staffers. The food was the same as it was in the states, thanks to frozen shipments and cookie cutter cooking techniques, and it was just as expensive.

Brayden noticed while dining there for the first time, that people would stare at the Americans as they devoured their appetizers, followed up by their entrées and topping everything off with dessert, all while sipping five-to-ten-dollar drinks. This was money that even most of the wealthier Colombians simply did not have to burn. It was very common to see a family sharing a large carbonated beverage, and splitting meals between at least two people to save money. Brayden vowed to remember this when conducting source operations, to avoid unnecessary attention at a time when he least needed it.

Eduardo opened his paper and began to read. Even if he were seen in the mall by someone that he knew, it would not seem out of place. He frequently visited the malls and small cafes in the area to people watch and read. He would walk around the malls sometimes in the early mornings, during the weekend or weekdays when he didn't have to work, as a form of exercise. He had seen this in an American television show and it fascinated him that senior citizens used malls for exercising. He thought it was brilliant, it afforded a certain level of security, and it kept you out of the elements, he became an instant fan.

Brayden, from his location in the café, could see Eduardo move into this position and began looking toward the entrances for signs of surveillance. Once satisfied, he finished his second coffee and monitored Eduardo for movement, before walking toward the escalator. Eduardo waited his full ten minutes before continuing his route. He was not aware that Brayden was now following him; he didn't even know he was there; his job was to complete the drop.

Anytime a source was to complete a drop, it needed to be monitored. You needed to ensure that it was actually your agent that completed the operation, and confirm that they hadn't been made while on the last leg of the movement. Obviously, if you observed someone you didn't recognize making the drop, you had a problem; and if your source was being followed, he had a problem. Even if the pursuers were not intending to interfere in an aggressive or active manner, you were still compromised and the entire operation was now in jeopardy.

As Eduardo entered a corridor just before the drop, Brayden noticed a man coming toward them that didn't quite fit in with the casual vibe that was in the mall at the time. He was wearing a full suit, expensive by appearance, which was unusual because most business professionals ate lunch at the smaller mall four blocks north; it had a nice size food court and wasn't as crowded during the day. This mall at the present time was family central, with kid-oriented stores and attractions specially catering for the grand opening event. That particular corridor led to the Movie Theater and video game lounge, the doors in that area of the mall only allowed you to exit; and no one with a suit would be watching a movie during this time of day, let alone playing video games.

As the distance closed between the three men, Brayden noticed the man removing a pistol from under his suit jacket, a silencer was attached. Brayden quickly ran toward the man and knocked the gunman's arm outward, opening his mid-section up. He throat jabbed him while maintaining control of the hand with the weapon and pushed him into the nearest opening away from the corridor, a women's restroom. Brayden grabbed the hand containing the pistol and began banging it on to one of the sinks in an attempt to dislodge it. He simultaneously released his neck and punched him in the groin. The gunman doubled over and with his left hand, reached for a knife in his boot. Brayden kneed him in the face and used his momentum to turn his hand into him and put him on his back on to the floor. He continued rolling his hand into him until it was pointed at his left shoulder and he squeezed the man's finger, pulling the trigger and shooting him. As the man relinquished control of the pistol, Brayden took a firm hold of it and shot the man again in the head.

Brayden wiped the pistol down with his shirt tail and threw it into the trashcan. He looked briefly under all of the stalls to ensure no one was present during the struggle. He attempted to calm down before exiting the bathroom, but he was shaken up by the experience and worried about Eduardo and the possibility that the gunman was not alone. As he exited, he looked around for signs of curiosity from passerby's, trying to get a feel for what commotion could have been heard, no one was fazed. He continued to the drop point, a small plant near the video game section in close proximity to the movie theater entrance. He knelt down and re-tied his shoelace that ironically was untied, dug around in the planter until he found the drive and continued out of the side exit from the mall.

At least Eduardo was able to make the drop, Brayden thought. That meant that he hadn't been picked up before leaving it, so he more than likely was clean. *Were they targeting me?* Brayden pondered while pulling out his phone to call Eduardo. He attempted to call, but it would not connect. Eduardo was not getting a signal in the parking garage and he had no reason to be expecting a call from Brayden. Brayden walked his route through the city, frantically thinking about what had just occurred. He called his driver and gave him instructions on where to pick him up, they went straight to the embassy.

Brayden explained everything about the mystery encounter to Mitchel before retiring to his office to write his report; it would likely take the remainder of the day. Unlike the movies, in the real world there is a great deal of reporting that is required after any type of communication with an asset. Moreover, you generally don't continue to work in an area after an altercation that ends in the loss of a life; Brayden would await Mitchel's verdict regarding his stay. If it were found that Brayden was being targeted, then he would have to be temporarily reassigned.

As he replayed the events of the day in his head, he began to wonder if he or Eduardo had been the mark. If there had been two attackers, surely Eduardo would not have been able to make the drop. He stopped typing, pulled out his phone and called Eduardo.

"Hello?" Eduardo answered the phone.

"How long did it take you to get back to work?" Brayden asked.

"About an hour, traffic was still pretty crazy." Eduardo replied.

"Ok, keep your phone on and if you think something is going awry text 191 to my phone." Brayden snapped.

"Are you alright?" Eduardo asked.

"Yes, I'm fine, thanks, I have to get back to work, take care."

Brayden hung up the phone quickly, switched out his sim card and removed the memory stick from his pocket. He abandoned his report for the moment and walked down the hall to the DIA office. They had an information technician on staff he had met when he first arrived in country, although he couldn't remember his name. He wasn't a technical surveillance analyst, but he was capable of exploiting digital media and right now Brayden needed anonymity. Brayden handed the man the device and asked if he could take a look at the contents, the man obliged and told him he would have the results in a few days.

"Once you have the results give me a call, I don't want this to be seen by anyone else until I've had a chance to look at it." Brayden said.

"Ok, no problem, you spooky types are weird." The man chuckled.

He locked the drive in his safe, to ensure it remained secure until he had the chance to exploit the contents. Brayden returned to his office and finished his report.

Eduardo had just finished up helping with the Learjet's landing gear, that came into the shop that afternoon. It needed a part they didn't have on hand so there was nothing more to be done until it arrived. He enjoyed working on aircraft and was very good at his job. He had never done anything else in his life. His father was a pilot for the Colombian Air force and also flew privately. Eduardo had always loved airplanes, but never got around to learning to fly himself. He had applied for the Air force to follow in his father's footsteps but being colorblind was a problem for the military flight program, and it was not waiver-able. He decided that working on planes was the next best thing and began helping out at a small local airport near his hometown. He eventually saved enough money to pay for formal training and applied for a job as a civilian working on military aircraft when he was twenty-two.

Eduardo packed up his bag that he carried daily with his coveralls, earmuffs and steel-toed boots. He could leave the items in a locker on site, but it was his ritual, plus he liked to wash his coveralls in preparation for the following day; they were his only pair.

On his drive home, he thought about the secrecy of the day and felt good about the fact that he may be of some help in an effort to finally bring an end to the wide spread corruption in his country. He hadn't thought about what he would do if he were successful in uncovering a conspiracy involving the company that he worked for; this had been his livelihood for several years. He would never find a job with as many benefits, and it paid better than anything he would find that was Colombian owned. He drove home pondering his options, wondering how useful he would be to people he helped at the embassy if he no longer had a job. It was a scary proposition, but so was the thought of cartels growing any stronger. Maybe he would apply for his visa to the United States, he thought Brayden might even help him if the information paid off.

The next morning, Eduardo arrived at work on time as usual, punched his card and began walking toward the main office. He reduced the speed of his stride when he noticed that just about every employee of the hanger was standing in, or just outside of the office. Eduardo slowed his walk even further and wondered whether he should turn around and leave, run even, and call Brayden and let him know that he had been made. Surely, everyone was standing around as some computer technician explained what Eduardo had done, and they were waiting for him to arrive before detaining him and calling the police or worse. He would be made an example of for all the remaining employees after his termination. As he reached the door, several people looked in his direction, Eduardo's throat went dry as he thought about what he would say in his own defense. He really hadn't done anything wrong; he was allowed on that computer. He did however use some kind of program that allowed him access to a restricted portal. He pulled out his phone slowly and prepared to text Brayden, hoping he could get him out of this predicament. As he moved closer and was able to see into the office, he saw a well-dressed man that he had never seen before; he introduced himself as a member of upper management.

"Hello Eduardo, I suppose you have heard the unfortunate news." Said the man.

"No" Eduardo replied,

"I have just arrived; I am not sure what is going on."

"Raphael Sandoz was murdered last night at his home. It appears he was strangled in his kitchen with some type of wire after retrieving his mail yesterday evening. His home was completely ransacked, we have no other details right now."

Eduardo was stunned. Why would this have happened? Did someone think that *he* had stolen the files from the computer? How would they have known that a file or two had been downloaded?

Trenton Industries had key loggers and keystroke recorders on every one of their computers. The programs were managed remotely by an administrator and used to keep track of who logged on at what time, and which information they requested during the course of their business. Raphael had access to certain information on the portal, as he was implicit in some of the activities that took place within the business; he also knew the kind of people he was in bed with, Eduardo did not.

Eduardo figured that it would only be a matter of time before whoever killed Raphael would be on to him. The entire shop was given the day off with full pay; Eduardo couldn't leave fast enough.

Eduardo called Brayden as soon as he was away from the airfield and convinced that he wasn't being followed. He was panicked from the ordeal, and now beginning to fear for his life. If the people that killed Raphael started to suspect that he wasn't actually the one to download the information. It wouldn't take much of an investigation to figure out who was there at the time the material was stolen. After the sixth ring he cancelled the call and immediately called his wife.

"Hello." His wife answered the phone sounding a little shocked he was calling so soon after leaving for work.

"Pack a bag for us and be ready to leave in fifteen minutes." Eduardo's voice was shaky.

"Why? What's going on? Are you on your way home now?"

"I don't have time to explain, I just need you to listen to me, and don't let anyone into the house until I arrive. If you see anything out of place, call the police."

Eduardo hung up the phone without waiting for his wife to acknowledge what he had told her. He again dialed Brayden's number, pleading with the handset for him to pick up.

"Eduardo what's up?" Brayden answered.

"I'm in trouble. The hanger manager was found dead in his home this morning and I think it was because of me. They are going to find out and kill me. I need to get my wife and I out of here, today." Eduardo was almost hysterical at this point.

Brayden held the phone for a second allowing what Eduardo had just told him to register. He thought about his options and the fact that *he* may actually be forced to leave the country soon.

"What are you doing right now?" Brayden asked.

"I'm on my way home to pick up my wife and then we are going to drive into the city. I don't know where to go but I can't stay in my home and wait to be murdered. We will have more anonymity in the city." Eduardo rattled.

"Go to the Essa Hotel and let me know when you are there." Brayden told him.

Brayden hung up the phone and walked to Mitchel's office to give him a full report. If he wasn't fully convinced that there was something shady about the way the company conducted business, he was now. Mitchel promised to help and told him he would assign one of his handlers to

Eduardo's case and protect he and his family the best they could. Brayden didn't tell him about the thumb drive however; he wasn't sure how much he could trust him at this point. The CIA had a way of stealing your good sources if they began to produce. Brayden didn't know it, but that wasn't the only reason he shouldn't trust him.

Brayden submitted his paperwork through the Theater Special Operations Command, and sent a copy of his findings to Mitchel as a courtesy. He included a relocation request and justification for Eduardo and his family, even recommending him for transfer to the U.S. and wished that he could remain in Colombia long enough to see it through. He was being reassigned after a brief visit stateside for some obligatory psychological testing.

Brayden knew that bad things happened in the world all the time, but until he had experienced it first hand, it was just another form of entertainment on the television. Moving through the jungles with an indigenous force, ready to make contact at any moment was one thing. You know the enemy is on patrol as well and is protecting something or someone, so exchanging lethal greetings is expected upon discovery. However, a great deal of underhandedness took place in cities, districts, towns and villages all over Colombia, South and North America and other developed, developing or impoverished countries around the globe. You will seldom find armed guerrillas in that environment, there you will find deep rooted corruption, drug running, prostitution rings filled with women brought in through human trafficking and contract killings; but it had never occurred to him that he would actually see that side of it up close and personal. He wasn't even convinced that he had. He needed to know what was on that drive, could it really be that revealing? Really? Something pulled off a computer in an airplane hangar? Brayden didn't want to believe it, but two men were dead, and more than likely because of it.

August 2001

CHAPTER 20

BRAYDEN HAD OFTEN HEARD the phrase "Being beaten to within an inch of your life", but had never quite understood what it meant until now. As he slowly regained consciousness, he noticed that he had been moved from his metal box and now lay on the floor of what looked like a make shift cabin. He struggled to make sense of the sequence of events thus far. He had been beaten multiple times over multiple days and no one had spoken a word to him except the mystery man with blonde hair. Surely someone was looking for him, but until now he had no way of leaving signs of life.

To his surprise, he had been dressed in his tattered and stained BDUs, minus the ghillie portion of the garb. He almost chuckled aloud while thinking of these hardened criminals redressing his deadweight, ragdoll like body. He was not restrained at the time, but it didn't matter as he was in no position to attempt an escape. There was a glass of water and plate of food on the floor in front of him, but even if he could slide himself to it, he didn't think he could eat or drink it because of his likely broken jaw, and the accompanying severe swelling to his mouth. He suddenly heard movement behind him but he could not position himself to see who it was. Two men gently put their hands into his armpits from behind and pulled him up into a chair. His body shuttered in pain as he flexed from the movement, he suspected he had broken ribs, and possibly internal bleeding. He was surprised that the men were handling him with such care. As the men backed away the blonde gentleman came into view. Brayden looked at the man, trying to focus through the haze of pain, and locked eyes with him in utter and pure disbelief.

It was his sponsor, the man that helped him submit his packet to attend the Special Forces Assessment and Selection. The same man that he had later met in Australia, sometime after the Special Forces Qualification Course, to attend a technical surveillance course called Brimley. He knew he had been an operator, but he thought he had long since retired to a farm somewhere in Middle America. The last time he saw him was at a course he was enrolled in, not dissimilar to SERE, taught by the Joint Personnel Recovery Agency. His name was Steve Landers; and he had considered the man a friend. He was six feet tall even, had blonde hair, blue eyes and a medium but muscular build. His age was starting to show, but by no means did this make him appear less of a threat.

"I would ask you how you're doing Brayden but I pretty much know the answer to that one." Steve said with a slight chuckle.

Brayden didn't say a word. He sat as still as he could muster staring at Steve as steadily as he could. He was starving, angry, confused, and hurt. He wanted to leap forward and have a futile go at him, but all he could muster was a stream of tears. He felt betrayed, but at the same time, somehow relieved that Steve was there; even though he suspected he had to be working with the cartels now.

"What is going on?" Brayden muttered through his injuries, faintly, feeling now with the first words he had spoken since the beatings, that he was possibly about to lose a few teeth. Still, trying to speak as clearly as he could, all while trying not to burst into tears.

"You tell me." Steve said in a calm and soothing voice, showing very little emotion. Brayden felt helpless and ashamed as he considered telling him the nature of the mission. If he did, it would violate everything he was taught in his training about hostage situations. "Remain in your circle." It's what you learned in SERE school, to only give the information that is required to remain a legal combatant in accordance with the Geneva Convention. If caught during war, you really only needed to hold out for a few hours, at a minimum, long enough for your unit to know you were taken hostage so any plans you were aware of could be changed. It was a fallacy that you could hold out forever. He remembered hearing that in movies, but now knew it to be impossible.

Being a peacetime hostage was different, and Brayden had been to several courses that prepared him for the rigors of being detained by a country in which the U.S. had no status of forces agreement, but were still bound by law to treat you in the same manner they would a criminal in that country. Or, by being remanded by entities that did not recognize any common thread laws, like terrorist cells, cartels etc.; which was the worst situation you could be in, and was his current predicament.

He had been caught while conducting a non-U.S. sanctioned action, with the U.S. able to claim plausible deniability and captured by a non-state actor that had no legal or moral binding to affect his safe return. The only hope he had was to be allowed to write a letter home, as a proof of life; or to be put in front of a TV camera, to be broadcasted to the world. Neither was likely to happen. Steve had been to the same training as Brayden, probably more. He understood how the system worked and so far as Brayden could tell, he had no intentions of allowing him to leave or be found.

Brayden lowered his head deliberately and let the last shred of hope leave his body, visibly seen in his posture as he dropped his shoulders in defeat.

"I was sent to kill Javier Rolando," said Brayden.

Rolando was a mid-level member of the southern cartel that called themselves Tiko's Gentlemen. They were known for kidnappings for ransom, drug trafficking and massive marijuana grows; they started in the late 80's. In the early 90's they began standing up para-military groups, most were unsuccessful due to the lack of guidance or direction, but by 1999, they had organized themselves into full fledge members of the Revolutionary Armed Forces of Colombia or the FARC. The FARC had grown to be a legitimate, lethal fighting force with numbers escalating to and through the thousands thanks to the safe havens President Casper negotiated to keep the peace in Colombia. By 2000 the FARC had successfully aligned cartels and provided them the security force that they needed to openly defy the country's laws. Large cocaine manufacturing facilities began to crop up in the unpopulated jungles of Colombia and they were permitted to operate for the most part untouched. The DEA at the time did not have the ability to fight this problem. The environment was harsh, they were outnumbered and the firepower was overwhelming. The U.S. Special Forces (USSF), also known as Green Berets, had been operating in Colombia and other countries in South America for decades. Their mission was and is, to train and advise their target countries military or in some cases para-military force, in Unconventional Warfare techniques to effectively combat enemy factions with the potential to affect U.S. interests. It also gave leverage to policy makers when negotiating foreign strategies. The SF teams working in Colombia were experts in jungle warfare. They lived, ate, slept and patrolled with their counterparts during their three-to-four-month rotations, with a roughly six-month re-fit back at their home station. Although not approved to conduct combat operations, they frequently encountered pockets of resistance while on "training missions" with their host nation counterparts, and on occasion, they were given a green light to conduct clandestine operations other than war. Brayden had been assigned by higher headquarters to conduct one of these missions.

The train up was minimal, as his team had been operating in this particular area for the past two years. He had graduated the Special Operations Target Interdiction Course, SFs version of the U.S. Army Sniper School, less than two years ago and kept his skills honed post-graduation. He loved working as a small element, and even though a Special Forces Operational Detachment-Alpha or SFOD-A is only 12 men deep at best, he enjoyed the added intricacy of deploying as a one or two-man team. The decision to move into the over watch position solo was not taken lightly. The SFOD-A conducted an exhausting amount of planning before allowing that particular course of action to play through to fruition. It came down to minimizing exposure, maximizing stealth, coordination of required assets and non-negotiable abort criteria. Everything aligned so the mission was a go. Three detachment members and a platoon (-) of Colombian Army would remain in a Mission Support Site or MSS. The MSS is a defendable position, usually in the form of a triangle, terrain dependent. The most casualty-producing weapon, usually a heavy machine gun, is oriented on the most likely avenue of approach. The other two tips of the triangle should have a light automatic machine gun minimum. Everyone else would fill in the space on the line between these systems. If you were to remain overnight in this position it would then be finished with shallow firing positions, aiming stakes, range cards and a slit trench for relieving one's self. This is commonly referred to as a patrol base. But this was temporary.

Each element had their contingency plans worked out, radios set to the proper frequencies easing the ability to coordinate amongst each other, higher command, and all supporting assets. Colombian support and attack aircraft would be put into an orbit and a ROZ or Restricted Operating Zone would be established in the event close air support was needed. A ROZ allowed military aircraft to occupy airspace without the fear of monitored commercial or private traffic entering it. It also provided the aircraft controller on the ground an invisible cube of space to position all military aircraft that he controlled, limiting the area that the aircraft operated in. This made it easier for him to bring them in during an emergency. Close air support is the ability to have air nearby, able to respond to an expedient exfiltration, air to ground attack fires, or medical evacuation.

All SFOD-A members were in the Colombian Army uniform, and outfitted with standard issue Colombian Army equipment, to include weapons. This allows for complete U.S. government deniability should a mission go sideways. Each of them knew the risks and collectively they accepted them. They infiltrated the area on foot with their indigenous partner force, established the MSS and pushed elements forward into a Release Point, or RP. The RP is used when multiple elements have departed the MSS. They navigate to an easily distinguishable point, and separate to move to their final respective positions. Depending on the scope of the mission, a contingency security element can also remain in the RP as a quick reaction force, should an element need to break contact and fight their way back to that point. Brayden would depart the RP and move the final two kilometers on his own.

The remaining half of the platoon of Colombian Army Commandos would remain in the RP with one SFOD-A member and establish a Casualty Collection Point. In the event it was needed, they could defend this position for a short time until moving back to the MSS; there they would have a reserve element, the remaining platoon and SFOD-A members, to combat a pursuing force. The distances between these operational hubs can vary, and for this particular mission, and the current environment, they were great. The separation was needed to maintain a low operational signature in the target area.

Brayden continued, "The intelligence that we received suggested that he was next in line to head up a new crop of drug labs being established just outside the safe zone that Colombia and the U.S. had negotiated with them. The strategic thinking? If he were to be taken out, it would slow momentum and possibly halt operations temporarily. Honestly, that's all I know."

Brayden spoke slowly; he figured there was less harm in starting out with the obvious. Perhaps Steve would let it go at that, honestly, he knew better but it was worth a try. At least it would buy him some time. Steve stared at him without blinking or moving a muscle. He looked as though everything he was hearing denied all rationale. He let out a quick breath, and shook his head slowly, almost as if to say he didn't believe anything that he was being told. He glanced away for a brief second, cracked a very slight smile, and then looked back up at him and coldly replied with a response that made Brayden sick to his stomach,

"Brayden, the man you killed was not Javier Rolando."

September 1999

CHAPTER 21

THE LIGHT BAR AT the tail of the C130 turned from red to green. The ramp at the aft end of the aircraft was already open, and looked like a giant television screen showing a picturesque scene of the sun setting beautifully behind the ocean's horizon. Brayden didn't remember seeing anything as beautiful while he was learning to jump in Yuma, Arizona while in High Altitude Low Opening or HALO school. The barren desert that you stared at while making jumps was nothing special to see, and while you were a student you were more concerned with body position and remaining stable while falling than anything else. Jumping during the day was just ok; jumping during the night was downright scary. With full combat equipment, consisting of your rucksack, weapon and night vision goggles so you could see where to fly; it felt like it was only a matter of time before you were a human lawn dart. Brayden enjoyed flying, and he absolutely loved to scuba dive, but conducting a HALO jump from a perfectly good aircraft while in flight was not for him. It was a necessary means of infiltration, which is the only reason why he continued to do it.

The flight from Florida wasn't that bad, he had slept for most of it and only within the last hour and half had he and the rest of the team began moving around the back of the aircraft. They checked and donned their parachutes, and ensured that their oxygen masks worked before the pressure was lost in the tail end of the aircraft, in preparation for opening the ramp. They checked their boats that were rolled and strapped down to wooden pallets and ensured that the parachutes attached to them were hooked up and ready to deploy once pushed out of the plane. Nap of the earth flying had ended and the aircrew began the climb up to 25,000 feet as they prepped to depart. They would slowly begin decreasing speed to a safe pace that would allow the team to exit without incurring injuries. They began moving toward the door, checking the Draeger underwater breathing apparatus one last time before the fall. Now, as he stood looking at the beautiful scene, he was ready to put all of his training and preparation to use.

The SFOD-A methodically began exiting the back of the plane flying a steady flight path at 27,000 feet, and one by one each of them began establishing a stable arch position for the remainder of the fall. They formed up and continued their descent toward the ocean, checking their altitude as they fell, in preparation for the pull. After almost two minutes of freefall, at 5000 feet above ground level, they began to deploy their parachutes. The men stacked in a stair case like manner and corkscrewed toward the ocean, each following the other. Just before preparing to land, they fanned out to their own piece of real-estate and pulled downward on the toggles to slow themselves before making contact with the water.

Immediately upon touch down they activated their floatation devices, removed their oxygen masks, disconnected their chutes and began swimming to the three bundles that had been pushed out by the aircrew before they followed them out of the plane. Each pre-determined four-man element quickly retrieved their bundle and began cutting away the parachutes and nylon straps that held them in place. The enclosed zodiac combat rubber raiding craft, with engine was inflated via a pre-staged and connected single cylinder scuba tank. Once inflated, they boarded the craft and put the engine into operation. At fifteen miles off shore, no one would be able to hear the specially designed 55 horsepower engines from land.

Each boat signaled that the other was up and ready, and began traveling on azimuth to the infil point. At five miles off shore the engines were stopped, the men removed their HALO harnesses and packs, donned their fins and masks, and ensured the dive surface valve on their already rigged and attached Draeger re-breathing system, was closed in preparation to turtle back. Each boat took turns splashing divers and once they were all in, they tactically sank the boats. They formed into two, six-man teams, each with one navigator and they began their surface swim to shore. The compass man positioned the nav-board on his chest as they swam on their backs toward the objective. Once inside two kilometers the men stopped, purged their pure oxygen closed loop dive system of all carbon dioxide, gave each other the diver down signal, and went sub-surface. A bud line connected the six-man element to each other. The navigator swam in front with the other five individuals staggered behind him to give enough room for fin travel.

As they moved along in symbiotic harmony through the warm waters, Brayden thought about arriving to his SF Company as a Navy diver. He wore his bubble proudly and assumed that since he had been to dive school that he would be immediately assigned to the dive team, and he was. He walked into the team room of SFOD-A 715 with his Navy credentials leading the way. His achievements were instantly deflated; he may have been a diver, but he was by no means a combat diver.

The Combat Diver Qualification Course, or CDQC was in sunny and beautiful Key West Florida. Brayden arrived in shape and ready to train. The grueling five-week course was nothing like the scuba school he attended in the Navy. The first two weeks, called pool week, covered events including Navy drown-proofing, equipment recovery, sub-surface knot tying, buddy rescue, and the dreaded weight belt swim. If you were still around after that, you began your open and closed-circuit swims. Diving was one thing, but swimming horizontally with dive equipment for time and accuracy, while maintaining a transit depth of no deeper that twenty-five feet, attached to a swim buddy and still able to hit the beach and walk for miles to the actual objective; was a completely different animal. Brayden enjoyed the challenge, and was glad to serve with like-minded men. Now, off the coast of Central America, he put his school-trained skills to the test with his entire combat diving SFOD-A.

Just as they had practiced in the schoolhouse and on subsequent training missions, each six-man team had their own azimuth to swim, a point fifty meters from each other on the beach. Once they were close, they conducted tactical peeks to ensure they would hit the correct spot. At one hundred meters out, a two-man clearing team was sent up from each six-man element. They removed their three-day assaults packs at depth and prepped their weapons for the assault. Each clearing team purposefully exited the water, with their weapons at the ready, and cleared the beach while simultaneously looking for their linkup point.

They could see a vehicle on a road no more than two hundred meters away. One of the men signaled with two flashes of a concentrated beam of light and the vehicle responded with four, the correct response. The scout swimmers gave the safe signal to the remaining divers and they made their way ashore. The SFOD-A moved tactically toward the vehicle and gave a verbal bonafides before actually conducting the meet. They moved toward the vehicle and began removing their gear as another vehicle moved up to assist in carrying the weary detachment. "Welcome to Costa Rica." One of the sister team members said, as he helped remove gear and place it in the back of the truck. They would be staying with another team from their company that was in country conducting training with the Costa Rican drug enforcement police. They had to come in under the radar, as Costa Rica would not allow more than twelve USSF members in their country at one time. Nor did they want any personnel with their level of training roaming around the country without a formal dossier; because of the way they entered, they couldn't be identified. They also did not know they were there to augment the DEA and assist in intercepting drug runners. The detachment made their way to the safe house that had been coordinated for them and made comms with the DEA before getting some much-deserved slumber; they would need it for the coming days.

CHAPTER 22

COSTA RICA WAS BEAUTIFUL, and enjoying it from a beachfront safe house sitting on fifteen acres, was amazing. Brayden woke up early and took advantage of the ocean that was lapping up onto the shore a mere fifty feet from the back balcony. He grabbed his swim gear, consisting of fins, mask and booties, and made his way out into the clear water. He found a small natural reef not far off the shore and headed toward it. The reef sat at a depth of only twenty feet, so diving down on a breath-hold was not a problem. The coral arrangement was riveting, switching back and forth between white, green, yellow, brown and fire red. Eels, seahorses, parrot fish and other aquatic creatures swam around in their ecosystem completely oblivious of the one just above them.

Brayden swam around the reef, diving down and searching for sand dollars and uninhabited shells as if he were on an island resort, without a care in the world. It was moments like these that made him wonder why man was so greedy. The need to explore and exploit the surface had driven men into a perpetual fight for resources. Powerful countries had good reason to interfere with the affairs of developing or poverty-stricken nations; to keep them resource poor in order to continue building and strengthening their own superiority. Besides, not everyone could live on the scale of the current super powers, as the world's resources couldn't support it. Battling against corruption and greed was the premise that many powerful nations used in order to invoke their will on the masses. Ironically though, the same men entrusted to better the plight of the people they represented, also used that trust to exploit a flawed system and make themselves more powerful, and usually by any means necessary. Here however, just twenty feet below the surface, was a pure, synergetic community, that thrived off of a strong survival instinct, but without the flaws of imperfect reasoning and intelligence; called greed and deceit.

After a quick glance at his watch, Brayden knew that the fantasy was over, and it was time to get back to his known reality, the world marching on above him. He swam back to the beach just in time to meet the DEA team that his detachment would be working with. As they made their introductions, each one extending their right hand for the requisite nice to meet you hand shake. While purposely waiting until both parties' hands had clasped, to commit to removing their G-man sunglasses from their faces in a vain attempt to appear more personable, Brayden's gaze stopped instantly on the only female in the group. As she turned her attention to Brayden, her facial express changed to a look of almost horror. Brayden, squinting through the sun that was virtually blinding him, shining directly in his eyes, focused just well enough to see the only woman on the planet that he wished he could forget; Lisa Tippis.

June 1990

CHAPTER 23

IT WAS A GORGEOUS summer day in June and the only day that really counted all year as far as Brayden was concerned. June 11th, which was Brayden's birthday, had been spent with family every single year up to this point in his life. He would receive his presents from his parents, open them and truly be grateful for what he received, and then go to his grandparent's home to relax with them for the remainder of the day. It was an observance that he could actually see the meaning of. All other holidays had lost meaning to him long ago. Yes, his family taught him the importance of Thanksgiving, Christmas, Easter and the like, but the nation at large looked at those days as a way to increase consumer spending, increase consumer debt thus further adding to the stressors of life. His birthday was a random day. It was impervious to commercialism, couldn't be exploited by the news media, didn't contain any must see sporting events or parades. It was his private anonymous moment, something that he and his family could celebrate for the true meaning; being thankful that you had lived yet another year that was not promised to you. He relished the purity of it.

This year however, he would be spending it with the love of his life, the girl that he would love into adulthood, and eventually wed, grow old, and die with. The notion of marrying your first love seemed foreign to many, but to Brayden it seemed like the natural progression of life. Too many people wanted more than what they had, leaving behind the one that mattered, the one that truly played their heart strings, only to later be lost and searching for the soul mate they once had and let go. Brayden was by no means a romantic; he had two wonderful role models in his grandparents. Young lovers that knew they were a perfect match, married just before his grandfather shipped off to World War II now still married, with seven offspring, forty years later, just as in love with each other as the day they said *I do*.

He was a realist, and to him what he felt for Lisa was as real as feelings got. Everything around him disappeared while in her presence, he loved to converse with her about anything, even disagreeing at times, strengthening their bond while working through their differences. They laughed, loved, and cherished each other more than anything they had up to that point in their young lives, but Lisa wanted something more; or so she thought.

Brayden bid his parents farewell as he left the house in route to his girlfriend's. He arrived at her house around noon and was surprised to see a few cars already in the driveway; their alone time would have to wait. Upon entering the house, he immediately noticed the effort she had put forth in the birthday décor. It brought a smile to his face that increased into pure giddy when he noticed a couple presents and a giant card and balloons in the living room. Lisa met him in the main living space as she heard him come in and jumped in his arms and kissed him.

"Happy Birthday sweetheart!" she whispered in his ear.

Brayden eased the tension in his arms to allow her to fall away from him and plant the tip toes of her feet back onto the floor, just enough to look her in the eyes, then he pulled her close again to give her a meaningful kiss. A few friends that had already arrived came up from playing pool in the basement and wished Brayden a joyful day as well.

It wasn't long before the music was blaring, beer bottles were opening, and the grill was sending up delightful fragrances. Brayden was the chef for the day, churning out marinated chicken, burgers and hot dogs. As the driveway began to fill up with members of the schools various sporting teams, club members and their guests, Brayden was starting to miss having the hostess by his side. He turned the grill over to one of his teammates and wondered off into the sea of hormones to find his girl. After a sweep of the main living areas, he walked down the stairs to the basement. As he made his way down the stairwell, he ducked slightly to allow his head to pass under the floor joist. As he cleared it and was able to peer through the enlarging opening to the ceiling of the lower half of the home, he saw Lisa on the couch in the arms of another boy. She was sit-laying across his lap; Brayden loved when she did that to him; kissing him with full tongue. Brayden stopped on the stairs and watched in silence not able to think of what words could be uttered at that moment. They must have noticed him in their peripheral when they came up for air. They both looked his way as Lisa's face turned from delight to trepidation, she quickly jumped up from the boy's lap and began heading in his direction with excuses. The boy she was kissing was a tennis player that had received a partial scholarship to Kent University, the same college Lisa was attending. A small, scrawny, almost sickly-looking kid, that excelled at swinging oversized flyswatters at doggie chew toys. Brayden was mortified. It was the first time in his life that he had ever reached a point where he wanted to cry for emotional reasons instead of pain, and there was a difference. When you took a hard blow on the football field, the kind that would cripple a normal human being, a hit that leaves you lying on the field for some time after the play. A tear, or ten, may stream down your face, brought on by the sheer magnitude of what your body had just endured. Men understood those tears, they could relate, it resonated deep in their manhood, understanding that pain can bring a warrior to his knees. But emotional pain cannot be seen, so the act now looks weak and feminine. This was not acceptable, so Brayden had no choice but to leave quickly and deal with what he had just witnessed at a later date.

As he drove home, he wanted his heartbreak and disappointment to turn into rage, but it wouldn't. He wanted to gear himself up for battle and treat the boy to a public ass whipping, but he couldn't. All he could do was think about how much he cared for her, and the fact that it would never be the same.

His birthday had lost its thrill. The school year was over; he would never see Lisa in that setting again. He wouldn't return her phone calls, and he departed for college without making any attempt to see her. He often wondered over the years if it was the way he ended up with her that was his downfall. After all, he had dated another girl with every intension of dumping her for Lisa at his earliest convenience. It was karma and he knew it, and from that day forward he promised to never use his ability to influence people he cared about for his own personal gain. He dated other women as he got older and had steady girlfriends for varying lengths of time, but he could never get Lisa out of his mind. Everyone was compared to her; no one could live up to the shrine he had built for her in his mind. He accepted the fact that he would never see her again, thus never having to revisit that chapter. He was over her he thought, just waiting to meet the right woman to settle down with and completely bury her once and for all.

Now he was standing face to face with her, with waves of emotions beginning to overcome him. After all those years he still loved her and he knew it; perhaps now he could get some closure.

September 1999

CHAPTER 24

BRAYDEN EXTENDED HIS hand and firmly shook Lisa's.

"Lisa, how have you been?" Brayden said confidently with an amazingly genuine smile.

"Fine." She replied timidly.

Everyone looked at the two of them as if waiting for the back-story on how they could possibly know each other. Brayden could see the anticipation building on each of the onlooker's faces and decided to break the awkward silence.

"Oh" said Brayden in a matter-of-fact manner,

"We went to high school together."

Lisa could not believe the man that she saw in front of her. Mature, handsome, incredibly fit, and apparently over the incident he had witnessed in her basement.

The group continued to familiarize with each other as they setup a time for the DEA to bring the SFOD-A up to speed on the problems they were facing and the reason the team was needed there in the first place. Brayden dismissed himself so he could get dressed for the day and prepare for the aerial and sea reconnaissance the agents had planned for them that afternoon, to better orient the detachment to the situation before developing a plan.

The detachment split into two teams, one would take the boat ride, the others would get the aerial tour. Brayden was with the half that traveled by helicopter and Lisa was with his group. As they traveled to the nearby helicopter landing zone Brayden came to the realization that he and Lisa would have to talk at some point, there was no way they could spend that much time together and not bring up the past, but for now it was all business.

They boarded the aircraft and departed in route to Puerto Carrillo. It was suspected that drugs and money were being moved by air from Colombia, with a brief stop in Panama, then terminating the air portion in Puerto Carrillo. It would then move by submarine from there up the coast to Isla Plato, an island not far off the coast of Flamingo Mexico, and then put into cigarette boats and moved up the coast of Mexico to the U.S. border. From there it could be hauled or 'muled' into the United States with very little resistance from the Mexican authorities, who were busy with their own civil unrest, and of course get over the U.S. boarder with no problem. Catching them was difficult but not impossible, stopping them was simply not an option for the DEA alone. They needed personnel trained to confront an aggressive force head on, with the firepower to level the field, and the USSF fit the bill.

Their plan began with observation. The DEA had been trained in surveillance techniques, so they could aid in developing pattern of life for the areas they suspected were being used as crossover points. Once they had successfully pinpointed the smuggling routes and their link up points, they could exploit the weakest point and hopefully inflict enough damage to at least disrupt the flow long enough for them to feel it financially. Successfully destroying equipment, product and even hard currency could set the cartels back months if not years if done correctly and succinctly. It would also force them to replace key leaders within the organization either because of attrition, lack of trust, or the loss of confidence in their abilities. Either way it would slow the flow of drugs into the U.S., and give the Colombian government a chance to strike the cartels while they were on their heels. Disrupting their freedom of movement was first. This tactic would likely demand the larger players to surface, if only for a brief moment, to settle any problems and get the smuggling routes working smoothly again; they would be risking their identity, but they would have no other choice.

Once back at the safe house the team began to plan. They studied nautical charts, tides, waves and current data along with moon phases to help them plan their dives. The submarines would be their least vulnerable and most valuable assets, and worth the risk involved to destroy them if they could find them. The detachment surmised that they must travel at night in order to avoid detection, but they had to be stored somewhere during the day. The DEA believed that they sank and camouflaged them during the daylight hours and when they were not in use. Covering them with something to help them blend into the ocean floor. Perhaps they ran some sort of small business, or at a minimum owned the area where the vessels were stored, which would explain not being able to find them despite their, what one would think, obvious presence.

The DEA would patrol the shore in teams, aboard non-attributable marine vessels, posing as fishing charters, tour-guides and pleasure cruisers. Hopefully they could identify some areas of interest and limit their pattern analysis to those key locations. They had four months to achieve effects, after that, the joint federal and department of defense experiment would be over.

October 1999

CHAPTER 25

AFTER ONE MONTH of constant observation, they narrowed their efforts down to one location, Mr. Ripper's Fishing Charter. This was the only charter in the area without steady business. The charter had made one outing in the past month, compared to the fifteen to twenty charter average for the other services in the area. Lisa and another agent even attempted to book an outing with them. It was cancelled because they hadn't met the minimum number of passengers required for an expedition, likely intentionally.

Initially the DEA had worked up a plan to emplace a listening device in the main office. This would require entry into the building either clandestinely or overtly, the latter not being feasible as no Americans really worked in that area; and as a tourist you were limited to the holding area in the front of the office. The detachment didn't want to take the chance of a surreptitious entry, as being detected would likely cause the group to go to ground, closing operations temporarily or opening another ratline that would take them months to find. They operated the charter for a reason, so the target would be the boats. The dive team devised a plan to install tracking devices onto the bottom of the vessels. This would allow them to track their movement patterns without devoting personnel to the task, increasing the risk of compromise. The devices were magnetic which was not necessarily a good thing when dealing with marine vessels other than naval ships, the benefit to them was that the magnet was electronic and could be controlled remotely. If the power source to the magnet were terminated via a radio signal, the device would fall away reducing the chance that it could be found if a sweep of the boats bottom was conducted.

Brayden was very familiar with ship bottom searches. He had conducted hundreds. Boats came in all sizes and each provided its own set of problems. The first thing they would have to overcome was the resin that the boats were made from. The magnet would not work on these surfaces, and tacking the device down would defeat the purpose of its design. The most obvious place to put a device was directly on the bottom, it would be detected within seconds of splashing divers. Brayden suggested affixing it to the aft portion of the vessel near or in between the screws. This area usually had some sort of metal plate to add to the stability, decreasing the amount of torque applied to the transom during acceleration and tight turns at high speeds. Additionally, it was near the working end of the vessel, no diver really liked to remain in that area for any significant amount of time, regardless of the status of the moving parts, because of the rare but possible chance it was fired to life.

The team agreed on the method and began researching the type of boats Mr. Ripper's operated in preparation for the mission. Six divers led by Brayden would swim into the marina through the harbor on Draeger's and attach the devices onto the three boats they had tied there. A second device, called the trigger, would be installed on the lower portion of the dock, out of sight from the surface. The trigger is a larger device designed to remain stationary and emplaced in a location where its rather large battery box can be hidden. If the tracking device moved out of a predetermined radius, the trigger would active it, and send a signal back to the rover device which would audibly let the observer/tracker know that his or her target was on the move. This reduced the amount of battery power that was required by the tracking device, and was required when the tracking device was on a constantly moving object like a marine vessel, or else the battery would die in a matter of hours. The only thing holding them up was an execution confirmation from higher headquarters.

CHAPTER 26

MANY ORGANIZATIONS THAT hadn't worked well with each other in the past, were now working in unison to disrupt the processes that were making the cartels successful. The particular Line of Operation or LOO that the SFOD-A and the DEA were currently working under was called Operation Thunder Dome. Thunder Dome had many moving parts, and each one was compartmentalized, meaning if you had no operational need for the information that the left hand was collecting, then you, as the right hand, would not be privy to that material. Funding worked in a similar manner. Defense spending bills, which budget for what is needed to ensure that each of the services continued to function in much the same manner as they had the previous year, was different than funding for special missions and projects. The monies used for covert and clandestine operations were practically limitless, and depending upon the lethality or influence potential of the organization you were trying to quell, it was just about endless as well. As long as an agency could tie itself into a particular special mission LOO, they could tap into the associated funding. Each entity had its own marching orders, some collected signal intelligence, others employed agents and sources to collect human intelligence, and the action arm was employed once all the information had been analyzed and they could pin point with a fair amount of accuracy, a particular area of interest or AI. When an AI was identified and it was found to have some validity to the overall success of the mission, it was then made a Line of Effort or LOE. These nested with the LOO and supported the overarching campaign. The LOE that the joint team was working was called Running Man. Intelligence had brought them to that area, and now they, as the action arm, had to confirm or deny the findings. Their higher headquarters did not appear to be able to work as well together as the ground elements proved to. Each organization wanted to keep the information that they discovered through their systems close hold, forcing the other agencies to waste time and money employing their own methods only to eventually reach the same conclusion; redundancy at its worst. This exercise in futility was now threatening to hold up progress on the ground.

CHAPTER 27

THREE DAYS HAD passed since the initial request for approval to conduct operations. The dive team had meticulously planned to dive each day, only to be told to stand down each evening before launch. The mother craft that they had intended to launch from, only had two days left on its lease; the team was spinning its wheels.

Brayden decided to take advantage of the unintended down time and finally talk to Lisa about the events that took place on the eve of his eighteenth birthday. Each night after dinner, he noticed that she would walk out to the beach alone and sit in silence listening to the calming sounds of the waves breaking and crashing along the beach. What Brayden couldn't know, is that she was all the while waiting and hoping that one night Brayden would join her.

He walked out into the resort like setting with a bottle of red wine and two glasses. He had no idea whether Lisa drank wine, or drank any alcohol at all for that matter. It had been over nine years since he had last seen her, and they obviously had not kept in touch. He had no idea what she was like as a woman, though he had thought about her off and on for years. As he watched her over the past few weeks, it was amazing to him that she was clearly not the girl he dated in high school, but she was still very familiar all the same.

He was nervous about the encounter, but built up the courage to carry through with it. The sound of the ocean masked any noises that Brayden might have made as he approached. When he walked up behind her, she jumped slightly, as she had not been seriously expecting him to ever join her. He sat down next to her and buried the bottle of wine in the sand between them. He reached over and extended his right arm toward her with an empty wine glass without saying a word. She took the glass and smiled, as Brayden grinned at her slightly; looked away, and into the direction of the ocean. He sat there staring out into the sea for a minute as Lisa intently gazed at him. She really had never stopped loving him and all the feelings she had been repressing over the years were rushing back to the forefront. Brayden reached into his shorts pocket and pulled out a corkscrew, without looking over at Lisa; he grabbed the bottle of wine and opened it. He gestured in her direction with the bottle, and she willingly brought her glass up to be filled. He poured her glass, and then his, buried the bottle again, took a few long sips, and then spoke.

"I never in a million years thought that I would see or speak to you again." Brayden started.

"Brayden, I…" Lisa began before he cut her off.

"Lisa" he said as he now turned to look at her,

"I would like you to please just listen for a moment." He continued,

"I have been waiting a long time to finally tell you how I felt that evening, and even though it may be trivial to you now, I would like to get it off my chest and move on. That night meant a great deal to me. What I intended to tell you that evening after my birthday party, is I was going to give up my scholarship and follow you to Kent. I felt as though I could accomplish anything as long as you were by my side. Obviously, I was a dreamer back then, heck I still am, and I'm probably too optimistic with my outlook on life in general. Anyway, I knew that you were uneasy about us having to attend separate schools and even though it seemed I was always blowing you off when you wanted to talk about the subject, I was truly listening. If you are anything like you were then, I know you are making someone a very happy man. You taught me a great deal about myself, about love, and about pain; and I think it had to happen that way to make me the man I am today. I have always wished nothing but the best for you, and I hope that you have that. I loved you then and I still care deeply for you now. You will always be my *first* love."

Lisa sat in silence with tears slowly running down her face. That night in her basement she was trying to preemptively fill a void that she knew was coming. Brayden was a football star and for the life of her she couldn't believe that he wanted anything to do with her. She loved him with all of her heart, but wanted to cut away before she could be hurt. She knew Brayden was going to go off to college a hundred miles away from her and be popular with the girls there. She had watched him date a few girls in high school; he even dated her best friend. So, in her mind, once they were apart, their relationship would eventually end. In time the visits would stop, the calls would get fewer and she would have to deal with the pain on her own. Now she sat in disbelief, listening to the jock she pushed away, regretting the manner in which it happened. What Brayden hadn't seen that night, was after the guests had left; she sat in the basement and cried herself to sleep, alone. She was relieved that the inevitable break up was over and that it had happened on her terms, she went off to college and did her best to forget Brayden.

"Brayden", Lisa began,

"I didn't mean to hurt you, but I panicked at the thought of losing you to the college experience. I was plain in high school; I didn't play any sports or belong to any clubs. For the life of me I couldn't understand why you wanted to be with me. I was truly surprised that we even dated for as long as we did and I just wanted to end it before we inevitably went our separate ways. I didn't even like the guy I was kissing; I didn't plan for you to catch us; I thought it would just get back to you from one of your friends. Either way, I wanted us to end before you had the chance to break up with me. It was selfish, I know, and now I realize we should have just talked about our future, but we were young."

Lisa reached for Brayden's hand, as tears continued to run down her face. Brayden took her hand and held it firmly, he had noticed the wedding ring shortly after shaking her hand when they first arrived, but he ignored it.

"There will always be a place for you in my heart Brayden." Lisa said, as they looked each other in the eyes.

Brayden wanted to lean over and kiss her, but fought the urge. He knew she was vulnerable at that moment and he didn't want to show any disrespect for the bond that she had formed with another. As he sat up and slowly pulled his hand away from hers, one of his team mates came running up behind them, "THE MISSION WAS APPROVED, IT'S A GO!"

MENDACITY

July 1999

CHAPTER 28

THE PREDATOR UNMANNED aerial drone was put into use around 1995. Primarily the United States Air Force and the CIA used it. Its principal use was for reconnaissance until the CIA began outfitting them with hellfire rockets to test its effectiveness as an offensive weapon. They were flown in multiple theaters; they caught the tail end of the Desert Storm engagement in Iraq, and were used heavily in countries on the continent of Africa, the Philippine's, Central and South America.

With a cruise altitude of 20,000 feet, a range of just over 400 nautical miles and a station loiter time of fourteen hours, they made a fierce and deadly weapon that could be used almost without detection. Many were housed in hangers all over the world, flown mostly at night to avoid detection from workers and aircrews and could be piloted from a remote location within the U.S.

Eduardo had not seen any predators while working for Trenton Industries, but he knew they existed and one day wanted to see one. He was very interested in the propulsion system, as a mechanic he wanted to see what powered it for such long duration flights. How did the fuel system work, what were the potential stress points in the airframe, did it take a beating on landing. Eduardo was curious, but not curious enough to go poking around in the many *off limit* sections of the airfield and right now that was the last thing on his mind.

Eduardo Manteo had been assigned a new handler and he and his wife were to be moved out of Bogota, Colombia, to wait in a safer location until heading to the U.S. The paperwork for their visas had been expedited through a few back doors of the embassy channels because of the nature of their situation. Eduardo was to meet his new handler in Girardot to discuss the manner in which they would be moved out of Colombia and into the U.S. He showed up to the office building that he was told to meet in and waited for someone to show up. A short in stature man that called himself Jim showed up to give Eduardo his instructions for departing Colombia.

Eduardo saw the headlights of the only other vehicle on the dark and desolate road, pull up behind him and stop. His wife was very nervous, not knowing what was happening. Eduardo had not divulged much information to her since their frantic and hasty move to the city. He was only an aircraft mechanic after all. He leaned over and kissed her and ensured her that everything would work out, "the Americans will take care of us." He told her. He exited the vehicle and walked up to the building where Jim was already standing, holding a flashlight under his chin and fiddling with multiple sets of keys until he found the right one to open the front door. Once inside the rather small office Jim introduced himself.

"Hello Eduardo, I have been assigned to your case. I hope you didn't mind me having you move your family down here on such short notice, but we have an opportunity to get you out of here tonight." Jim started.

"Is it just you and your wife? You don't have any children or extended family that you may be leaving behind? It's very possible that you would be putting them in danger." Jim added.

"No, it's just me and my wife. We never had children and our family consists of distant cousins as our parents have long since passed away. We haven't had any contact with the extended family in years." Eduardo replied.

"Great, I hate to ask, but did you make any copies of the information that you were able to retrieve from Trenton Industries? We would hate for that to fall into the wrong hands and make you a target again after all of this effort." Said Jim.

"Copies of what? I was only able to log into the computer and access the information. I wasn't able to download or make any copies of anything. You guys could take action if I had."

Jim already knew the answer to the question, but wanted to make sure that nothing was out there that could come back to bite the agency in the ass. What he didn't know, was that Eduardo had said exactly what Brayden told him to if asked directly about obtaining any data. Brayden didn't know what was going on yet and didn't want to put Eduardo at any more risk than necessary.

"Awesome." Jim replied. "I have your passports and visas to the United States here. I also have a little bit of Panamanian currency for you to use, until you board your commercial flight departing Panama. You will not be able to use any credit cards that you have now, so I will take those. I will also take your identification cards and give you new ones to match your passports. You will receive your final identities and financial accounts once

MENDACITY

you have reached your contact in the states. Once stateside, you will move to the baggage claim of your final destination airport and look for someone holding up a sign for The Carters. Do you have any questions?"

"No, I don't right now, thank you so much!" Eduardo said with a hint of hope coming through in his voice.

"Ok, I just need you to collect up your credit cards, identification and any other identifying information like bills, photos and business cards for both you and your wife, I'll give you your paperwork and boarding passes and guide you to your departure point." Jim said with a smile.

Eduardo walked back out to the car and retrieved his wife's things. He walked back inside, now moving with vigor and new life, and gave up all the requested documents. Jim gave him two envelops with their temporary new identities, passports, visas and boarding passes for their flight out of Panama.

Both men walked back outside, Jim stopped to lock up the office while Eduardo handed his wife their packets through the passenger window.

"I'm going to put an "X" on the top of your vehicle in a night vision friendly material to identify you as friendlies for the inbound aircraft. They will be flying blacked out to avoid detection but will see this under night vision goggles. Don't be nervous when you board the aircraft, it will not be like a commercial flight. You will likely have uncomfortable nylon seats, but it will get you to Panama safely and anonymously." Jim told Eduardo with a smile as he placed the mark on the roof of the car.

Eduardo didn't care, he was ready to leave and feel safe again. He was sad to leave his country, but relieved that the Americans had pulled through for them. Jim pulled his vehicle in front of them and together they departed the office. They followed him out to a nearby jungle landing strip. Eduardo and his wife were excited, busy talking about all the sites they would plan to see once settled in the states. Eduardo had always wanted to see the Wright Brothers Museum in North Carolina. He wanted to learn more about the rich history of flying and view some of the aircraft that flew during that period. His wife wanted to see Washington DC, walk through the art and history museums and the famed building housing the declaration of independence, the document that, when upheld, made America the greatest country on earth.

As they parked in the grass a few hundred meters from the strip, Jim walked over and said his goodbyes. He wished them a safe journey and said he would look them up when back stateside. Eduardo almost came to tears while shaking his hand. He couldn't wait to track down Brayden and thank him for making sure they were safe and well taken care of.

As Jim drove away Eduardo and his wife sat in their car on the edge of the strip happier than they had been in a very long time. They gazed in each other's eyes, not even fully able to comprehend the chapter that was closing and the one that was unfolding before them. Eduardo took his wife in his arms and whispered *I love you* into her ear just before their vehicle was struck by two hellfire rockets and vaporized. The only thing remaining was an engine block.

The predator pilot called tally target just before releasing his ordinance. He was able to clearly identify his target by the "X" that was marked on the roof in iridescent paint.

"The source marked that thing perfectly." The predator pilot exclaimed. "I can't believe those guys risk their lives like that to paint cartel members for us." He continued.

The virtual pilot had completed his mission for the night, and began heading back to his assigned airstrip. For he and other pilots like him, the war on drugs was hell.

Jim made his way back to Bogota, pleased that he was able to help out a family that had been risking their lives for their country. He enjoyed his work and enjoyed when it worked out for innocent people even more. He was making a difference and it motivated him to continue his sometimes-depressing work. "If I can help save Colombia one family at a time." He thought to himself. He would return to the embassy and write a full report before retiring for the night. Jim, and the pilot, were unwitting participants in the roles they played. They legitimately had no idea what had actually just taken place.

June 1999

CHAPTER 29

SEVERAL PERSONNEL WAITED in a briefing room, to hear about the continued progress of a few special projects that had been initiated by the CIA. Ten people, from varying levels of government, sat up in their seats when an older gentleman with a slight limp walked across the threshold and into the room. He sat at the head of the table in front of a thick folder that lay before him. He reached into his outer suit jacket pocket, the one that should hold a neatly folded handkerchief, and pulled out his bifocals. As he opened the folder a man to his left began to speak.

"Sir, we would like to bring you up to speed on the Trojan Scimitar and Missing Lynx programs."

Trojan Scimitar was a decade old program that was finally starting to show its usefulness. The premise, was to take applicants from the CIA analytical studies that clearly were not cut out for the monotony of sitting behind a desk, and push them into the field course, preparing them to be operators. OGAs had been around for years under various naming conventions and, at times, housed a very efficient and effective action arm. But they, along with the Special Activities Division or SAD, were witting participants for the CIA. They understood most operations, and even if they were not fully read onto a particular line of effort, they understood the premise under which they conducted these operations. What they needed were individuals that could be scattered throughout the selective services that had been trained in black ops. These individuals could then be used unwittingly to carry out operations all over the world; they would have the skills needed to be successful, without the additional level of cover involved for traditional operators.

All potential candidates were continuously interviewed and psychologically tested at different times during the training. Those with military backgrounds, or thinking about future military service were sought out, especially if serving with an elite unit was on their list of jobs to obtain if not employed by the CIA. The initial portion of the program had a sixty percent success rate. Sixty percent of those chosen for the program had ended up serving with the Navy Seals, Army Special Forces (Green Berets), or some color-coded organization belonging to the DoD or State Department. Those that did not make it into the ranks of one of these elite organizations needed to fulfill the CIAs requirement, were none-the-wiser, and at best had stories to tell about their experience that likely would not be believed anyway; and most certainly couldn't be corroborated.

Twenty-five personnel had already been used successfully around the world to carry out CIA sanctioned missions unwittingly. They had the know how to do it, the access to get them into the right locations, and the placement to make it completely believable. The program gave the CIA complete deniability, as the individuals conducting the operations had no ties to the agency. They didn't even need deep, or non-official cover, because they were actually living their status. It gave the CIA visibility on information that they would not have been able to attain otherwise. Target sets could be created and pushed into these organizations for them to take ownership of and execute without CIA involvement. But the best insurance it gave them was the ability to shift blame if something went terribly wrong; and the asset couldn't tie it back to them. After all, they didn't even know they were working for them.

This meeting was to discuss the funding; it was postponed while congress was dealing with a budgeting issue, but was recently turned back on; the program was in its eleventh year.

Missing Lynx was a super secretive ratline program that went live a couple of years ago. It was used off and on to put agents into the field and bring them out again without anyone being able to trace their whereabouts. The CIA wanted to expand its use. They just needed to find a work around for potential security issues.

"We have several missions using Trojan Scimitar personnel that are underway as we speak. Funding delayed a few, but I suspect the word to continue with planned missions will be trickling down within a day or so. Most of our missions are taking place in Lebanon, Mali, Semar Islands, Costa Rica and Colombia. All individuals have been given their orders except one, as we were told specifically to wait until we had spoken with you Mr. Gaul. He is currently involved in the Running Man LOE. The Missing Lynx brief has been sent to you on the high side Sir, we are awaiting your approval before moving forward."

James removed his glasses and looked up at the briefer. Every single person involved in the Trojan Scimitar program had their orders delivered to them by various means. Some were on singleton missions and easily directed through their higher command. Others were imbedded with teams and needed to have their directives activated through more unconventional means. Brayden, when it was time, would be activated using a special satellite computer system that could connect to the high side. This was a system that was classified higher than the secret level. It required a minimum of a top-secret clearance, and even then, the information pushed down was compartmentalized with a need to know. Brayden was the only member of his team at the time with a Top Secret-Sensitive Compartmentalized Information or TS-SCI clearance level. The laptop that he was issued before departing on the mission could connect to a satellite approved for that specific level of information. During his time in Costa Rica, he was required to sign in at least once a day and retrieve any awaiting messages. No one was privy to the information that he pulled; he only knew that it was for special intelligence or SI, which could help shape the current or future missions. Brayden popped up on James' radar while he was assigned to the embassy in Bogota, Colombia. He could have been used there before his mishap, but now that he was involved in the Thunder Dome LOO; James was particularly interested. Brayden had not yet been activated.

"Have we fixed our security concerns involving Missing Lynx?" James asked.

"As far as we can tell, we should begin moving individuals through the system before the year is out. The test group has not finished their training just yet."

"Keep me informed." James replied.

October 1999

CHAPTER 30

THE TEAM CONDUCTED last minute checks of their dive gear and prepared to splash off the tail of the well-appointed leased yacht the *Marianna*, courtesy of the DEA. The movement from the inlet, through the harbor and into the marina was fairly long, so they intended to use Diver Propulsion Vehicles or DPVs.

DPVs came in all shapes and sizes. The Navy Seals had specially designed vehicles that could carry up to four divers. They even had their own built in breathing system so that you didn't waste your individual resources while in transit. Brayden and his team, had experienced them while training with a seal platoon in Virginia Beach. They were great to play on but unless you had a dedicated driver, they were a serious pain in the butt. SF had two propulsion vehicles that they used. A two-man vehicle equipped with moving map navigation instrumentation and a small single man device. The latter is what they would use as they were easily cached, and if they needed to abandon them, their relatively low procurement price made them expendable. They could also carry two divers for a short distance, before the battery would be negatively affected with the additional weight. The DPVs would be hidden at the bottom of a channel marker with two team members remaining with them. Brayden and his swim buddy, with the remaining team, would continue on to the marina and emplace the tracking devices.

The six-man element entered the water and descended to their twenty-five-foot transit depth. Three DPVs were used carrying two divers each, one driver/navigator and one passenger/observer. They moved through the channel without difficulty, having planned their movement time for the slack tide and being careful to remain at least one foot above the sea floor once inside the channel; in order to avoid discarded trash from uncaring boaters.

As they reached the DPV cache site, Brayden collected all the pieces he needed from the divers remaining at the site and crammed them into his assault pack. He and his buddy swam on, carefully navigating their way into the marina. The second dive team swam to the mouth of the marina to create a diversion in the event compromise was imminent. Here they swam smoothly and deliberately to avoid disturbing the surface of the water. The vessels used by Mr. Ripper's were in the front of the marina, nearest the shore. As they made their way to the boats, they started to faintly hear commotion coming from the surface.

"Hurry up, we should have been out of here thirty minutes ago!" Said one of the men on the dock as he threw his duffle bag down in the aft end of the boat. Five other men hurried their way down the dock to the boats and gathered around to quickly discuss the urgency of their departure.

Fifteen feet below the surface, Brayden had installed the trigger, and began emplacing the tracking devices. He started with the boat closest to the rear of the docking area, emplacing the device between the inboard/outboard twin screws. His buddy remained planted against the sandy bottom with a line attaching him to a pylon. He kept slight tension on the bud-line that connected he and Brayden, in the event he needed to pull him away from a prop quickly. The men on the surface began boarding the boats and powering the electronics, checking the fish finders and navigation charts before starting the engines. Brayden noticed the increased rocking of the vessels, signifying that someone had boarded. He hurriedly placed the last of the devices and as he flipped the toggle switch to hibernate, the screws started to move slightly just before they roared to life. He pulled his hand away quickly and was just as swiftly pulled down by his dive buddy. He avoided being struck by the prop, but his mask had been dislodged from his face and began floating up toward the surface. The divers watched helplessly as the mask broke the surface and the glass began catching light from the docks and shimmering in the night. The boats were untied and began pushing away from the docks; luckily the occupants where too enthralled in conversation to have noticed the stray mask. As the vessels made-way out of the marina, Brayden slowly surfaced and completed a 360-degree check of the area with his silenced pistol drawn. No one had remained on the docks. He moved slowly to his mask and retrieved it, before gently making his way back to the bottom.

CHAPTER 31

PAUL SHRIVER WAS the lead DEA agent on the ground. He remained at the safe house with the remaining SFOD-A members. He was sitting at the table that the rover was perched atop, legs swung to the side to accommodate his six-foot frame, staring intently at three red dots that began to move out of the channel.

"They did it, we actually have movement!" He yelled at the team as they were currently talking through what types of demolition charges would penetrate the hull of a submarine. Setting down their equipment they moved from the faintly lit, narrow strip of grass next to the driveway, into the screened in rear portion of the house and huddled around the screen next to Paul. They all began watching the dots move atop the digital navigation chart on the screen, exiting the channel and heading out into deeper waters.

The boats stopped at a position nearly one hundred miles off the coast. As the men watched the dots secretly hoping they would tell them what their target was doing at that precise moment, the returning team pulled up, parked and began removing equipment from the vehicles. Paul remained at the screen as the rest of the guys helped the returning divers and agents organize their gear.

"What's the status on the tracking devices, the boats started moving as soon as we had them installed." Brayden questioned.

"Right now, they are stopped about one hundred miles off shore!" Paul yelled out the back door having overheard Brayden's inquiry as the men continued to unload equipment.

Brayden broke away to set up his high side laptop and retrieve any awaiting messages. He also wanted to report on the events that had transpired for the day, to include the successful emplacement of the tracking systems. Only one envelope appeared in his in box. He clicked on it and read the contents.

SM1356, identify smuggling route and report. Do not intercept at this time. Do not interfere at this time. Direct engagement is not authorized.

Brayden exited the mail program, closed the laptop, broke down his satellite antenna, and returned to the house. He purposely didn't report their success, and instead asked the team to send it up through the normal reporting channels. The next 24 hours would be interesting.

November 1999

CHAPTER 32

JOHN O'BRIEN SAT AT his desk looking at the calendar next to his computer screen. It had been almost a year since he had seen his family. His wife and children had hair just as red as his, with green eyes and minor freckles dotting their cheeks. John was a thin man that stood just under six feet tall. His weight fluctuated in Colombia as he tried to maintain his eating habits as a vegetarian. He frequently made his own meals and seldom ate out for fear of animal fat being used during preparation of the food. His time as an information technician for the defense attaché was coming to an end. He was ready to return stateside.

As he sorted through his work, organizing projects and preparing to handover to his successor, he noticed the thumb drive that had been given to him by Brayden Smith. He had forgotten about exploiting it after Brayden had been abruptly reassigned. He pulled it out of the safe and removed it from the plastic electronics sleeve he had placed it in. He stuck the drive into his computer and pulled up the contents. Most of the documents were financial reports, highlighting significant earnings and disbursement among the holding companies. Makes and models of various aircraft with their tail numbers and service hours, but nothing that really stood out. He decided to run the documents through a program that could detect additional encrypted information. He didn't expect to find anything, but it couldn't hurt. Several locations on multiple pages brought up hits. Buried deeply in certain periods and comas was an abundance of additional information. John clicked on several of them and discovered additional encryption. Upon cracking the extra cypher layers, he was presented with lists of latitudes and longitudes, account information with currency and exchange rates, and the names of miscellaneous individuals.

John pushed slightly away from his desk and thought about what to do with this discovery. On the surface it didn't really seem like much, but he couldn't help but wonder why someone would go through all that trouble to hide something that seemed so trivial. *This has to mean something.* He thought to himself. He then grabbed two recordable disks, slid them both into the large compact disk burning machine next to his computer, and saved the relevant documents to them. He picked up the picture of his family that he kept on his desk and removed the back carefully from the frame. He inserted one of the disks along with a note to his wife, re-attached the back to the frame, and shoved it into a large padded envelope. He removed the other disk from the machine and slid it into his pocket.

He walked down to the mailroom, still not really sure what he was doing or even if it was necessary; but the secrecy that he created made him feel like a spy. He reached the window and smiled warmly at the woman behind the counter.

Hello." He said to the mail clerk as he presented her with his envelope.

"I would like to mail this back to my home in the U.S., I always break things like this when I'm packing." He said in a nerdy, matter of fact manner.

The mail clerk looked into the envelope in a cursory fashion before sealing it up and throwing it into the pick-up box.

"How much longer do you have here?" She asked.

"I'm under a month now." John replied sincerely, clearly pleased that his time was ending soon.

He returned to his office, ejected and removed the thumb drive, slid it back into the protective sleeve and headed to the Sensitive Compartmentalized Information Facility or SCIF. There, he could access the high side and send the data to the information analysts at the DIA in Washington DC. He remembered that Brayden told him not to divulge the data to anyone but him, but he was sent back to the states a few months ago and John just assumed that someone else would be working all of his cases. He had done his due diligence by sending him a copy of the CD, so he would in a sense, be kept in the know.

John loaded the disk and drafted a brief message about the circumstances surrounding the gathering of the information to the best of his knowledge, which didn't amount to much. He explained how he had exploited the data to give clarity to the analysts and possibly assist them in further subjugation. After sending his message, he visited the CoS's office and gave him the original device, along with the CD that he had burned. Surely the information would be of use to the new operator that was filling Brayden's role.

"Hey Sir, I was preparing for my turn-over with my counterpart and came across this drive. Brayden Smith recovered it from an asset a while back and asked me to check it out. I was able to pull some information from it but I am not sure if it's of any importance. I'm not really an operations analyst, so I've already sent the data forward to the DIA for further manipulation."

Mitchel extended his hand and accepted the package from John.

"Ah yes, I had almost forgotten about this." Mitchel started.

"I appreciate you tying this up before heading out, it should help in our continual battle against the cartels. Is this everything?"

"Yes Sir, that's it. I made a copy of the drive so that I could transfer it to the high side." John clarified the addition of the CD in the envelope.

"Have you sent this information to anyone outside of the DIA analysts?" Mitchel inquired.

"No Sir, other than my high side message, you and I are the only ones that know about it". John replied.

"So, when are you finally out of here?" Mitchel questioned.

"I have just under a month remaining. It's been an awesome experience here, but I am ready to return home." John replied.

John smiled, then threw his hand up and waved as he departed Mitchel's office. As he walked down the hall back to his workstation, he wondered why Mitchel would mention the cartels? He hadn't heard anything about Trenton Industries having any ties to them. However, they *were* in the air industry, and airplanes moved drugs and money. John chuckled to himself at the absurdity of a legitimate and successful business risking everything to conduct illicit activities.

"I've definitely been here around these spy types to long." He said to himself as he sat back down at his desk.

Mitchel pulled the CD from its protective case and slid it into his computer. He opened the files and began to scroll through the data, clicking back and forth between documents. He clicked on the page that contained names and phone numbers, then one that contained locations in lat./long. He paused briefly while staring at the screen and then reached for his phone. He pulled his Rolodex toward him with his left hand, as he picked up and held the receiver in his right. Finding the contact he was searching for, he slowly punched in the numbers. After ringing several times someone finally picked up.

"Hello?"

"Hey, it's Mitchel, you need to intercept a message sent on the high side this afternoon to the DIA concerning some data Brayden Smith stumbled upon while he was here. When Brayden left here, I had no reason to believe that there were physical copies of the information, but it appears I was wrong as I was just handed one by an information technician of all people. I think we may have a problem."

October 1999

CHAPTER 33

AS THEY NAVIGATED toward the coordinates that the fishing boats had visited, Brayden began prepping his gear for the dive. This would be a dive deeper than the rest of his teammates were qualified to make. The dive to the 140-foot depth would require the use of Trimix, a mixture of oxygen, helium and nitrogen. The helium was needed to reduce the effects of nitrogen at depth. Nitrogen narcosis can occur in as shallow a depth as 70 feet of water. The gas, if kept at the 21 percent ratio, has an almost narcotic effect on divers. The deeper you push past 100 feet, the more exacerbated the effects.

He began to set up his rather cumbersome equipment. Twin eighty-cylinder tanks would be back mounted, connected together with a single manifold. This would be his main air source during the start of the dive. The harness that he wore, consisting of a back mounted buoyancy compensator, which helped him achieved neutral buoyancy during various stages of the dive; was specially designed to attach multiple scuba cylinders. Two additional tanks were attached under each arm, with separate first and second stage regulators. He would switch to these tanks once he ran out of air on his primary source. He carried three light sources. One as his primary, another as a backup system, and the third as his emergency, the military believed in the two is one and one is none theory. Most technical divers, military or not, live by this motto and practice this redundancy for all dives, no matter how simple. He carried two masks, one that was worn; the other was shoved into a large pocket on his wet suit. The waters in Costa Rica were fairly warm, but because of the depth of the dive he knew he could get chilled. He wore a 7mm in the core with 3mm extremities wet suit. His Seiko automatic diver was positioned atop his wetsuit using the diver extension band so that he could use the rotating bezel to accurately time his various phases of the dive. He also had a digital timer to keep track of the demolition charge once he placed it. He carried extra time fuse initiators in one of his dive suit pockets in case one was damaged during his descent to the bottom, and the demolition that he would take was prepped and ready to go in a three-day assault pack. The dive would be very equipment intensive, but he was used to the load.

It had been almost 48 hours since the vessels had been tracked to that location, and according to the rover, they had not returned. Brayden's teammates jeered him for being the only one technically qualified to emplace the demo charge should the submarine be found in that location. He thought back to his days in the Navy diving mixed gases, staging on a decompression trapeze. Breathing a clipped off oxygen bottle once at a safe depth to lessen the possibility of getting bent once on the surface. Unlike those dives, he would not have the added safety of an ascent / descent line going from the surface to the bottom, something that he could hold on to and allow him to guide himself toward the depth, and then ascend in a controlled manner. Most of his diving in the Navy was during daylight hours, sometimes you would even have additional lighting, to aid you while you worked, but you always had the light of day to assist you to the surface. Because of the nature of this dive no lines could be rigged, so he would have to conduct a free descent in the direction of his target, and strictly control his buoyancy during ascent. It was a crescent moon so the illumination was not ideal, he would need lights to aid him during his dive.

As he finished assembling his scuba gear, checking his primary and back up air sources, ensuring that he had the proper amount of lead weight and picking out the spot where he could connect his additional equipment bag; he thought about the dangerous marine life lurking below. He usually never worried about a shark attack or aggressive barracuda, but now, in the dark of night, preparing to conduct a deep dive on his own; he briefly visited those fears. The only threatening shark encounter he had ever experienced up to that point was a brush with hammerheads in Panama. The team was conducting a daytime navigation dive on Draegers. They had only been at transit depth for thirty minutes when a large school of prey fish darted through their formation. Normally this would not be a big deal, they usually dart back and forth, almost whimsically as you swim along and eventually, they move on. This time they did not hang around, they continued moving in one direction quickly until out of sight. The team almost came to a complete stop as they watched the fish moving away as if being chased. After a few seconds they looked in the direction they had swam from and noticed a school of hammerhead sharks. Almost in unison the team began to give the ascent sign and move toward the surface. Once on top they quickly came off of the Draeger system and began frantically flagging down the safety boats as dorsal fins began to surface and circle very near their position. They all made it into the boats safely, no one was injured, but it was a hair-raising experience. That was during the day; he could see the threat closing in. In the conditions he was about to dive in, his initial introduction would likely be a bump.

He pulled his wet suit up, zipped up the back and attached the hook pile tape at the neck. He began to stretch in it, conducting several knee bends and arm extensions to loosen up the neoprene. His teammates helped him into his gear, holding the tanks so that he could slip into the straps and tighten everything down before receiving the full weight. His additional cylinders were attached under his arms while he was seated and everything was checked by one of the diving supervisors on the detachment to ensure everything was properly connected and that the air was on and available to him. Once completely kitted up, he was assisted to the edge of the dive platform on the non-descript DEA boat and prepared to enter the water.

He entered the water with the giant stride technique. Because of the added weight of his extra equipment, it felt like he had sunk to a depth of 10 feet before being able to fin back to the surface to give the O.K. signal. Before going subsurface he checked his connections once more and tested each of his regulators to ensure they were delivering air properly. Lisa knelt down close to the water's edge and handed him the three-day assault pack containing the demo. In that moment she saw that he was still the adventurous athlete that she had dated in high school. He was doing what made him happy, she was both envious and proud of his resolve.

With no diving aids, he would have to bounce down to depth, confirm or deny the existence of the submarine, set the charge and return to the surface. Keeping track of his time at depth would be crucial to avoid going into a decompression scenario. He would only have minutes to identify places to set his charges, initiate them and return to the surface. Honestly, he knew he would blow the table, but at that moment he tried not to think about it.

He gave the diving supervisor the descent signal before conducting a murky water surface dive and transitioning into a head down posture to start his slow and methodical descent to the bottom. Even in his almost seven-millimeter wetsuit; he could feel the chill of the deeper waters setting in as he passed through multiple thermoclines. His light penetrated forty feet in the direction he aimed it, the visibility was decent but it could have been better. The ocean floor was flat with nothing but sand for miles. The only thing that kept him on course was a large object that barely differed in color from the bottom. It was just enough of a variation to stand out as he passed through one hundred feet. He looked at his depth gauge as he continued to steadily fin toward the bottom. He enjoyed the peacefulness of diving. All he could hear was the audible melody of his second stage regulator, as the diaphragm gently flipped back and forth with every inhalation and exhalation. The soothing sound of bubbles venting passed his head as he motored to the bottom. As he got closer, he noticed netting held in place by large firmly planted poles. *How much money do these people have at their disposal?* Brayden thought. As he swam under the tent like covering, he could clearly make out a submarine, though it was like nothing he had ever seen. Brayden had heard of narco-subs before in documentaries and on the news, but he never thought he'd see one first hand. The smuggling machine was at least seventy feet long, and meticulously kept. It hovered off the ocean floor with lift bags that were inflated enough to make it buoyant; and it was tied off at four points to stakes. Lighting was rigged to large polls that were buried deeply in the sand. They were powered off of portable battery packs that the traffickers must have brought with them. He swam down the body of the sub in awe, starting at the tail and making his way to the nose. He pretended for a moment he was Jacques Cousteau, discovering some long-lost WWII submarine; perhaps damaged in battle and never found. Brayden came back to reality, checked his air gauge, and began pulling out his demolitions. He was not there to sight see; he had a mission to conduct.

The plan was to emplace three charges, one to damage the propulsion system, another to attempt to breach the hull, and one to destroy the antenna mass. Individually these things could be fixed in a relatively short amount of time. Combined however, it would pose more of a challenge, increasing the likelihood of a major player showing his face. Brayden prepped the charges and began planting them around the submarine. He pulled all of the ignition systems activating the time fuse, and began his ascent. When building the charges they factored in the ascent time from 150 feet plus ten percent. Brayden knew he had plenty of time, but followed his second to slowest bubbles just to be sure. He would rather get bent than eat a water amplified demo charge.

On the surface the remaining team members remained silent and vigilant. The chop from the ocean was beginning to pick up, but sound had a way of carrying while out on the ocean at night. All lighting from the vessel had been turned out with the exception of a small red light that was shining in the cabin to allow the boat captain, Paul, to read the nautical charts that he had laid out on the table. As the crew grew more anxious, one of the SFOD-A members thought he saw boat navigation lights in the distance. Against the backdrop of faint city lights, it was hard to tell. After a few more minutes several other members of the team began to see what looked like multiple lights heading in their direction.

"We are going to have to move and quickly." Paul suggested.

"Roger, Brayden knows what to do." Said one of the SFOD-A members. "And we'll know real soon whether he found the submarine or not." The man continued.

At about thirty feet from the surface Brayden heard what he assumed was the DEA vessel start up and instantly go to full power heading out to sea. He looked at his air gauge and panicked at the decision he was forced to make. Absence of the safe signal is always seen as a sign to abort when planning. For this mission, the DEA planned to black out the boat and launch at full power out to sea if they believed they might be compromised. They knew that Brayden would hear the boat going to full power even at depth and know that more than likely something was wrong on the surface. It didn't necessarily mean his portion of the mission was compromised; but it did mean his survival went from probably successful to Vegas odds within seconds. The only thing he could do was head back down to a depth where he wouldn't get hit by a boat prop and expedite his movement away from the blast area. He leveled out at thirty feet, dropped all additional gear except his back mounted twin eighty's and began swimming in the direction of land as hard and as fast as he could. Never swim so hard that you hit a hypoxic state was one of the lessons taught in the CDQC. Right now, however, he had to get out of the kill radius of the charges he had just emplaced.

He could now hear multiple sets of screws turning above him, although he could not make out what direction they were moving. He continued to swim, checking his air gauge every few seconds on his final tank, only to see the needle moving toward zero right before his eyes. He knew that he couldn't remain at depth, so he started his ascent while still maintaining expedient movement away from the sub. At fifteen feet from the surface, he began loosening his straps and disconnected his gauges from his buoyancy compensator. At five feet he ditched all equipment and as he exhaled fully, purging his lungs as much as he possibly could, he broke the surface. He could see two boats in the distance over the sub. He was actually a pretty good distance away, far enough that they would never see him without an intense search. He remained there with his ears out of the water in anticipation for the explosion. As the divers from the Mr. Ripper vessels made their way into the water and began descending, the charges detonated.

Brayden felt the shock wave of the subsurface blast. He was starting to feel nauseous, possibly from the increasing swells that were just about high enough to break. He tried to keep focus on the boats and watch as they pulled the likely injured divers from the water and back aboard. The boats weren't damaged, as they were able to speed away back into the direction of shore. Surely the divers sustained, at a minimum, ruptured eardrums he thought.

Brayden decided to do what he was trained to do in a circumstance like this, and began surface swimming back into the direction of land. The furthest he had surface swam for any school or real-world event up to this point was seven miles. He now had just shy of one-hundred miles to swim before hitting land. He was sure the DEA vessel would remain blacked out to decrease the chance of detection until the Ripper boats were out of the area. If they were not able to find him, his only chance would be entering a shipping lane and hoping one of the tanker or container ship deck hands could see him. He started to faintly hear a boat moving closer with the ear that he had planted in the water as he swam. He paused to look around and as soon as he went vertical in the water, he began to cramp. He had experienced cramps from dehydration and over use of the muscles during long arduous swims, but this was different. They were intense and debilitating. Something was seriously wrong. He put a little air into his buoyancy compensator while he could still breathe deeply, and turned on his emergency beacon light. At this point he didn't care who picked him up. If he remained in the water he would perish.

In all of his time in the Navy, with literally hundreds of dives under his belt, Brayden had never even come close to having a dive injury. Now he lay on the floor of the DEA powerboat, motoring full speed toward shore, suffering from decompression sickness type one. They needed to get him to a chamber and quickly. The team had a portable, collapsible chamber back at the safe house for emergencies, but that required time to set up, and time is something they didn't have. The crew reached the dock area, removed Brayden from the vessel, and loaded him up in one of the SUVs. They knew that this would risk the entire operation, but at the moment Brayden's health came first. As they made their way to the medical treatment facility, Paul thought about the second and third order effects of the actions they were forced to take. Whenever operating under the radar or in a covert manner it wasn't usually a large-scale mistake that got you compromised. It was the little things, wearing something that gives you away as an American or even as being associated with the military or U.S. government. Saying something revealing while conversing benignly with a local national, that could start them probing for more information. Or by showing up somewhere that you shouldn't be and drawing unnecessary attention to yourself, which is what they chanced at the time.

He was taken to the Clinica Biblica, a private hospital that had a hyperbaric chamber on site. It was used specifically to treat diving injuries.

Decompression sickness type one or DCS 1, is a result of dissolved gasses coming out of solution in the form of bubbles inside the body. This can cause pain in the joints and other areas of the body where the bubbles could become lodged. The injured diver would need to be placed inside of a recompression chamber and taken back down to a simulated depth or *pressed*, at a minimum, to the deepest point of their dive. They would remain under that machine-recreated pressure for a specific length of time, giving the bubbles that have formed a chance to shrink back into solution and pass through the blood stream and other tissues they had formed in; normally. Brayden needed this procedure immediately.

Once inside the hospital he was rushed to the hyperbaric room, striped to his shorts, carefully put inside the chamber, and pressed on what they call a table three ride. After the excitement and scurrying around died down, the realism that they were being exposed set in. The medical staff began to look over the occupants of the room, and glance at each wearily as they contemplated who these people were. They did not look like tourists as they were too well built, and considering no charters offered night dives in that area, it was extremely late for a diving injury. The staff turned on the television that was located in the room in an attempt to hear something on the local news about a diving mishap or other activities that would explain the presence of the strange group. As one of the nurses began to slowly pick up Brayden's clothing, a time fuse initiator fell from the neoprene pocket of his now tattered wetsuit. Everyone stared at the device with varying thoughts. The medical staff wondered what this military like device could be; the team wondered why this was happening to them. A detachment member peeked through the window of the chamber at Brayden and saw that he was actually coming around. He looked at the operator and asked him to begin bringing him up.

"But Sir, he has not made it completely through the table."

"I understand that, but we just don't have the time, there is somewhere that we have to be." The SFOD-A member replied.

The staff began to look around puzzled at each other as the room fell to an uncomfortable silence. Only the newscaster was speaking at the moment, in Spanish, about the beautiful weather that was in store for the remainder of the week. Each member of the team began pressing their hip slightly with their elbow to ensure they were still armed with their pistols. Obviously, they would not use deadly force on an unarmed and innocent civilian, but they knew that the area was home to some very hardened and experienced criminal organizations. *Spies are everywhere*, Paul thought. The decision to pull Brayden up was difficult under the circumstances of his injuries, but absolutely necessary.

It didn't matter; it was time to leave and the decision would have been made for them sooner or later. As the operator began fulfilling the request, the now suspicious medical staff began pondering what actions to take next. They obviously couldn't deny medical treatment as they had taken an oath to help anyone needing attention regardless of the circumstances; but they still had an obligation to report what they deemed as suspicious activity. Paul noticed one of the nurses grab her cell phone and quickly disappear behind a partition.

"Start gathering his things and get ready to vacate the premises quickly." Paul said in a low whisper,

"You three" he pointed at several of the SFOD-A members, "head out and get the vehicles ready, I think we're going to have to leave in a hurry."

As Brayden was coming out of the chamber, they could hear commotion coming from the waiting area down the hall. They assisted Brayden into surgical scrubs, and headed out of the chamber room and down a long corridor toward the exit. As they made their way to the door, they heard the nursing staff in the hyperbaric room begin yelling at a group of individuals in Spanish. The SFOD-A figured that the personnel that had shown up couldn't be law enforcement by the tone and subject of the conversation. They pushed through the exit as the men started heading in their direction. Once outside a team member ran and flagged the vehicles over to them as they quickly moved across the lawn toward the road. Their pursuers emerged from the doors leading out of the hospital and brought their weapons up in preparation to engage. They were unable to, because of the potential for collateral damage and the inevitable follow-on inquiry by the authorities. They instead ran to their vehicles to continue the chase.

As they sped through traffic lights, weaving their way back to the marina, they wondered what plan they could come up with to the get themselves out of their current predicament. The team bickered back and forth; half believing the boat was the ticket out and the other wanting to return to the safe house. For now, the safe house had not been burned, and if it stayed that way the sister SFOD-A could take care of it before they re-deployed back to the states.

They made it to the marina and began preparing the boat for launch. Brayden still had minor cramping but was now able to move under his own power. He made his way onto the vessel and laid down on a bench as part of the crew sanitized the vehicles for any information that could be used to trace who they were, in the event they were broken into and ransacked. They also activated the emergency homing beacon on them to alert the U.S. consulate that the vehicles needed to be recovered. The remaining members began preparing the weapons mounts on the boat and distributing the small amount of ammunition to those locations in the event the chase turned hostile.

Everyone was on edge, if their pursuers decided to take their operations kinetic; it would mean major attention could be brought onto them, likely causing an international incident. If the local law enforcement were to get involved, it would escalate the situation to news worthy which would raise the hairs on those that signed their paychecks. And if one of them were killed, captured by the opposition or arrested, it could halt efforts in multiple countries and possibly highlight the already known fact that the U.S. was working to combat cartels and their enablers. This would be revealed shortly after they pieced together the fact that they had just destroyed a submarine, presumably used by the cartels; and it wouldn't take Sherlock Holmes to make that stick.

As they pulled away from the dock, they could see vehicles pulling up, presumably full of the men that had been following them. They appeared to be weighing the decision to continue their pursuit. The SFOD-A began hastily developing an escalation of force plan to deal with the threat should their pursuers continue the chase. They continued through the harbor at a pace well above the recommended no wake speeds, toward the mouth of the channel.

Once through the channel and heading out to sea without followers, Paul called a member of the sister team on the satellite phone to notify them, minus details; of what had just transpired. He was informed that the authorities had already been in contact with them and were on the way to their location; Paul and crew would likely be forced to find an alternate way out of the country. The medical staff had informed the authorities of the events that took place and the description pointed to the SFOD-A, the only one legally in country. They would be able to explain their way out of it, but it would probably mean the end of their trip. The dive team and DEAs gear would be fine, even if the sister team were kicked out of country, they would be able to pack it up and take it back with them along with completely sanitizing the safe house, the embassy would help with that. However, they could not help the dive team if they were taken into custody. Paul hung up the phone with a flabbergasted look on his face. He jokingly told the group what their quandary was. At least the submarine wouldn't be reported to the authorities, that was an internal problem for the cartels. Brayden slowly sat up on the bench he had laid on and asked to use the phone.

He had never called James for anything, not even to say hello, even though James told him when he was departing the program that he could always call him at any time. People always said that as an obligatory gesture of kindness; it was almost expected. And in this instance, he was going to test that theory. Brayden called the only number for those past programs that he could remember by heart, the one he was first given while training in Virginia, to call in case there were an emergency during an exercise.

"Hello", a woman answered the phone and Brayden could hear the digital disturbance of the recording device as it started.

"Hello, this is SM1356",

S and M were the first two letters of his last name and the following four numbers were given when he enrolled in the secretive training program. Ironically, it was the exact same number given to him when he applied for his high side account after his SCI read on. He just figured it was what they did in the more elite organizations, he never questioned it; why would he?

"How may I help you?"

"I need to speak with Mr. James Gaul, I know its late ma'am but this is an emergency."

After a brief pause the woman replied.

"Wait one Sir as I connect you."

Brayden suddenly got butterflies in his stomach. He was nervous to speak to James. He knew that he wouldn't be upset or yell, but just like in training, he would be able to hear the disappointment in his voice.

"Hello Brayden" James said in an upbeat and surprisingly cheerful voice.

"Hello Sir, I desperately need a favor."

"Ok, I'll see what I can do, what seems to be the trouble?"

"Well Sir, I am aboard a DEA vessel and we are afloat off the coast of Costa Rica. We cannot return to our safe house and I think our sister SFOD-A will be getting kicked out of country soon. By now, air travel it out of the question. I'm not sure if you can help, but we are running out of options."

"Hmm, let me call you back Brayden, I have the number."

James hung up the phone and Brayden and crew sat in complete silence. Only the sound of the engines could be heard as they continued to motor further out to sea. Each member of the team began looking at the other.

As they stared each other in the eyes in disbelief, trying to make sense of the events that had taken place in the last few hours they each began to quickly realize their mortality. No bullets were flying; no eminent threat was on the horizon, just the realization that at that moment, for the first time in many of their careers they had absolutely no plan. The DEA could pull some strings maybe and get them a bird from Costa Rica to Panama. If they were detained while making their way to the airport, they would likely spend quite a few nights in a Costa Rican Jail. If the smugglers got a hold of them, a few might be held for ransom, but the majority would likely be killed. The U.S. would not be brokering any deals on their behalf, as that could damage relations. They were on their own.

Ten minutes later the satellite phone began to ring.

"Hello", Brayden answered.

"You're in luck kid, give me your current position. You will have to get that tug boat you're on out into international waters. There is a carrier group in the area performing maneuvers. Heck, I'm surprised you can't hear those top gun idiots flying all around you doing their touch and goes on the carrier deck. You'll need to signal code to them with a bright light once you've made contact. Hope somebody on board is familiar with morse code. Take care of yourself and next time you want to say hello, please do so at a reasonable hour!"

James hung up as Brayden collapsed the antenna of the sat phone and laid back down on the bench. Everyone was in awe that he had arranged a rescue, looking at each other inquisitively wondering with whom he had been speaking. Maybe he would tell them later, but for now he just needed to rest; and pray one of the gray floating cities had a chamber.

August 2001

CHAPTER 34

BRAYDEN STARED AT THE FLOOR and pondered what Steve had just told him. *This doesn't make any sense.* Brayden thought to himself. His mind flashed back to the files he had studied while he was preparing for the mission. Extensive surveillance had been done, nothing was left to chance, and multiple individuals and agencies had vetted the information. Brayden replayed the scenario over and over again in his head while Steve leaned back in a posture suggesting he had as much time as he needed. Nothing was adding up and Brayden had questions of his own. What exactly was Steve doing associating with the cartels? Perhaps he was deep cover? If that were the case, why would he pursue him and ensure his capture? Shouldn't he be happy we took a major player out of the equation? No matter who he was? Brayden had heard about former SF soldiers getting out of the military and going to work for the cartels. It was talked about frequently because of the serious consequences it posed to conventional U.S. forces if ever put on the ground in the Colombian jungles. If some of America's most elite soldiers were now teaching tactics to one of the most ruthless organizations on the planet, the lives lost in an armed conflict with the FARC would be astronomical. The FARC was already outfitted with gear that rivaled what SF was issued, and in some cases their technology was better. Arms dealers have no allegiance, they sell to whomever has the required funds. Money wasn't an issue to the cartels and they ensured that their personal army had the best. This included training and they paid handsomely for ex-operators to bring that knowledge to their training camps. Other than being morally and ethically unsound, once you had sold your soul to turn a quick buck with the cartels, you were in it for life. If Steve was now working with them, why was he keeping Brayden alive? Brayden was of no informational value to them and he knew it. Steve understood the conditions in which SF worked in that region, so prolonging the inevitable would only increase the chance that he would be found. The U.S. had very sophisticated air assets they could push in that direction and collect atmospherics that would allow them to triangulate Brayden's location based on his last communication, and the cell signals of those they were tracking. The ground forces that were in place during the operation surely went into their caged eagle procedures and would eventually come bursting through a door and rescue him. But Steve knew all of this information too. The only other scenario was that no one was looking for him.

"I don't know what you're trying to do Steve, but you know the team is out looking for me as we speak. It's only a matter of time before I'm found." Brayden said.

Now that he was conscious, he could leave signs in inconspicuous places for his rescuers to find and use to guide them to where he might be. At a minimum it would prove that he was still alive and that the search should continue.

"Brayden, do you really think you are here by accident? Did you learn nothing from your brief experience in Virginia?"

At this point in Brayden's career, he had only been to Virginia for one thing, to briefly brush arms with the CIA. As far as he was aware, no one knew about his stint there. It didn't even come up when he applied for his clearance; it was as if it never happened. He hadn't met Steve until he joined the Army. He met him at Pathfinder school and they remained in contact off and on until Steve retired. Even with the highest-level of clearance you can attain in our government, certain material is still need to know. So how would he have come across this information? Brayden thought back to his final hide site, the one from which he shot Javier. As he picked up to move to his extraction point, he remembered how odd it was that his aggressors had gained so much ground on him and the speed at which they did so. The only logical explanation is that they were already there, was he set up?

"How did you know where I would put in my hide?" Brayden asked.

"It's exactly where I would have put mine." Steve answered.

"Brayden you weren't sent here to assassinate Javier by chance." Steve continued.

"They never intended to extract you."

Steve motioned to the man guarding the door; he walked into the room and threw down a bag containing some type of gear. Steve reached into the bag and pulled out the SPIES rope that was used to extract Brayden, his harness was still connected to the attachment point. He slowly pulled through the rope until he reached the clevis that connected inside the aircraft. The rope was intact, the cutaway band that attached the clevis was sliced clean through, it was clear he had been cut away.

Brayden had heard all he could stand. His head was now spinning thinking about the circumstances under which he would have been cut away by the crew chief of the aircraft. He was getting nauseous and his mental state was quickly unraveling. It was surreal, all of it, he still couldn't really believe that he had been caught, beaten and now sat talking to someone that he had met years ago, and thousands of miles away from where he currently sat; that was likely going to kill him shortly. He anxiously thought of a way out of his current situation. *Desperate times call for desperate measures.* He thought to himself. He was untied, but didn't think he had the strength to fight his way past at least the three men that he was aware of, possibly more. The one thing he was convinced of is that he was not leaving there alive if he stayed. Escape was worth a try.

Brayden reached back with his right hand and grabbed the side of the chair, gripping it to make sure he had the strength to at least pick it up. Steve leaned forward in his chair placing his elbow in his knees, and favored in as if to start speaking again. At that moment Brayden stood up, swung the chair around in his right hand, reinforcing his grip with his left hand, and continued through, planting it into Steve's side. Steve had little time to react and raised his left arm in an attempt to block the attack. He was knocked out of his chair to the ground and Brayden immediately went for the pistol at Steve's waistline. The two men fought as Brayden sought to gain control of the firearm. The man that had brought in the gear bag returned and attempted to move the chairs that were blocking his pathway to assist Steve when a shot rang out and he slumped to the floor. Brayden had gained control of the pistol, aimed it directly at Steve and was now backing away from him toward the door. Steve stood with authority, as if the pistol posed him no threat. Brayden continued to back toward the door, never taking his eyes away from him and actually contemplated shooting him before turning and running out. The third individual was waiting in a vehicle parked just outside. He had not even attempted to move. *They must have planned to kill me.* Brayden thought as he reached for the driver's side door. He opened the door and put the gun to the driver's head and simultaneously pulled him out of the SUV. Steve, and the now wounded guard, made their way outside in time to watch Brayden expediently assist the driver to the ground with a kick to his back; enter the already running vehicle and begin driving away. Brayden had no idea where he was, but he had successfully escaped; so he thought.

November 1999

CHAPTER 35

JOHN HAD TWENTY-THREE days left before he could board a commercial flight back to the good ole US of A. His replacement had just arrived and they were starting the handover process. If everything continued as planned, he would actually have a few days to do some shopping for souvenirs before he left for home.

He was dropped off at the entrance to his five-star hotel after work as he had been for almost a year. He took the elevator to the 17th floor and then walked leisurely to his room. He stayed in a suite, as most U.S. embassy workers did, that had a kitchen, two bedrooms and a modest living room. Staying in the hotel was not by choice, it was because of the security concerns of staying elsewhere in the city. The kidnapping of U.S. persons abroad in South America was on the rise, and in Colombia it was just about guaranteed if you strayed too far off the reservation without understanding how to read your surroundings.

John walked into the living area and tossed his bag on the sofa. He sat down in the chair next to the window and turned on the television. The bombings in Israel had been the hot topic on the news for the last few days. "I wish I was someplace exciting like that." John said as he walked into the kitchen. He opened up his cupboards and fridge to peer into each at the same time and decide what to get started for dinner. He decided leftovers it was and pulled them out to start heating. As he flicked on the range, he reached back into the fridge and pulled out some orange juice. He squeezed it himself every few days into a glass pitcher, he only drank natural fruit juices that weren't frozen or from concentrate and with no preservatives or other additives. Just about everything he could get in Bogota was processed. He poured the juice into a glass that he re-used to keep from piling dishes in the sink and returned the pitcher to its place in the fridge.

He sat back in the chair and sipped down his cool beverage as he began flipping through the television channels. He stopped on an old rerun episode of Sesame Street. At that moment in the show Bert and Ernie were discussing whether or not to eat cookies in bed. He remembered hearing something about the crumbs causing you to itch, as being the number one reason against it. He hadn't paused on the program because he liked the children's show so much that he wanted to catch up on the gang's charades; it was because he was paralyzed by a strange sensation coming over him. He had just ingested a lethal amount of arsenic trioxide.

Arsenic trioxide is widely used as a wood preserver in the U.S. and Malaysia; most other countries around the world have banned its use because of the chemical's expedient and lethal effects. Signs of ingestion include digestive problems, vomiting, severe abdominal pain, bleeding, convulsions and death. This can all happen with as little as a pea sized amount. John has just ingested almost three times the lethal dose.

As he moved his hand toward the coffee table to set down his drink, his stomach convulsed violently causing him to drop the glass. He felt as though he needed to vomit, but nothing would come up. He fell to his knees and tried to catch himself on the table, but instead brought it crashing down next to him. He continued his current trajectory and fell flat on the floor landing face down. His brain was racing, thinking about what could possibly be happening to him. Had it been a severe allergic reaction? He hadn't had anything except the OJ? Could he have been poisoned? Who would want to harm him and why? John began to foam at the mouth and convulse uncontrollably. He knew that if he didn't receive medical aid he would likely be unconscious in a matter of minutes. What John didn't know or want to believe, is that he was essentially already dead.

CHAPTER 36

BRAYDEN LAID IN his bed relieved that the ordeal was over as he replayed certain parts of the mission in his mind. He was given two weeks of convalescent leave to allow him to rest up after his dive injury. Luckily the ship that picked them up in the Pacific Ocean had a recompression chamber on board. He was able to restart the process on a table four and finish decompressing appropriately.

He decided to climb out of bed at the crack of noon and move his lounge party to the couch in the living room in his small condo. He heard the post fall through the mail slot in the front door and figured that that was his cue to start the day. As he walked into the kitchen to get a pot of coffee started, he wondered when he would hear about the decision to destroy the submarine. He had, after all, been given a direct order not to interfere with the smuggling line. He poured water into the reservoir, inserted a filter and coffee grounds into the brew basket, and hit start. As the aroma of fresh coffee filled the room he walked over and started picking up the mail. He slowly began sorting through it.

"Bill, bill, advertisement, junk... Katie O'Brien?"

Brayden starred at the package that he had just received and looked puzzled at the name of the addressee.

"Um, right address, wrong person."

He headed to the door to see if he could catch the mail person. They had just dropped his mail not long ago, and it usually took them awhile to deliver to everyone in his particular unit. As he walked out of the front door he noticed the mailman at an adjacent Building. He yelled and flagged him down as he ran across a small patch of grass; tip toeing to avoid the dog business that no one ever bothered to pick up.

"Sir, I don't think this was intended for me." He said as he approached within a few feet of him.

As he stretched out his arm he read the name on the back of the package along with the return address. *From: John O'Brien, U.S. Embassy, Carrera 45 No. 24B, Bogota Colombia DC.*

"Oh crap, I'm sorry, this is for my girlfriend, I still haven't gotten use to the fact that she has actually moved in with me!" Brayden offered as he withdrew his surrender attempt of the package.

The mailman waved and smiled, Brayden reciprocated the gesture and made his way back to his condo.

Brayden remembered John from the IT department at the DIA in Bogota. He had given him a thumb drive that he recovered from his source and wanted him to take a look at it before he was forced to send it to an analyst. He wanted him to extract any information he could from it and give it to him without involving anyone else from his office. John was especially talented at exploiting digital media devices, though he rarely let on that he could. He wasn't an analyst, or a Technical Device Specialist (TDS), so he didn't have to report to anyone about defeating equipment or software. Brayden had intended to retrieve the results himself a few days after he gave it to him, but his hasty reassignment interfered.

He sat at his kitchen bar, opened the padded envelope and noticed the picture of John and those who he presumed were his family. He pulled the picture out, propped it up in front of him and looked into the packaging. There was a very small note that said "I love you." *Did he really put the wrong address on here?* Brayden thought. He walked around the partial wall containing the bar, grabbed himself a mug from the dishwasher and poured a cup of coffee. All the while thinking about the oddity of the package. He stared at the picture wondering why John would send it to him. He wouldn't have written his wife's name and inadvertently scribble the wrong address. He was certain that John didn't even know his address, so he had to actually look it up and purposely send it to him. Brayden sipped his coffee and moved closer to the counter. *And if he were actually sending it to his wife, he surely would have included a note that said more than I love you, right?* He thought to himself.

He grabbed the picture, turned it over and began removing the back. "Ah, that's more like it." He said out loud. A CD had been placed inside the frame between the picture and the cover stand. He retrieved the disk, laid the back of the picture frame on the counter and headed back to his bedroom toward his computer. As he sipped his brew he inserted the disk into the CD drive. After the computer took its time recognizing the newly inserted media, he clicked open the file and began perusing it. The contents looked benign; financials, aircraft stuff, grid coordinates and a list of random names. As he looked at some of the names associated with the holding companies, he almost dropped his mug. He didn't know any of the people, but he had heard some of the names mentioned on CSPAN. They were political figures and representatives from all facets of government, along with ethnic sounding names of people probably of Spanish and middle Eastern descent.

Brayden set down his coffee cup, stood and pondered what this could mean as he walked around his bedroom. He returned to his computer and printed out the documents with grid locations. On the wall near his desk, he kept a map of South America that he could look at periodically to help him remain oriented on his area of operation. It was a gift from one of the commandos he had helped train in Tres Esquines. He looked at the map and tried to place some of the grids but nothing really stood out. The map was nice for names and known locations, but he would need to head to work and enter them into a much more robust mapping system. He ejected the disk, stuck it into the backpack laying on the floor by his desk, and returned to the kitchen. He sat back down at the bar and while sipping his coffee, began to put the picture of John's family back to together. He wondered what John was up to; he would have to thank him for remembering to extract the contents of the drive. For now, he needed to find a place to hide the disk.

CHAPTER 37

BRAYDEN KNEW FROM his training that if you wanted to hide something and not get caught; you had to do it while off the grid. To the layperson it might seem like too much effort when you're talking about a minute percentage of a chance. But to the informed, any chance is enough reason to take extra precautions. Brayden wasn't sure if anyone knew he had received this disk, but he didn't want to chance being caught with it.

He decided to try a trick he had only seen in the movies. No one taught this, and he figured it was because of the over use in blockbuster movies. There was an old Amtrak train station about fifteen miles from his condo. There were no cameras inside and it had very little foot traffic. The train was still in service, but the station was mostly used as a museum of sorts. People would stop and take pictures and read the history posted on the outside of the building while visiting the city's downtown area. Brayden decided this was the perfect spot to start.

He dressed inconspicuously and decided to ride his mountain bike to the station so that his car would not be seen in the vicinity. He parked outside in the bike parking area and looked around casually judging the atmosphere and number of potential onlookers. It was a weekday so most people were at work. He walked into the building and was prepared to make small talk with the window agent, but no one was there. He opened one of the public storage boxes and dropped off an envelope containing bank statements and information for an offshore bank account in his name. If found it might look interesting enough to consider the search a success, allowing the requestors to call off the remainder of the hunt. His real package, containing the photo of the O'Brien family, and the CD, remained hidden in his backpack.

As he closed up the locker, an attendant entered the building with his Subway lunch in hand and disappeared behind the counter. Brayden walked up and rang the bell. The man, an older gentleman, walked out of a back room still chewing on his lunch and offered his assistance.

"How may I help you young man?" He said as he continued masticating his sandwich.

"I would like a ticket to the airport please." Brayden requested.

"Ok, that will cost you ten dollars. You know that the line doesn't take you directly there, you will still need to take a taxi or walk." The man informed him.

"Yes, I am aware of that, thank you."

Brayden received his ticket and waited the fifteen minutes before his train arrived, sitting on a bench outside near the tracks. As the train pulled in and began slowing to a crawl in anticipation of coming to a halt, Brayden pulled the hood up on his sweatshirt and walked to the yellow boarding line. As he boarded, he looked over his map of the train's routes that the station agent had handed him when he purchased his ticket. He glanced at the airport exit, where he was scheduled to get off, and studied the additional exits nearest the Beach Haven Mall. The Mall was the stop he intended to take in the first place.

Like most mass transit areas, the mall also had a bank of storage boxes. It was usually crowded with people intent on minding their own business but instead of worrying about making it to their connecting gate on time, they were enjoying the temporary high of consumerism. All that mattered to Brayden, was that he could place his contents there without looking like he was trying to hide something.

At the moment though, he noticed a man three rows up that was looking suspicious. He had already glanced at him twice and the last time they made eye contact, the man quickly looked away. Brayden hadn't remembered anyone getting on with him, and definitely no one wearing a suit. He peered at the man for a few minutes before reeling in his active imagination. *I just received this package, there is no way anyone knows about it yet.* He thought. *Don't over think this, just stick to the plan.*

As Brayden neared his stop, he checked the man over once again. His briefcase was still open and he was looking through papers that he had balanced on his lap, he was not ready to exit the train. Brayden stepped off the train and moved around a corner near the entrance to the platform. He waited there momentarily to see if the man would be following behind him, no one was trailing.

He walked the mile and a half to the mall and entered the ground floor, which held the storage lockers. He walked around the relatively large bank of boxes checking to see how many were in use. He counted twenty-five.

Great, he thought, *at least there were other boxes being put to use*. Teenage girls used most of the storage boxes in malls. They would smuggle in their more revealing clothing articles and hide them there to allow a quick change after school. All this to peruse the meat market for the under aged, the mall's food court.

He locked up the remaining contents of his backpack and departed the mall. He decided to walk the five miles into the actual city of Beach Haven. From there he hailed a taxi and took it to an antique store just outside of Stanton, the city that he lived in. He perused the store and even purchased an old corncob pipe that came with a display stand. He walked the three miles back into the city and decided to stop and grab something eat. He ate on the patio of a sandwich shop so he could watch the train station, and bid farewell to his $1000 mountain bike, as he would not be retrieving it. He chalked it up as a charitable donation. No one of any interest showed up. *Man, I am getting too paranoid*, he thought.

April 2000

CHAPTER 38

TIME HEALS ALL wounds, and most diving injuries. Brayden returned to work and after a thorough dive physical, he received a clean bill of health. He arrived back with his team just in time to begin planning for their upcoming trip to Colombia. He still hadn't heard anything about the submarine, but he couldn't imagine that it would just go away.

The drug wars had been going on for decades. He remembered seeing Nancy Reagan on television talking about the countless lives ruined in the U.S. due to drug use. Drugs had been pushed over the boarders of Mexico in the U.S. for as long he or anybody else could remember. Marijuana and cocaine had been main stay drugs through the 60's and 70's, but recently the scene started moving toward harder substances. These were made with cocaine or heroin as the base with additional chemicals added to deliver the drugs to the system quicker and with more intense experiences. Also, at this time the cartels were introducing their armies, and they were proving very effective at attriting Colombian forces. Brayden just happened to enter into this very turbulent time with the addition of the FARC to the already ruthless drug kingpins. They were large enough to begin to project serious power, and because of the sanctuary they had enjoyed in the jungle for years; they were now almost uncontrollable.

The Aregano Feta Organization or AFO was a merciless band of brothers and associates that had grown very powerful in Colombia, Ecuador, and Mexico. Their span and reach was growing and their illicit activities were increasing. They went from drug trafficking, conspiracy and money laundering, to aiding and abetting violent crimes. The latter is what caught the attention of the State Department. They weren't members of the larger, more influential cartels; they instead provided disappearing services for them that would allow them to remain detached from the overt business of killing. Drugs were one thing, but you couldn't risk moving large quantities of drugs *and* carrying out murder yourself; especially the killing of respected members of the community and the politically connected. That was an instant recipe for disaster, as all agencies would focus on you until they effectively shut you down.

Murder for hire however, allowed everyone to get a piece of the game and keep each line of criminal activity separate from the other. The AFO was already under investigation, but they sped up their take down timeline when they began to target U.S. personnel abroad that were working in embassies, aid organizations and contract companies. Several successful killings had taken place and their efficiency was improving.

Brayden was to once again be assigned to the embassy in Bogota while the remainder of his team conducted training for the Colombian Lanceros', their equivalent of Army Rangers, in a neighboring city. Broderick Chapman was the new CoS, and unlike Mitchel, his tolerance for military personnel was zero. He didn't particularly like USSF personnel conducting source operations in what he believed was his area; and made it perfectly clear to Brayden upon his arrival. Brayden took the hint and decided that avoiding him was the best policy. He was technically not required to answer to him, so he actively ignored him.

Brayden got busy tracking down an associate of the AFO that was willing to inform on the organization's activities. They were set to conduct a meet in a hotel on the other side of town. Brayden booked three rooms; two to conduct the meet, and the other to house two members of his team in case he was being set up.

The meet rooms were wired for sound, several microphones were hidden in various locations around each room. Cameras had been installed in light fixtures and wall décor and several electronic devices were prepped to collect information from his cellular phone. Two members from the detachment were staged just down the hall in the third room, they now called it their operations center. It contained the monitors for viewing the video feed live, and amplifying equipment for picking up even a whisper. They were also heavily armed in the event that the meeting took a turn for the worse. Brayden used this particular hotel because one of the individuals at the front desk was a trusted agent. She would check the potential source into the hotel, and issue him a room key in a familiar and random appearing manner, but ensure that he would be staying in the predetermined suite. He would likely ask for a view of the street, so that he could attempt to observe Brayden enter the hotel, this had already been factored in. The second room would only be necessary if he suspected something and returned to the desk to request a different room; this ensured that they had their bases covered. Once the subject was in the hotel, she would call Brayden and tell him which room he was occupying. Brayden would be able to receive the subject's status and posture confirmation from his team members that were observing the room, and then make his way into the hotel from a bar across the street.

His name was Ruffelo Guzman; his associates called him Ruffy. He owned a trucking company that moved chemicals for water treatment plants all over Colombia. By the nature of his business, he had access to the neighboring countries, as he would pick up contracts here and there as an attempt to expand his reach. He was persuaded to work with the AFO after making a large delivery to one of their warehouses unwittingly. He moved what he believed to be water treatment supplies, until they were revealed as cutting agents for cocaine production by the AFO. They blackmailed him with the information, by having a member of the authorities on their pay role intercept and observe the shipment. He would be charged with criminal activity if he refused the AFOs offer. He accepted, as he would instantly lose his business while he was being investigated. Even if it settled in his favor, he would lose hundreds of thousands of dollars in the process. Or he could continue to work with them in a similar manner, on what they said would be a limited bases, but earn a substantial amount of money doing so. Ruffy agreed.

He was making more money that he knew how to hide and was offered a way to launder his new earnings, furthering his implication. Eventually they began using the cross boarder access he had, to move women to be sold into the sex trade; but it's the kidnappings of U.S. personnel that drew the line. The organization began targeting Americans working in small, outlying rural areas. They would switch drivers, or send along an associate to direct the trucks where to go to take these individuals hostage. They would then be sold to the cartels and hidden in the jungle under FARC control to be used later for negotiations. Ruffy was prepared to help Brayden orient to these men, in hopes of finally being freed of their malicious control. Brayden still questioned how deep Ruffy was actually involved.

Ruffy arrived to the lobby of the hotel at three o'clock. So far, he was following the timeline and instructions he was given. He checked in, received his room key, and proceeded to the elevators.

"He's on the way to the room, stand by."

Brayden said through an earwig to send word to the team already positioned to collect atmospherics. Brayden watched the man check in and head toward the elevator. Five minutes later, he observed the curtains opening in the room and Ruffy standing in the room looking up and down the street; so far so good.

"He's in the room and so far, he hasn't said anything, it doesn't look like he is going to attempt to make any calls." Said one of the team members.

Brayden waited ten more minutes, to allow the situation to develop, before walking across the street and into the hotel. He walked into the lobby and toward the front desk. He stopped in front of the counter and smiled at his asset.

"Do you have any messages for me?" He asked.

She walked over to a predetermined box and pulled out a hand written note and gave it to him.

"Here you are Sir."

"Thank you." He said as he continued to the elevator.

Once inside he opened the note as he reached for the button to the 7th floor. It read. *The man that checked in had a large distinguishing mark on his left hand.* Brayden had explained the details of a sizeable scar the man had on his hand. He needed to ensure it was actually him that showed up. He couldn't risk anything while dealing with a potential member of an organization that didn't play by the rules.

Brayden walked down the hallway, thinking of things that could go wrong. He wasn't nervous about the meet; he was instead anxious to find out if anything actionable would be derived from it. He paused in front of the room before knocking. He checked his watch, looked down the hall, and then knocked on the door. Ruffy answered the door and hurried Brayden in as if he were afraid they would be seen together.

"Hello Ruffelo, I'm Brayden, it's nice to meet you in person."

Brayden said as he extended his hand. Ruffy shook his hand and began walking toward the small seating area.

"Hi Brayden, nice to meet you too. You know you can call me Ruffy." He reminded him.

The men sat looking at each other for a few seconds, neither knowing how to begin until Brayden broke the ice.

"I understand how difficult this must be, but you know how serious this is." Brayden started.

"This organization will not just let you walk away. You are now implicit in their activities. You can volunteer as much or as little information as you want, I'm here to help."

"I don't know where to turn." Ruffy began.

"If I go to the police or government officials, I will be killed, they have connections. They have taken over my trucks and created new routes into places where I have never done business. They know that I am not happy with the direction they have taken my company, they have started to kidnap people, and they are now threatening my family. I have no more options."

Brayden pulled out a notepad and showed it to Ruffy to ensure his approval. Ruffy nodded in conformation and Brayden postured to take some notes.

"Tell me about your routes? How has the AFO changed them? Do you know what they're moving, when they're moving it, and where it's going?"

Ruffy began answering the questions and painting a detailed picture of how his company operates under their control. He divulged routes into and out of city warehouses, industrial parks, and areas in the jungle that were difficult to reach. Sometimes they would deliver to temporary holding locations, before transferring the cargo into a different mode of transportation. Often times, they would deliver to a runway in the middle of nowhere. Brayden's interest was piqued when he began discussing dirt strips in the middle of the jungle. He swayed the conversation in that direction and pulled a piece of paper from his jacket with lat./long. coordinates.

"Do you think you could find out if you deliver to any of these areas?" Brayden questioned, wanting to tell him rather than ask.

"Yes of course." Ruffy replied.

"Can I take this paper with me to verify?"

"Absolutely." Brayden said.

"Next time you have a truck heading to a desolate strip in the jungle, I need to know about it." Brayden said sternly.

"I will Sir, what do I do in the mean time?" Ruffy asked in a desperate manner.

"Continue to do what they tell you, this time we will be watching."

Brayden thought it obvious, but he followed up with, "Do not get caught with those coordinates."

Brayden knew that even if they could eliminate the entire network, it would only be a matter of time before someone caught up to Ruffy. He would do his best to protect him, but that was not his number one priority. As the meeting ended, Brayden asked him about his family and interests outside of work, to get him back in the right frame of mind before heading out of the hotel. After the brief bonding session, Brayden coordinated for the next meet, then excused himself and headed back to the office. Ruffy departed shortly after; the team sanitized both rooms then made their way back to their safe house.

Against his better judgment, Brayden summarized the meeting and sent it via his relatively new line of reporting on the high side. He included everything except the tasking he had given Ruffy of locating the remote airfields. He would rather beg for forgiveness than ask for permission. Once his report was sent, he moved back to his office and decided to check the messages on his standard secret computer. He had nothing on the high side, and likely wouldn't see anything until after his report was analyzed. After logging in and clicking through several windows to get his email up, he discovered one message.

Brayden, I hope this finds you well. I was finally briefed about the fiasco in Costa Rica. First of all, I'm glad I could assist in getting you all out of there in one piece. Second, I heard about your incident at the hospital. Why were you diving in the middle of the night? Didn't you take a portable chamber? This hasn't been received well, but I will do my best to put this issue to bed. Brayden, I will caution you with this son, learn to follow orders. James

Hopefully the fact that James brought up the incident and didn't mention anything about major equipment loss, means he won't have to hear about it again. Brayden wasn't about to get his hopes up; usually it doesn't work that way. For almost all organizations, crap rolls down hill and it still had a long, long way to go.

May 2000

CHAPTER 39

THE DECISION TO once again work with the DEA was not Brayden's. It was actually suggested by Broderick. Brayden knew that it was an attempt at projecting influence over his operation, but it was actually to his benefit. The DEA had the authority to seize drugs and currency; USSF did not. All they could do was destroy it, and he already knew how that could turn out based on his recent experience. He didn't plan to take any action on this particular mission, as that would most certainly put Ruffy in danger. He planned to confirm or deny the validity of the runway location and if it panned out, come up with a way to proceed.

Ruffy had held up his end of the deal. He sent Brayden a list of all the areas they traveled into that matched the coordinates on the list. Of the five total, three were actually accessible and not in the heart of FARC territory. Ruffy gave Brayden the information for the next pick up and drop off that was scheduled to take place at one of the isolated airfields. It was one that was on Brayden's list. They decided to conduct split team operations. This would allow one group to follow the truck from its launch point, and another to stage for an air insertion on to the target area once the location was identified. Brayden would be on the air infil, so he staged at a Colombian Army Airbase with half of his team and members of the DEA.

The group following the truck would have the riskiest part of the mission. At some point, they would have to affix a tracking device to the vehicle. It would be the only way to trace its position once off the main roads. Following the truck off-road, where vehicles didn't frequent, and where it merged to only one lane, would get them compromised or worse.

According to Ruffy, the AFO did not put heavy hitters in the trucks. Properly licensed truck drivers, most of whom Ruffy had hired himself, drove them. Everything was made to look as legal as possible. So aside from actually breaking open a properly marked container, it would pass most cursory searches.

From the location it was departing, the truck would have to contend with no less than four checkpoints. The Colombian police, whom USSF had no control over, ran three of them. The Colombian Army ran the other; that's the one they could influence. To ensure the device was emplaced properly, one of the members of the SFOD-A staged at the Army checkpoint in a host nation uniform. His heritage allowed him to blend in, as long as he wasn't required to speak for very long; his dialect of Spanish would give him away. While searching the vehicle, the soldiers would pretend to find something that would prompt a more thorough examination. This would require the truck to pull off the road into a temporary holding area and its occupants to get out of the vehicle. All doors, the hood, and all interior compartments would have to be opened for a more detailed search. This would give the time, concealment, and proper misdirection needed to emplace the device.

As the truck left the city of Cota, the team passed the license plate details to their teammate staged at the Army checkpoint. GUC-980 was sent as a text to his phone, along with a brief description of the vehicle. The surveillance team was split into two vehicles. This way they could rotate who took lead position behind the target and mitigate the chances of their surveillance being detected. They would also have to watch the traffic around the target and ensure no one was conducting counter-surveillance, actively looking for them.

They followed the truck for miles, setting up a box like pattern during brief stops, so that they could pick them up no matter which direction they departed. They rotated the trail vehicle enough to be easily forgotten. Once the truck began heading toward the Army checkpoint, they backed off in preparation for the change of responsibility.

The truck pulled up to the checkpoint and one of the guards began checking the undercarriage of the vehicle with a mirror, while the other spoke with the vehicles occupants, in order to verify credentials and load manifests. When the Colombian guard checking around the vehicle reached the rear, he confirmed that the license plate matched the number-letter combination he had been given. The truck was waved over to the side and into the traffic coned holding area so that it could be more thoroughly searched.

"Why are you holding us up? We come through here all the time and we've never had a problem." The driver began.

"It's just a routine stop." One of the Colombian Army guards started. "Every few days we pull over every third or fourth vehicle and do a more in-depth search."

As the men departed the vehicle, opening up all required spaces, the SFOD-A member moved into position to place the tracking device.

"Come on, hurry up." The driver said as he was becoming impatient.

The passenger continued to try peeking into the truck, to ensure that the guards were not going to steal any of their belongings. The team member was able to install the tracking device at the rear or the vehicle inside the bumper. As long as no one suspected anything, the device wouldn't be found. Once finished, he signaled to the guards, who ushered the men back into the vehicle and on their way.

Brayden and crew began picking up the signal almost immediately. They notified the Colombian Army pilots that they would like to depart within the hour, which would give the truck and any aircraft on the runway time to clear out. They conducted their pre-flight, topped off with fuel, loaded up and took off. The flight would be slow, as they did not want to spook the target or destination area with the loud and distinct sound of the old but reliable UH-1H Huey. The helicopter landed and staged in a small clearing nearly fifteen nautical miles away. The truck was still being tracked at the strip, so they waited for the transaction to complete and all parties to depart, before continuing into the runway area.

The helicopter completed a sweep of the area, checking all roads and small clearings in the vicinity to ensure they wouldn't fly into a guerilla-controlled area. Use of the Colombian aircraft was necessary to remain anonymous. The Colombians routinely flew over the jungle, varying their routes to appear to have a presence. More often than not, they were shot at a few times before returning to the base.

Once the aircrew was satisfied that the threat was minimal, they landed and allowed Brayden and the DEA to unload and walk around the airfield. It was a meticulously kept strip of dirt, with a small windsock hanging from a stake on the west side of the north / south running field. The area was just as Brayden had hoped. A strip in the middle of nowhere that was left unattended when not in use. Now that he knew this one actually existed, he could plot the others and fly them one by one.

Brayden stated his findings about the trucking company, Ruffy and the AFO. He was told to continue developing their pattern of life and report any new findings. What he left out was the fact that he had flown into one of the runway locations and that he had grids to most of them, courtesy of Trenton Industries. He was convinced, that rendering these private strips useless would most certainly cripple the cartels' ability to move large quantities of product. It would also give the Colombian Army the nudge they needed to begin seriously targeting the cartels and the FARC. All he needed now was approval.

The decision to take out a piece of a ratline was usually not taken lightly. Those serving at the strategic planning level viewed it as treating one of the symptoms, versus treating the actual ailment. The thought process was logical, if you destroyed a runway let's say, you may risk your target using an alternate location or another means of transportation. Which would force all agencies involved to restart the process of finding the line. This wasted time and money and increased the exposure of assets on the ground. Each major operation usually had a timeline and or events matrix that had to line up before the entire network was taken down in one fell swoop. However, at this point in Brayden's career, he did not care about the strategic picture. He wanted to see instant feedback from the rather perilous work he and his teammates were doing on the ground.

He sent an email through the secret side of the network to several individuals at the TSOC and ensured to courtesy copy the CIA liaison that worked there. His email explained the various runways in the jungle that were being used for unlawful activities and the fact that the CIAs OGA would be best suited to conduct the reconnaissance. After all, they were the best international detectives in the world. He also talked about the trucking company that was moving cutting agents for drugs, and the high probability that some of the kidnappings in the east were being conducted by the AFO. His recommendation was to continue observation, and pass any operations that might be conducted to the follow on USSF team or OGA. Broderick didn't like entities that tried to pass the buck or not pull their fair share, so he knew this would especially get under his skin. The liaison officer would have no choice but to forward this message to Broderick after reading it, as he was the CoS for the area from which the reporting was created. Brayden just hoped he would take it the way he wanted him to.

August 2001

CHAPTER 40

BRAYDEN CONTINUED RACING down the dirt road, thinking about nothing except putting distance between himself and Steve. His pain took a back seat to the new mission of self-preservation. If he were to succumb to his injuries now, he might as well pull the trigger himself. He searched the vehicles instrumentation for a direction-heading indicator; it didn't have one. It really didn't matter as there were no turn offs, and off roading in the jungle was not feasible. With his current direction being his only option, he worried about the speed in which they could send reinforcements. Hopefully he would at least hit a fork before much more time past. The fuel gauge registered almost half a tank; he figured that would give him a decent head start if he had to transition to foot; although he wouldn't get far with his injuries. He had been stripped of everything; all of his communication devices had been…"Communication devices", Brayden said aloud as he slammed on the breaks. He hurriedly looked around the vehicle for a cell phone and found one in the back seat. He stretched over the seat despite the pain to grab it, as he didn't want to exit the SUV. He flipped the phone open and it had power, but it didn't have a signal. He laid the phone on the passenger seat and took off again down the road. It seemed as though he had been driving forever when he finally came to a fork in the road. The choice to go right was made for him when he saw multiple vehicles moving toward him in the distance on the left. He hoped that they would have continued in their direction of travel, perhaps being too far away to notice a turning vehicle; this was not the case. Both vehicles paused momentarily at the fork before turning and following him. As he accelerated, throwing all notions of conserving petrol out of his mind, he heard the familiar, rhythmic, bass filled audio of a helicopter beating the air into submission.

"You've got to be fucking kidding me." Brayden mumbled to himself.

The helicopter flew over him, performed a very well executed, full tilt, 180-degree turn, and flew back over him in his direction of travel. It slowly climbed and started a turn back toward the cabin, Steve's location. Brayden knew that it was about to get very bad, very quickly.

He hated driving in traffic back in the states. Always being cut off by rude and inconsiderate drivers, or wishing the person in front of him would at least drive the speed limit; but at this moment he would have given anything for the anonymity. To have a chance at blending in and perhaps making it out of a chase in the midst of all the added confusion, as he had so many times in training. This, however, was futile. There was nowhere to go, on a straight road to who knows where with who knows what waiting at the other end. He was starting to have an out of body experience. He thought about everything that he had been through in his life and wondered was it really worth it to finally end up on this road, literally and figuratively. Had he really been that bad of a person that he would be left to die alone, in what he imagined after this stunt would be a violent and painful death? His predicament seemed so dire that it almost brought him to laughter. As his pain started to creep back up, and the pointlessness of his current escape attempt started to seep into his reality, he began to ease up on the gas pedal in preparation of accepting his fate. As he looked in the rearview mirror, attempting to judge the distance of his pursuers, the phone he had set on the passenger seat began to ring.

May 2000

CHAPTER 41

BRAYDEN WAS CALLED to Broderick's office twenty-four hours after he pushed send on his email to the TSOC. He walked in and had a seat in one of the club chairs that sat in front of his desk.

"Hello Sir, I heard that you wanted to see me." Brayden announced.

"Yes, I would like to speak with you about this runway in the middle of the jungle that you visited." Broderick started.

"I would like you to orient your team, along with the DEA, on building a pattern of life for these runways. I don't believe that we will be able to affect the entire area, but if you carefully select the most frequented strips, it should slow down the cartel's freedom of movement. It would force them to either patrol the areas more, or begin using zones that the Colombian Army can't actually reach and sustain combat operations in, at least for a while. Keep the operations low visibility and use the Colombian Army when you can to maintain deniability."

Brayden sat in silence with his legs crossed, actually feeling pretty smug about the fact that his scheme appeared to be working. He sat up in his chair and rubbed the back of his head as if he were pondering whether or not they were capable of the task.

"Ok Sir, of course I will have to clear this with the TSOC but I will alert the team and begin planning." Brayden replied.

Broderick excused him, as if he was his subordinate, and Brayden walked out of the office hardly able to contain himself.

Brayden stopped by the SCIF on his way out of the embassy for the day to check his high side account. He only had one message, and he was actually nervous to open it.

SM1356, prepare to meet source # NHL-023-001-98, his dossier and case file will follow upon acknowledgment. This is an asset validation and takes priority over all other tasks.

Brayden hit the message confirmation button and decided to walk down to the cafeteria and grab himself a cup of coffee. Depending on the amount of information in the file of this new asset, he may find himself at work longer than expected and wanted to begin fueling for it. He walked down the back staircase on his way to the centrally located eating area and noticed the mailroom was still open. He poked his head into the small room to accost the lady behind the half counter half door.

"Hello," he said as he waved to the woman.

"I always forget this place is in the embassy, I received a package from here while I was back in the states and it had the address stamped on it, kind of threw me for a loop." He said attempting to break the ice.

"Yes, I do get that a lot, after a few months when you want to send souvenirs home, we will be your best friends." She said jokingly. Brayden smiled and continued.

"I don't know if you can give it to me, but do you have John O'Brien's stateside address? He used to work upstairs in the DIA office."

"Oh yes," she replied.

"But I'm not really supposed to give that information out, stop by tomorrow afternoon and I'll see what I can do."

She said with a smile. Brayden thanked her and continued to the coffee machine. He poured himself a cup, added two sugars, one creamer, took his time stirring the contents so he could soak up the happenings in the large break area and then headed back to the SCIF.

Validating an asset was usually done just before recruiting them, or to test the accuracy of their reporting at different times during their employment. Usually, you gave them a task and used some sort of controlled means to test whether or not they were actually doing what you ask, or being deceitful. You could have them retrieve information that you already had the answer to, if they provide anything different you knew they were being untruthful. You could send them out with electronic surveillance, tracking devices, microphones, and video to monitor them and see if they were doing what you asked. You could have a validated and trusted agent watch them and report their findings, unwittingly of course. Or, you could task them with something you knew they couldn't accomplish; forcing them to do the right thing and return telling you it wasn't possible, or attempt to provide you false information. Brayden decided to use the latter.

Source number NHL-023-001-98 was actually a man named Miguel Felipe.

MENDACITY

He started his path into the criminal world at the age of 18 when he first began working for a cartel. He was a driver for an upper-level financier within the Cortez family. He progressed from menial work to personal protection and remained there until a heated blood feud ensued between the Cortez family and a rival faction. It was then that he made a name for himself, killing without mercy or any regard for his own personal safety. He excelled at this new job and became a professional hit man shortly after. Murder for hire was a much better living. He worked for many different organizations over the years. But like all good things, it came to an end when his wife and children were killed after a botched attempt on a Saudi mediator.

The Arab was supposed to be eradicated once the Tiko's Gentlemen had negotiated a cocaine deal that was intended for a Saudi prince. The businessman was a cut out to ensure the royal family wasn't exposed and shamed. The prince had past dealings with the organization in the way of prostitutes that he had obviously forgotten about.

Associates of the Tiko's Gentlemen had organized a shipment of prostitutes to service a very large and exclusive party and eventually pad his harem. The women were delivered in a shipping container and left on the dock because the prince had not made the proper coordination's to have them picked up. All ten women died, and the prince refused to pay because in his mind, he had never received his request. The members of Tiko's Gentlemen never forgot, and they wanted their revenge.

The prince's representative was to be killed and decapitated so that his head could be sent back to the prince. Miguel was hired for the job and given creative freedom to assassinate the man in the manner he chose. The drive by shooting should have been easy and it probably would have been successful if he had done it himself. Instead, he allowed two of his cousins that were following in his footsteps, to try their hand at the lucrative trade.

The location was perfect; very little traffic frequented the side road near the small coffee shop in Medellin. The two aspiring murderers waited at a corner for the man to exit the shop and get in his car. They slowly drove up as the Arab was starting the vehicle and fired several shots into the automobile. The first grazed his ear, the second grazed his left shoulder and the rest hit various places in the vehicle where they came to rest. An associate of the Tiko's Gentlemen was to take care of the decapitation, but when he arrived on scene to retrieve the body shortly after the unsuccessful shooting spree, it and the vehicle were gone. After the attempt on his life, the man made his way back to Saudi Arabia to explain to the prince how he was treated.

Miguel had been out shopping with his wife at the time and was completely in the dark when he showed up to collect his fee for the job. He was paid his full asking price and congratulated for a job well done. Two weeks later, he returned home after negotiating another contract, to find his wife brutally raped and stabbed to death and his kids hanging in their bedrooms. The note that was left, kindly explained the rationale behind the murders, and as he read it; he knew he wanted out. But walking away from the cartels was not that easy. Once you had woven yourself into the web they controlled, your only way out was followed by a funeral procession.

Brayden read Miguel's file entirely and began preparing his report for the tasking that he would give him. It was a long shot, but he intended to have him pull business affiliations from those he still associated with. He felt that if he could undeniably link a criminal organization to Trenton

Industries, that he would have found the ultimate smoking gun. But what would he do if his wild tale were true? He honestly didn't even know if it was worth pursuing. After all, just because Trenton Industries owned a bunch of land in the middle of the jungle, it still didn't prove anything. It's not like it was guarded and under friendly control when not in use. And the fact that a mechanic was flown out to service an aircraft secretively proves nothing, but someone did try to kill *him*.

Brayden struggled to gather his thoughts as he worked through his conspiracy theory. Everything still fell under the Running Man LOE as far as he could tell, so he couldn't get in trouble for working outside his purview. It really didn't matter anyway because one of two things would happen. Miguel would get killed trying to get the information, or he would return and tell him he was unsuccessful. Either way, Brayden would have accomplished his assigned mission. Now he had to tell his team that he was once again going solo.

CHAPTER 42

THE FOLLOWING MORNING Brayden made his way down to the cafeteria to grab a cup of coffee and see if he could catch the mail person. He had purchased some flowers and intended to deliver them, if it was the same lady he had met the day before. He held the flowers behind his back in case the gender of the day happened to be male. He gently knocked on the outside of the door, as it was already slightly cracked, and the same woman opened it with a smile.

"Good morning" Brayden offered. "I brought you some flowers to brighten your day. I know it has to get old staring at boxes and letters all day. You can enjoy a nice bouquet, for a little while anyway."

"Thank you so much, I have never received flowers here and I've been here a few years! Thank you, thank you!" She said with a big smile. "How are you doing today?"

"I'm fine thank you; I am the one that asked yesterday about getting John O'Brien's mailing address from you? He left some personal items and I would really like to send them back to him." Brayden told her.

"Of course, I remember you, I pulled his address out right after we spoke. I'm not supposed to give it out, but I have it right here."

She handed Brayden a piece of paper with the address on it, it had been pre-positioned, so obviously she planned to see him at some point that day.

"Thank you so much, if you ever need anything please don't hesitate to ask." Brayden said with a smile.

"Thank you, and thanks for the flowers, it really means a lot. Take care!" She joyfully replied.

Brayden knew there wasn't really anything he could do for her, but it always made people feel good when you offered. He slid the paper into his pocket and continued making his way to the coffee machine.

Brayden called his teammates once back in the office and told them that he had been given another assignment. Without giving too many details, he hinted that it was a source operation and that they had to conduct planning for the airfield reconnaissance without him. He wondered if Broderick would give them clearance to destroy the airstrip if they could prove that it was being used for smuggling. Whatever they did it would have to be quick and decisive. As soon as it reached the higher levels of command it would likely be shut down. But as long as Broderick approved it, they would be in the clear.

He finished his conversation with the team, logged off of his secret computer and prepared to log into a green or commercial unclassified computer to check his standard mail account. The activation for Miguel was a mainstream email account that had been set up months ago by his previous handler. He was trained on how to use it, and instructed only to use it for initial communication with his next manager. Miguel was required to check the account every Wednesday at 10am and again the same day at 5pm.

Brayden loaded the account with his email draft, that allowed Miguel to log into the same account and check for messages without having to send anything, thus reducing the risk of it being intercepted. Once contact was made with his new handler, the account would be closed and a new one set up again the next time he was put into a dormant status.

Brayden reviewed the time and location that was coordinated for Miguel; it was well outside of the city, and this time he planned to be more alert in looking for counter surveillance. This was a very dangerous time for source operations; cartels were catching on to their vulnerabilities and conducting their own counter intelligence operations. The result, agents were being killed at a high rate and he didn't want to be part of that statistic.

What Brayden didn't know about this new assignment, is that the CIA would be tagging along. His insubordination in regard to the debacle in Costa Rica had not been forgotten, and wasn't going away. The destruction of the submarine hadn't come up in any official channels as far as he could tell, but diplomatic intervention had been necessary, highlighting the fact that the U.S. might be conducting operations outside of what was being declared. Because of the sensitivity of the line he was flirting with crossing, the agency needed clarity on exactly what Brayden knew, or thought he knew. Although Brayden was used to in-your-face chastisement for doing something wrong or being willfully disobedient. He wasn't ready for a finger wag from an old, tried and true organization, that knew his tricks better than he did.

The agents assigned to Brayden wouldn't be there to help him or interfere with his meet; they were there to operationally test *him*, or so *they* thought. The agents assigned to Brayden had no idea what the real motivation behind their appointment to conduct surveillance on him was. And technically, they weren't supposed to be spying on an American citizen, even though the CIAs been doing just that since the 1950's.

They were given their orders, much like Brayden, and they didn't question the reasoning. All they did and were required to do was report what they saw and heard, no more, no less. They already knew where Brayden would be meeting his source, so they didn't have to actively tail him, they would be there waiting on him. And because they knew how long it would take him to travel there and back, they had plenty of time to search and electronically wire his suite.

Brayden made his way to Ibague for the meet. The drive through that part of the country was peaceful. The scenery once outside of the city consisted of sprawling farmlands, rolling hills, and occasional mountain peaks in the distance. He enjoyed the drive immensely, but he consciously kept tabs on vehicles that could be following him.

He arrived at the Creole Café; he smiled at the name as it reminded him of a place you would see in New Orleans. He'd never been, but it was on his list of must-see places to visit in the states. So far, he had seen more of other countries than he had of his own.

Upon entering he realized that the theme of the restaurant was trying desperately to mimic something you would find in the U.S. There was an old jukebox in the corner playing American music from the 1960's. The

MENDACITY

tables looked like they were out of an old country diner. Even the wait staff had American styled hairdos and dressed in clothing straight out of the sitcom Happy Days. *If only they knew the name didn't really fit the look* he thought.

He grabbed a table in the back of the café and waited for Miguel to arrive. His drive had been uneventful and he made it into the location without any surveillance that he could detect. He wondered if he had been paying enough attention as the landscape had engrossed him. Brayden ordered a beer to blend in with his surroundings and relished the taste of the cool beverage. They had several brands of U.S. beers on tap, but he wanted something local. He ordered a Costena, something he couldn't get in the states, plus it was cheaper than the imports.

Miguel pulled up to the front of the café and parked illegally. It didn't really matter in Colombia the warning signs were really just a suggestion, as they were rarely if ever enforced. He watched as Miguel exited his car with the confidence of an actor or politician, and almost looked like one. His hair was perfectly cut and combed, his clothes were clearly tailored, and his swagger suggested he was used to having things his way. Brayden paid attention to the street and surrounding shops and businesses as he entered the restaurant and was satisfied that he had arrived without being followed. Miguel was in his mid-thirties but once he was close enough to see the weathered look of his face, he appeared closer to mid-forties. Brayden suspected that the short life span of a Colombian hit man must be stressful, whether you make mistakes or not. He looked as though fitness was a priority in his life, likely so that fighting or running could remain feasible options.

"Miguel, it's nice to you, I'm Brayden." He said as he stood and extended his hand.

"Nice to meet you Brayden, I was actually surprised to be contacted. I have been wanting to speak with someone for a while." Miguel shook his hand and both men sat down, Miguel across the table from him.

He was nicely dressed in slacks and a button-down short sleeve shirt. His shoes were polished and broken in but not worn, and his watch suggested he was distinguished but not pretentious. Brayden was enthralled but had to remember that he was a hit-man that enjoyed killing people for profit. This was not a social call, he was dealing with a real-life sociopath, and he was only there to elicit information.

"I contacted you to ensure that you were still on our team, it's been a while since you had any interaction with us. I'll be handling your case now and just wanted to meet you face to face and make sure you didn't need anything. So, you say you have information for me?" Brayden said, opening the conversation.

"Yes." Miguel started. "I believe that the cartels are pooling money together for a very large-scale transaction. I'm not sure what it is, but I have been hearing about large cash shipments with police protection."

Brayden was coming to his senses and finally getting annoyed that he was taken away from a truly purposeful mission to meet with him. He understood why this guy had been dormant for so long. The conversation was beginning to remind him of the movie 'Heat', when Al Pacino asked the chop shop owner about an individual of concern and was told that he knew a guy, that knew a guy, that had gone to prison with him... Money movement was nothing new.

"Do you know what they are doing with this money? Where it is being stashed? To whom it will be delivered?"

"No, that's really all the information I have." Miguel confessed.

"Well, that's really good information Miguel, thank you. When you receive anything else regarding this stockpiling, please let me know. We would be very interested in what these funds are to be used for. Before we wrap up, do you have any other information that you would like to share?" Brayden said almost sarcastically. He was trying desperately not to be annoyed, but he just couldn't help it.

"Yes, actually I do." Miguel started. "I think the cartels are going to step up their game and begin targeting U.S. and government officials. A few of the larger cartels are nervous about how information is being obtained. I guess sometime last year, some kind of submarine was destroyed and it has them freaked out about leaks."

Brayden sat up in his seat and put his beer down. He hadn't even heard his own chain of command talk about the submarine, but the cartels are clearly concerned about it. He set a small note pad on his leg in preparation of jotting down pertinent information about this discovery without looking too obvious.

"Do you know where this took place? Do they suspect anyone in particular? Do you think they are pooling money for the repair or replacement of this sub?" Brayden responded excitedly.

"Somewhere near Costa Rica, it was their largest submarine and their having a hard time finding a replacement. Anyway, they are talking about revenge and in a big way. They know the Americans did it; they just don't know why." Miguel replied.

They didn't know why? Brayden thought briefly, but quickly moved past the thought because of his excitement. He was ecstatic and could barely hide it. He couldn't believe what he was hearing. He didn't even want to meet this guy and he was giving him some of the best news he had heard since he got back on his feet. He would have to change the subject of the conversation though, so that he would have something to write about in his report. There was no way he could divulge this information, but he couldn't wait to tell the rest of his team the effect that their operation had.

Brayden gained his composure, which he outwardly never appeared to have lost, and prepared to explain to Miguel exactly what he needed from him.

"Miguel, first I need to know if you have given this information to anyone else." Brayden asked sternly.

"No, I haven't." Miguel responded.

"Good, keep it that way. Anything else you find out about this would be helpful. If you need any tools to assist, please let me know." Brayden informed him.

Brayden sat back in his chair, picked up his beer and took another drink before continuing. He thought better of what he was about to ask, but his nature wouldn't let him leave it alone.

"Miguel, the reason I contacted you was to retrieve some information about a company called Trenton Industries, have you ever heard of them?" Brayden asked.

"No, I don't think I have heard anything about them. I can ask around though." Miguel replied.

"No, don't ask anyone, that could possibly raise suspicion. If you come across any files or documents with mention of them in your dealings, let me know." Brayden said.

He knew that it was a long shot that Miguel could find out anything meaningful about the company, not without getting himself killed anyway. But if he could make the link between Trenton and the cartels, it would further his theory and possibly allow the Colombians to severely cripple the cartels distribution, for a time anyway.

CHAPTER 43

HUMAN INTELLIGENCE OPERATIONS are really not that difficult. It requires a large investment of time, to gain a certain amount of knowledge about the subject of your operations and the ability to properly record their links or ties to organizations and individuals with whom they have dealings. This information, along with historical data containing past actions, whereabouts, motivations, and connections to personnel or systems; can be used as mechanisms and levers allowing you to prompt, measure and predict future actions. You then use the analyzed information to assist in controlling the subject; you could use them as a source of information, as a tool to assist in carrying out specific operations, or you could use the information to target and terminate them. Although basic, it takes training and years of practice to use effectively and it's mostly about the details and departure from the norm.

Most people don't look for things that are out of the ordinary as they go about their daily lives. They instead move along habitually in their routines, with predictability, following scheduled, patterned events and only if something truly extraordinary happens, does it even register on their radar. To the trained operator though, slight deviations from the norm are enough to set off alarm bells in their head and alter the course of their mission entirely. If for no other reason than to protect the true nature of their operation, they will change plans at the slightest anomaly. Other times its necessary just to remain alive.

As Brayden introduced himself to Miguel and began conducting his meeting, two men entered into room 1114 of the downtown Bogota Hilton. They were of average height and build, wore dark non-descriptive suits and blended in to the mostly American clientele that frequented the hotel. They walked in through the service entrance at the back of the hotel, taking advantage of the fast-paced hustle and bustle of the various departments and their staff during that time of day. The men made their way through the maze of preparation and storage areas to the delivery elevator. Once inside, they held the elevator momentarily while looking carefully around the area they had just moved through, to ensure no one had been overly curious about their entrance before pushing the faintly lit button to the eleventh floor.

As they exited the elevator and moved down the hallway, one of the men removed a blank piece of plastic resembling a credit card and entered it into the room's card slot. The card was designed to defeat that specific electronic locking device, allowing them to enter without difficulty. Once inside they began the long and tedious process of methodically checking through the contents of the room.

The subject's room was neat and orderly which made it easy to sort through. It also made it time consuming to examine, as the suites occupant likely knew which way labels were facing, and the exact spot that items were resting in. As they looked through drawers, closets, luggage and bedding, they made sure to keep track of the time, as they would need to conduct a thorough sanitization before departing.

The men used small cameras to take pictures of the room and the array of its contents, to assist in putting things back in the exact place they were found. The only items discovered that they thought might be of value, were folded papers with what looked to be grids and names. The men unfolded them and took pictures of the documents and placed them back where they had found them. After ensuring they had left nothing out of place, they departed the room, walked out of the hotel through the front door and headed back to their office. All relevant pictures that had been taken were used in their reports and the ones of possible value were sent up immediately via the high side to their higher headquarters.

Later that evening, Brayden returned to his hotel room and prepared to take his shower. Surprisingly, he was exhausted from his meeting. Perhaps it was the distance traveled, or the constant heightened awareness looking for possible surveillance elements. He thought briefly about returning to the office to type his post meeting report, but he really just felt like calling it an early day. He sat down on his bed and laid back looking at the ceiling, wondering what he would be doing at that moment had he gone to work with his father. He smiled at the thought of being bored out of his mind with the day in and day out monotony of a 9 to 5 job. He had already done more in the military than most people managed to accomplish in their entire lives. Sure, he could be making more money, but would it really be worth it? To be trapped in a life that was nothing more than a race to acquire more material objects than the person next to you; until you were finally laid to rest in a pine box, void of all your acquired possessions? He was happy with his choices thus far and had no regrets.

He sat up and grabbed the television remote to turn on the news.

Telemundo was the most popular station in that area and was the equivalent of any conservative news station in the U.S. As he removed his watch to lay it on the chest of drawers beside his bed, he noticed that every single drawer in the unit was pushed all the way in. He sat for a brief moment and stared at the dresser, wondering if he had somehow violated his own rule. *One or two drawers maybe* he thought, *but the entire unit?* He immediately walked to the nightstand and called the front desk.

"Hello Mr. Smith, how may we help you today." The lady at the front desk said upon answering.

"Hello, I would like to know if the maid service entered my room today." Brayden asked.

"Just a minute sir, I will have to place you on hold."

Brayden always kept the *do not disturb* sign on his door unless he was available to supervise the cleaning of his room. He only allowed them to clean once a week and at that time they changed his sheets, refreshed his towel stock, and any soaps and lotions that he had used. Everything else he did for himself, every day, so that he would always know, without a doubt, the status of his room.

"Mr. Smith?" The lady had presumably called housekeeping on another line and now had his answer.

"Yes, I am here."

"No sir, no one cleaned your room today, they said you strictly stick to a cleaning schedule. Did you want someone to come to your room now? Is there a problem?" The woman asked.

"No, there is no problem, thank you, you answered what I wanted to know." Brayden replied.

"Ok sir, enjoy your stay at the Hilton and let us know if there is anything we can do."

Brayden hung up the phone and walked to his dresser for a closer inspection. He carefully checked all the drawers and they had definitely been closed. He purposely left a quarter inch gap between each drawer and the frame so that from a distance, they looked to be shut completely. This way, he could tell if anything had been tampered with when he arrived back in his room. He walked into the bathroom and checked his toiletry bag. This was another routine he had become accustomed to and like the dresser; it provided him peace of mind that no one had been rummaging through his room. As he suspected however, it was completely zipped up, the space he purposely left between the zipper and its halt was gone. He moved back to the entrance of his room and checked for the scotch tape; it too was gone. He always left a piece of scotch tape sticky side up near the entrance in a natural area of shadow so that it couldn't be seen. It was a trick he learned from his grandfather actually, and Brayden remembered laughing about it when he told him as a kid. He had used it every time he stayed in a hotel room as an adult, after his grandfather explained it to him, and this was the first time it had ever been missing.

Obviously, someone had been in his room and he knew that they had to be trained, no one else would have meticulously returned his articles to their original place. After aimlessly walking around the room thinking about what he could have done to draw this much attention to himself, he thought about what he had left in his room that might compromise him. As he rummaged through his drawers, he found the print outs of the grid locations of runways and the list of names from the thumb drive.

"Shit." Brayden said aloud.

He quickly got dressed, ran out of the room and took the elevator down to the lobby. He called his driver while in the lobby and requested that he be picked up and driven to the embassy. While he waited, he attempted to calm himself down and think through the possibilities. The fact that someone had entered his room was disconcerting, but not surprising. He was after all dabbling in the spy game. As he thought through the alternatives, he began to calm down. No one was trying to kill him as of yet, which was relieving. Obviously, whoever it was, wanted to gather more information. *So, they don't have all the answers* he thought. As he attempted to remember all of his training, applying the principles behind intrusive surveillance, he began to relax again and think about it objectively. He walked into the hotel bar area, while waiting for his driver and ordered a scotch, neat, to calm his nerves. He knew it was time to change his tactics and procedures and began with throwing his phone in the trash. He removed the chip, broke it in half and threw it and the receiver into the bin that was next to the bar area. From now on, he would purchase his phones off the local economy instead of signing for them at work. He tried desperately to figure out who would go through his room so thoroughly versus just tossing it. He knew the answers, but couldn't bring himself to believe it just yet. The Administrative Department of Security or DAS was the Colombian version of the CIA. *It had to be DAS or the CIA*, Brayden thought; but he was leaning toward the Americans. He finished his scotch and walked outside through the large grand entrance of the hotel, to find his driver waiting for him with phone in hand. He was probably attempting to call him and let him know he had arrived, but

Brayden had already ridded himself of the handset.

Once at the embassy, he went to his office and checked his standard email, nothing had arrived out of the ordinary. He visited the SCIF and checked his high side messages, again nothing. He sat for a while, confused as to why he would be under such scrutiny. He assumed they saw the documents that he had left in his room. It was really too soon to see any fall out from it right now. It would take a few days for the information to be reviewed and pushed back down through the channels. How would he explain having the information? He never included the fact that he had retrieved information from Eduardo. He had already sent a report about the runway location they had found, based off of source reporting. Now they may figure out that Brayden actually tasked the source, to find a location that verified the information he had already received; from Eduardo. It was a long shot, but Brayden knew it was possible.

He decided to tell Broderick everything the following day. It may be the only way he could save himself from reprimand or worse, for not accurately reporting. In the meantime, he prepared to be observed at *all* times. Right now, no one was aware that he knew he was being watched, he would use that to his advantage.

CHAPTER 44

DARIUS PRICE WAS the team sergeant for SFOD-A 715. He was a gruff, compact, stocky and barrel-chested man from Oklahoma. His bright red hair and fireplug stature was menacing and could inflict intimidation immediately. The members of his team secretly nicknamed him the soul crusher, because if you showed up to his team believing you were one of the greatest men to walk the earth, he would immediately extinguish your internal flame. He had Ranger mentality through and through; was old school Special Forces, and believed in the true meaning of being a quiet professional.

Obviously, being on a Combat Diving detachment meant that you had to attend the CDQC in Key West, Florida. Darius allowed you two chances, which was more than fair, as no one from his team was sent without the proper train-up. If you quit, you were immediately banished from the team. Everyone that Darius sent to the school from his team, had to first pass his rigorous pre-scuba training and complete all of the events to standard. What you didn't know until you arrived in Key West, was that his standard was higher than theirs; everyone he sent passed. You also had to attend Ranger school if you showed up to the detachment without the qualification, no exceptions. If you didn't agree to the terms of his team, you were more than welcome and most times, verbally encouraged, to seek employment elsewhere.

Darius was hard but fair, and if you were one of the lucky eleven to share the team room with him during his tenure, you were guaranteed one of the best mentors and leaders in the Green Beret inventory. He didn't just teach you how to do something, he showed you why you needed to do it that way as well. He always ensured that the team's training and focus nested with that of the higher command, and if necessary, showed you how to deviate from what higher wanted to actually achieve the mission on the ground. Brayden trusted him with his life. He was one of the only leaders he had encountered thus far that he hadn't ever felt the need to question. He led with purpose, always from the front, and never without commonsense. In a world that habitually misplaced who to celebrate, he and many men like him were routinely overlooked, but without question the true role models.

The decision to first conduct the reconnaissance from the air using predator drones was Darius's. He knew they were being flown in the country to look for new drug labs and identify locations where hostages might be held. If he could somehow re-task the platform while it was on a mission, there was a chance it wouldn't be reported through higher channels. The only person that would need to be convinced was Broderick. Darius attempted to contact Brayden and let him know about their decision the night before, but with no luck. He left several messages, but he never returned his calls. He wasn't cognizant of the fact that Brayden had destroyed his phone.

Brayden arrived at work the next morning twenty minutes early, so that he could speak with Broderick before the hustle and bustle of the day set in. He knew that he always arrived early so that he could sift through his emails and be prepared to answer any questions that may be posed to him by the Ambassador. Having to say you hadn't checked your messages yet, was never a good start to any day with the new Ambassador.

Robert Nichols had replaced Jane Whitehall. The outgoing U.S. President Casper put him in place. He was commonly referred to as an asshole, and most believed he was as crooked as they come, but there was really nothing that could be done about it. Anytime anyone was close to connecting that he, the President himself or the President's brother, Ramon Casper, were aiding and abetting the cartels and assisting in the drug trade, they mysteriously ended up dead. Their connections to the extremely rich and therefore powerful made them practically untouchable. Broderick didn't want to give Bob any reason to be in his business; in his opinion he wasn't even qualified to fill the Ambassador position. He was a political appointee and as such, hadn't fulfilled any of the prerequisites that most would be required to complete, in order to be taken seriously. Broderick couldn't stand him.

Brayden entered his office and knocked slightly on the door as a courtesy before sitting down in front of him. Broderick motioned to a seat and Brayden sat down. Brayden stared, as Broderick continued to reply to an email without saying a word. Broderick, noticing him glaring at him out of the corner of his eye, stopped typing, turned and faced Brayden and sarcastically gave him his full and undivided attention; displayed overtly with his body language.

"Listen, I know you don't like me, well not me personally, I know you don't like USSF doing this job. That's fine, but I really need your help. I have to tell someone because I don't know how these games work. You've been doing this spy versus spy thing for a long time and I truly need some guidance." Brayden said very seriously.

Broderick changed his body position to respect the tone that Brayden was conveying. He minimized his mail program on his computer and prepared to actively listen.

"What seems to be troubling you?" Broderick said in earnest.

"I am being monitored. I am not sure if its DAS or CIA, but they were in my room last night, and I have to believe that they have been following me."

Broderick chuckled a bit and then quickly re-gained his composure. He never really looked at special operations personnel that conducted source operations as legitimate field agents; but at that moment, he remembered that he was speaking with an operator. A member of an elite community that earned the right to be there and that put themselves in harm's way on most missions, he deserved his respect and admiration. He obviously trusted Broderick as he brought the issue to him first.

"Close the door if you don't mind." Broderick said, understanding the angst that Brayden was feeling.

"How do you know they were in your room? Did you pick up any tails while in route to your meet?" Broderick questioned.

Brayden explained all the signs that he found when he returned to his room. He didn't believe he had been followed, but he couldn't be sure they weren't already at the meet location.

"Do you have any idea why the agency might want to pry into your life?" Broderick asked.

Brayden looked at him and thought long and hard before pulling out the papers. He wasn't sure who he could trust, but he knew he had to try to align with someone. He slowly pulled out the papers with the grid coordinates and names that John had sent to him. As he handed it over to Broderick, he hoped he was not making the biggest mistake of his life. He began to give him the brief background about how he came across the information.

"I had this pulled off of a thumb drive. It doesn't look like much, but it was hidden within financial documents and statements. The technician that pulled the information, found it buried in the code of a period at the end of a sentence. Why would anyone go through that trouble for a couple of strips of land in the jungle? Do you recognize any of the names on that list?" Brayden said now hoping he was placing all of his trust in the right person.

Broderick pondered for a minute while looking over the two documents. Brayden sat nervously, thinking about the possible implications of divulging this information to the wrong individual. He knew nothing about Broderick; the men following him could be doing so at his direction. He waited on pins and needles for some type of response from Broderick.

"Brayden, what if these names are not people that are involved, but people that can be held accountable, like a list of those that can be blackmailed." Broderick revealed slowly.

Brayden hadn't thought of that angle and now began to contemplate that perspective. He was relieved to hear him theorizing about the possible uses for the information, rather than questioning him on exactly how it was obtained. His explanation added clarity to why the information might be encrypted, and purposely hidden.

Broderick got up slowly from his desk and walked to his locker. There, he kept offensive gear, his go-bag, and sniffing equipment; consisting of a few weapons, his body armor and a medium sized bag enclosing electronic surveillance detecting equipment. He removed the latter from his locker and handed it to Brayden.

"Sweep your room for bugs and cameras and keep this between us, the less people that know about this the better. I will try to get some information from Langley on these documents. Go about your daily duties normally and try not to burn yourself." Broderick said as he handed him the bag.

"No one knows I have that information, I never included it in any of my reports." Brayden warned.

"I've been doing this kind of work for a long-time kid, I know how this game is played, I helped write the book." Broderick said with a smirk.

Brayden left Broderick's office feeling better about his predicament. Now, someone else knew about the information he had come across, who was actually in a position where they could affect it. Once he was back in his office, Brayden called Darius to find out what the team had planned regarding the recon of the other runway locations. Darius filled him in on the idea of re-tasking a predator either at the start of its mission or just before it returned to base. This way it kept all ground elements out of harm's way until absolutely necessary to walk the terrain, it also kept from burning the site. Brayden agreed and put it on his list of things to bring up that afternoon to Broderick.

June 2000

CHAPTER 45

BOB NICHOLS SAT comfortably at his desk; he was finally settling into his job as the U.S. Ambassador to Colombia. He had been at the post for a few months but really hadn't exercised his influence until now. He was given the post specifically to protect the President's financial interests in the country, and ensure that his brother Ramon Casper was able to continue assisting with the movement of drugs; unofficially of course. Ramon owned a fishing charter and a parasailing outfit along the coast of Costa Rica. The parasailing boats doubled as speedboats for running drugs up to Managua. From there, they could be loaded onto shipping vessels and brought into the U.S. directly, or trucked into Mexico and brought in by coyotes.

Ramon frequently flew into Colombia privately via Trenton Industries chartered planes. He dealt directly with certain cartels and unofficially assisted in brokering the peace deal that allowed the cartels to grow at an alarming rate. His latest plan was to help the Saudi's move precious stones into the U.S. for sale on the black market, a very lucrative scheme that would net him millions. What he didn't know, is that this was the guise they were using to smuggle fundamentalists into Canada, to ignite civil unrest and help steer their government away from striking an oil pipeline deal with the U.S.

At the moment though, Bob was reading email traffic from the CIA concerning drone use in certain areas of the country. The peace deal that was struck between the growing FARC, the cartels and the government, was to allow them a safe haven in which the government would steer clear allowing them to operate freely. The cartels were threatening to step up operations outside of this area because of the increasing drone use.

As Bob finished replying to his contact in Langley, Broderick made his way from his office to the Ambassadors wing. He hated having to speak to him about anything; he was arrogant, narcissistic and aberrant. Everything about him was wrong, but he couldn't put his finger on the real problem. Influence and control could do strange things to some men, especially when they have an abundance of it and Broderick had witnessed first-hand what giving in to corruption, greed and abuse of power looked like.

Broderick had been witness to a Non Official Cover list, or NOC list release that ended with two agents killed and others making it out of their locations just in time to avoid peril. The NOC list contains the names and identities of field agents that are operating without an official cover. An official cover, provides the operative with a job that explains why they would be operating in that particular area, like an embassy worker. An operative on a NOC is illegally operating inside whatever country they are assigned, so in the event that they are captured, the U.S. has complete deniability and can essentially write them off.

While working in El Salvador, Broderick witnessed the deliberate release of a NOC list because one of the operatives refused to help the appointed

CoS move money for a major warlord. The deal involved soviet weapons, mines and demolitions and would have made the CoS over $1.5 million dollars. The CoS didn't have access to the area, but had agents that did. He contacted them and tried to unwittingly have them make the sale and deliver the money, but one of them caught on through a knowledgeable sub-source. In an attempt at self-preservation, he burned several agents that were in the field. The CoS was not aware of who all knew about his scheme, but needed to cover his tracks. Broderick was one of the agents that made it out, and was later called on to testify about the ordeal. Despite that experience he continued to stay on with the agency in an attempt to right some of the problems. From that point on he only worked in an overt capacity.

Broderick arrived at the Ambassador's office and notified the receptionist that he was expected. She smiled and waved him in. He walked to his doorway, stood in the threshold and knocked on the already open door.

"Broderick, good to see you." Bob said energetically as if he hadn't seen him in years. He stood and extended his hand to shake Broderick's who begrudgingly shook it fighting the urge to roll his eyes.

"You said you wanted to see me?" Broderick replied in a very matter of fact way.

"Well, right down to business then." Bob fired as if he was offended that Broderick didn't care to socially interact with him more than necessary.

"I know that there are predator drones flying in this country. I'm not sure how many are here, which I intend to find out, but from now on I need to be briefed on when and where they fly. Also, I will be the final approval for if and when they fly at all." Bob informed him.

"We have four in country at the moment, and they fly within ten areas of interest. The flight plans are published each week and pushed out to all relevant agency members and tactical controllers. I will publish the flight plans to you from now on. I do not control the route that the birds fly. I give input on what areas are of importance and what we are looking to obtain if the bird is pushed to those locations. If no tactical ground control element is directing them, they will fly the preplanned operations boxes and report any activity that they see. If you wish to adjust the frequency in which they fly, you would have to take that up with whoever has enlightened you about the program. I am not sure what your interest is with the predator flights, but they are a major help in fighting the drug problem and other illicit activities. You are the Ambassador to this country, so I am sure you have your reasons, and orders." Broderick said calmly.

"So, you don't control them from this location?" Bob replied honestly not understanding how the drone's work.

"No, we don't, we only give input for the areas that need to be flown based on intelligence collection requirements." Broderick said.

"Well, how do I stop these flights? At a minimum how do I control what areas they are permitted to fly into?" Bob said now clearly frustrated.

"I am not exactly sure why you would want to cease the flights, as I have stated they are definitely a valuable asset. The aircraft fly at an altitude that make it nearly impossible for anyone on the ground to be made aware of its presence, so what areas would be off limits?" Broderick was beginning to lose patience with the Ambassador.

Bob was beginning to accept the fact that this conversation was going nowhere with the little information that he had. "Fine, let's start with sending me all information regarding upcoming flights." He replied.

Broderick shook his head slightly as he stood up and walked toward the door. He paused briefly in the doorway to button his coat. He removed his glasses, wiped them with a handkerchief from his pocket before putting them back on. He looked back over at Bob who sat at his desk upset and utterly embarrassed, that he hadn't gotten all of the facts before attempting to assert some authority.

"Mr. Ambassador, you needn't worry. I will tell you everything that I think you have a need to know from now on. Obviously, because of the nature of my work, I can't divulge everything, but again, I assume you must already know that."

Broderick walked out of his office with a smirk, smiled at the receptionist, who smiled back, and returned to his office.

CHAPTER 46

TRENTON INDUSTRIES started as a small U.S. three-plane business operating in Mexico that grew into a multi-million-dollar empire. They now had multiple aircraft operating on three different continents. They had proved their worth and solidified their existence shortly after a major guerilla conflict in the jungles of Colombia, combined with a natural disaster in the same region. Several small, unused patches of land throughout the jungle, were painstakingly converted into areas that could be used as landing strips. The Colombian Army's Corp of engineers, with U.S. advisors, improved the areas and built most of the strips. The cartels built some of the others throughout the contested areas, capitalizing on the success of the government, and attempting to create their own hubs.

Trenton Industries was the only company already poised to fly into the hazardous areas and deliver food, rations and temporary shelter for the thousands of people displaced by conflict or victims of natural disaster. They also provided a way for U.S. aid workers and Peace Corps personnel to reach remote areas. They could even conduct resupplies by pushing small bundles from low, slow flying aircraft, for those working in remote and isolated areas. The service they provided had become invaluable to both governments, almost to the point of rendering them untouchable.

When the predator drones proved their reliability and worth, they began flying in larger numbers. The need for covert oversight in the areas that the FARC controlled, eventually necessitated the use of the platform in Colombia. The Colombian government finally agreed to the drones after they assisted in the location of several smuggling routes used by the cartels. The ability to achieve such precise reconnaissance without endangering ground operators, was an undeniable selling point. Trenton Industries stored the drones, and provided a cover story by way of legitimate contract jobs for the personnel that maintained, launched and retrieved the drones.

With other operations preparing to take place in Africa, utilizing the access and placement Trenton Industries had forged; they were almost too big to fail. Even though it was suspected that the cartels were somehow using the company to their advantage. Routine maintenance and servicing of aircraft was necessary to prolong their use and increase safety and Trenton Industries was the only company providing that service at the time. How deep the connections went, no one knew or cared to say, nor were they in a hurry to find out because of the instrumental service they provided.

Broderick had a feeling that the corruption ran deep within Trenton Industries and if Brayden were being watched because of what he may have found, it would confirm his suspicions. But, he couldn't allow that to stop him from doing his job, and it wasn't to focus energy on Trenton Industries. Between the FARC, the cartels, and what USSF was stirring up, he stayed busy enough. The latest request that he found in an email from Brayden for predator support just about made his day, considering the conversation that had just taken place with Bob. He sent a warning order to Langley about a possible deviation to the predator route in the coming days and sent Brayden a reply requesting more information on the areas he was interested in.

August 2001

CHAPTER 47

BRAYDEN LISTENED TO the phone ringing while managing several tasks that were dividing his attention. He was visually keeping track of where his pursuers were, audibly counting the number of rings from the phone, and coordinating his dexterity and motor skills whilst in pain; all while trying to remain on the road. His vision was blurry from squinting through the sun light past severely swollen eyes. The adrenaline rush from the escape was wearing off and the pain from his mid-section was becoming unbearable. Each breath that he took was now a concerted effort; he was tired of running. Besides, if Steve was right and he didn't shoot Javier Rolando, and he was actually cut from the helicopter like he had suggested, then the conspiracy went deeper than he would be able to run from.

He thought about the fact that Steve and his men were already positioned. Brayden knew that a great deal of drug labs were actually like large and complex tunnel systems on the inside. They had hatches that opened up in various parts of the jungle. Drug making was a serious, lucrative and often times for the workers, dangerous business. If something went wrong with the chemicals, the workers needed a way to escape before the entire facility exploded. That still didn't explain the precision and speed in which they oriented to him; it was as if Steve had actually been watching him the entire time.

If the target wasn't Javier, then who the heck was he and why did all of the intelligence that Brayden and his team focused on, have him listed as such? If they did have his exact location, why didn't they stop him before he killed that man? Steve was former USSF, he understood sniper and counter sniper operations and could have taken Brayden out before he understood what was even happening. Brayden was not expecting any resistance in that area let alone a tracker, and honestly, he was not even looking for it.

He now wondered what his team was doing, he knew he had been away from them for a while doing the military liaison thing, but they were brothers. There was no way they would betray him, but where did they go? There was so much fire power in that part of the jungle that day that there is no way a couple of cartel members could have snatched him up and gotten away without them being able to react. Multiple aircraft, to include attack platforms, were on standby and would have been in that area within minutes.

Brayden knew the gravity of the situation. He currently was not on a U.S. sanctioned mission, and unless he was reunited with his team, he didn't really know who he could trust. He reached over and picked up the handset from the passenger seat and looked at the caller identification screen on the front of the flip phone. He didn't recognize the number, but why should he? He peered up into the rear-view mirror at his followers and for a second swore he could once again hear the blades of the helicopter closing in on his position. He flipped the phone open with his right hand and slowly brought it up to his ear. "Hello?"

June 2000

CHAPTER 48

THE PREDATOR FLIGHT was successfully flown over the areas of interest that Brayden, Darius and their DEA counterparts had identified. The information gathered was plotted on a digital overlay and projected on top of a map of the area. Another overlay, containing known and suspected drug labs, was placed on top of that. Combined with the routes used to service guerilla-training camps and holed up locations the actual network was appearing right before their eyes.

The decision to move on one of the locations was tricky. The fact that seventy five percent of the runways were built to support legitimate air operations like aid delivery, troop movements and allowance for future expansion, meant that an aircraft would have to be caught in the act in order for anything to be accomplished. Sort of like a field in Humboldt, California that everyone knows is being used to grow marijuana, until you actually visit the field with the crop in full swing, it's just another empty field.

The plan was to recon a strip that was near the impoverished town of La Balsa. The town was known for its almost complete detachment from the

Colombian government, because of arduous terrain and its close proximity to the border of Ecuador. Because the coca was actually harvested in this area, it would have to be flown from its location near the city to a manufacturing plant in another region. Everything was separated into distinct compartments, the harvesters, the cocaine production labs, and the money moving and laundering operations, all separated to avoid a catastrophic loss should one of the pieces of the cartel's operation be discovered and eradicated.

A vehicle movement into the La Balsa area from the Commando base near Bogota, would take over three hours and would leave plenty of time for any early warning networks to alert essential personnel to their movement. Instead, they planned for multiple helicopter lifts to the vicinity of the border region city and about six miles away from the intended landing strip. This wouldn't look out of place, as aid was routinely dropped in that area by Colombian Army helicopters, as well as NGO flights with medical supplies and pop-up vaccination points. Once on the ground, they would walk to the target, the terrain was brutal and unforgiving but it was the only way to infiltrate undetected.

The helicopter portion of the infil was uneventful. All chalks made it into the landing zone as planned, conducted link up, and began the slow movement through the jungle. The Colombian Army Commandos took the lead. The first man in the file was strictly used to cut a path through the thick areas of the dense foliage. The second and third men were responsible for his security. The machete man would cut for around thirty minutes before needing relief. The soldiers would continue to rotate through the squad, ensuring to keep a fresh lead man. Everyone carried a machete as a survival tool, whether they intended to use it or not. It was light, took up very little space and it was better to have it and not need it, than the other way around.

Movement was slow and the longer they walked the more frequent the breaks became. They were averaging one mile per hour with three down and three to go. They hoped to make it into a MSS before nightfall. At least any enemy resistance would be unlikely, meaning noise discipline was all but lost on the part of the Commandos. It was their country and they understood it better than any foreigner could ever hope to.

Five hundred meters from the runway clearing, the terrain began to slope away from them, down into a slight bowl. The vegetation was beginning to thin and they could see the vast clearing in which the runway sat. The ODA assisted the Commandos in setting in the MSS and set out to begin the long arduous process of clover leafing the objective.

Clover leafing an objective was something frequently used by maneuver units to gain a better picture of what was happening on the target. It would allow the unit to get a better representation of enemy numbers, types of equipment, weapons systems and placement, and ingress and egress routes. This would allow better risk management and mitigation when planning a raid or ambush. Before the invention of digital cameras and UAVs, men drew rudimentary pictures of what they saw, complete with distances and directions to ensure accuracy, at least in the eyes of the observer. As the teams returned with their sketches, it would be compiled by the platoon leader and used in conjunction with a sand table to plan the assault. The Vietnam War proved that the use of this technique was paramount in the jungle, and because lessons learned in blood are rarely forgotten; it is still being engrained in infantrymen to this day.

Two teams of four were sent in opposite directions to move around the runway and ensure that no enemy patrols were in the area, or more likely, that no civilian activity was observed that could complicate and possibly compromise the mission. No NGOs were scheduled to be in the area, so they were optimistic that no activity would be detected. As they moved in closer to the clearing to observe any activity, they were amazed at the size and magnitude of the runway. It was incredible, like a dirt version of a commercial airfield. At the east end of the runway there was an aircraft that appeared to be a 747. It was partially covered by camouflaged netting that someone had taken the time to fit with large leaves and palms. Nothing had been seen in the UAV footage that would have suggested an aircraft on the runway, so the attempt at concealment actually worked. It was completely stripped of all markings; it was solid white and didn't appear to have windows. Darius, who was with one of the recon teams, wondered what an aircraft of that magnitude was doing parked in the middle of the jungle. And more importantly, why was it sitting there, by all outward appearances, unguarded?

As the teams finished their complete 360 of the clearing, they conducted link up on the far side and radioed back to the DEA and the rest of the team at the MSS, their findings. The decision was made to occupy the runway, and search the aircraft. From here they would send up their report.

Darius assisted the Commandos in setting up security on the only entrance and exit to the airfield. This would be the most dangerous avenue of approach, and other than an air infiltration; the only likely way anyone would move into the area. Darkness was now covering them like a veil so they decided to report the finding and securing of the field, and wait till daybreak to exploit the aircraft. They made camp just south of the airfield and kept a rotating recon element watching it and the plane.

CHAPTER 49

RAMON CASPER was a blonde haired, blue eyed, debonair looking man. His Kennedy-esque build, stature and dress, projected money and power. Being the brother of the most powerful man on the planet, gave him access and advantages that most people could only dream about. Even the obscenely wealthy couldn't buy themselves into some of the circles he found himself in. He was single by choice and never stayed in one place for a great deal of time. Despite his charming outward appearance, he was a cold and calculating businessman, and most of his dealings were illicit.

At the moment he was seated on a yacht in the North Pacific Ocean very near the Cocos Island National Park. It was a lush and beautiful island, that was protected from the treacheries of man by the Costa Rican government. He had arrived by speedboat and was greeted on the very large aft fan deck by Mayo Garcia. Mayo was the largest illegal trade transporter in Central and South America. He owned trucking, fishing, helicopter tour, and parasailing companies along the coast of multiple countries on the continent. Though the businesses themselves actually generated revenue, they were all fronts for moving various goods for anyone able to pay his extremely steep fees. He had the right palms greased in both the law enforcement and political arenas, and remained loyal to those that he conducted business with. He didn't even require disclosure of what was being delivered. His people needed a location and contact to pick it up from and a location and contact to drop it off with, period. He started his business by allowing the cartels to move large shipments of cocaine up the coast, hidden in the fishing bins with the vessel's catch. At that time, no one was willing to dump that much money in fish just to check for drugs. As things began to heat up and U.S. law enforcement started targeting this and other methods of movement, he switched to multi stage movements using a combination of fishing and speed boats. Word of his success quickly got around and soon he was moving everything from drugs, guns, and people to cash and counterfeit goods up and down the western coast. He built an empire on logistics, but was now facing an issue with a multi-platform acquisition deal that went south. He needed an alternate means of acquiring what he needed. Ramon might be just the man to secure what he needed; even though he had his own operations in Costa Rica.

"So why have you summoned me here?" Ramon wasted no time getting to the point of the meeting. He was perturbed that he had been called out for the meeting in the first place. He was supposed to be in Martha's Vineyard with a woman that he was courting at the moment.

"Ramon, my intent was not to beckon you. I invited you here as a friend and confidante. I trust your counsel and needed your help in resolving a matter." Mayo countered.

"So, what is this *matter* that you need help with?" Ramon inquired.

"You see that island over there?" Mayo asked as Ramon rolled his eyes. He hated when people got philosophical. It rarely meant anything to the individual that was being spoken to. In fact, often times it would elicit the complete opposite reaction than that intended by the speaker. Unless a parent or grandparent was delivering it, the gesture was lost.

"Yes, I see the island over there." Ramon replied in his most satirical voice.

"The waters around that island are home to some of the best fishing in the area. The groves that you can see off to the eastern edge, those are used to this day by fisherman that are caught out here during bad weather as holed ups until the storm passes. It was there, under those groves that I got my start in this business. A fellow fisherman was trying to save his boat from sinking, and while bailing water he asked if I would take his cargo. It was too heavy and if he wanted to get his boat back to the mainland, he would have to lighten the load. When we had finished moving the cargo to my vessel, he handed me a piece of paper with lat/long coordinates. He told me to go to that location and wait for someone to meet me and take the cargo. I had a myriad of questions that he would not answer. When the storm lifted, he steamed in the direction of the mainland, and that was the last time that I ever saw him. When I delivered the goods, the men that were there to off load it, asked who I was and why I had been sent instead of the normal individual. I told them the only truth that I knew and that I would never tell anyone what had transpired. I thought they were going to kill me Ramon, but they didn't they actually employed me." Mayo looked over at the island reminiscing about his humble beginnings. Ramon was not as touched.

"That was a great story Mayo, really, but what exactly is it that you want from me?" Ramon was upset. Even though he was a powerful man in his own right, he was not the *most* powerful man and that bothered him. His brother would never have been sent for in this manner. All business came to him, and Ramon strived to have that kind of influence.

"Yes of course Ramon I apologize, let's get down to business." Mayo began. "A few months ago, I was set to purchase two container ships and one submarine from a couple of the cartels. They were running into too much heat and could no longer feasibly move their own goods. Without legitimate businesses to disguise their shipping, it was beginning to get impossible to use the waterways. The submarine had been very effective for them, but it was aging and needed a great deal of work, something that they are not interested in pursuing. As the deal was being finalized, the submarine was somehow severally damaged. This is a loss for everyone, as the submarine could move large quantities of merchandise which we could cross-load to the container ships after their inspection. This transaction was worth a great deal of money, and I have a lot of it hanging in the balance waiting for a solution."

Ramon didn't say a word, he was still waiting patiently for the pitch that he knew was coming.

Mayo continued. "I know that you have connections, deep connections and I was wondering if you could source me another submarine to purchase?"

As Ramon looked off into the distance, Mayo could sense his resistance to help. But it wasn't for the reasons Mayo was thinking. Ramon was very resourceful and sometimes he would manage to pull off what seemed to be impossible but this, even for him, was a stretch.

As he scrolled through his mental rolodex of black-market movers and shakers he was stumped at a request of this magnitude. He knew the man that he could call and likely accomplish the job, but he couldn't get his brother involved at this level. Nor did he want to hand him all the credit when he successfully delivered. There was someone else that he could possibly call. This individual was buried deep in the bowels of the government. Entrenched in the fabric of dark politics, by laws that he could shape if they didn't exist. He was not to be mistaken as a friend and he most certainly couldn't be trusted. But if Ramon could convince him that he would somehow benefit greatly, he just might pull it off.

May 2000

CHAPTER 50

BRAYDEN SAT at the bar of his hotel with his backpack at his feet containing the sniffing equipment that Broderick had given him earlier. As he sipped on his drink, a two finger pour of Gentleman Jack Daniels neat, he pondered how to put it to use. The act of sweeping for listening devices and cameras was not foreign to him, he had done so in training numerous times. The trick was doing so without the individuals observing him realizing what he was doing. If he were only concerned with listening devices, he could get away with quietly moving about the room in a somewhat normal manner, using only the light indicator as his confirmation. Before his training, Brayden saw this done in spy movies all time; turn on some loud music and let the games begin. What they don't tell you about this technique, is that if you don't listen to music at that volume and regularity all the time, you will instantly raise suspicion. Cameras make it even more difficult for obvious reasons. Of course, you could leave everything concealed and meander aimlessly around your room stopping in front of miscellaneous objects waiting to hear a confirmation tone through your connected earpiece, but again; to the trained observer, that would look suspicious. Everything that you do is a pattern, humans are creatures of habit and those that make it an art form to study it, will instantly see a divergence. If you change your pattern of life, you *will* raise suspicion.

As he took his last sip of whiskey, he was certain he had formulated a plan that would allow him to maintain a semblance of his routine and accomplish his task. Although it wasn't his usual day for having his room cleaned, he figured he could manufacture a reason to have it done early. He was very particular and would use this to cause some commotion in his room.

As he slid his keycard into the door of his room, he smiled slightly at the thought of how ridiculous what he was about to do would look to an onlooker. But, his pride didn't matter right now, he needed to confirm or deny the presence of eavesdropping equipment in his room; this would determine how he behaved for the remainder of his stay. All of the gear in the backpack was switched on in the elevator, and he had inserted the earwig and checked that it was properly configured to deliver tone alerts. He had no way of checking to ensure it all worked, but he had faith in the fact that Broderick took exceptional care of his equipment.

Once in his room, he slid the backpack off of his shoulder and dropped it into the chair nearest the only window in his room. This was something that he did with any bag he returned with, until after he had taken his shower. He sat down on the end of the bed and removed his shoes, but as he did, he devoted an unusual amount of time studying the floor. As he pulled off his left shoe and set it near his already removed right, he jumped off the bed in a manner that would suggest surprise at what he was noticing on the carpet. He stood back and bent down slowly at the knees to again inspect the area and then quickly backed up completely to the door. He skirted the walls and furniture to the nightstand containing the phone as if avoiding a ferocious animal, picked up the receiver and frantically dialed the front desk.

"Hello Mr. Smith, how may we help you today?" The front desk person said.

"I know that today is not my usual cleaning day, but I have ants in my room and need to request service immediately!" Brayden almost demanded.

"Yes Sir, right away Sir. Please give me a moment to call the cleaning staff and someone should be there momentarily."

Brayden hung up the phone, and departed the room to standby in the hallway. This way he would not have to keep up the ridiculous charade while waiting, and it would legitimately appear that he didn't want to be in the room with the fictitious colony that had seemingly moved in.

The two-person cleaning crew arrived with the usual supply cart and vacuum; neither spoke English. Brayden led them into the room and began hurriedly showing them the problem, exaggerating his gestures and giving them little time to evaluate or respond. He insisted that his bed sheets and towels be replaced and that they thoroughly vacuum the room. As the ladies began their routine, he grabbed his backpack, as though to remove it from being in their way, and began placing it around the room as if to avoid interruption of their progress. As he moved from the clothing dresser, to the bed, to the pull-out sofa couch, to the coffee table and so on, he was intently listening for the tones that would confirm the presence of concealed audio and visual devices. He received four hits. After the women finished and he was satisfied that his infestation had been eradicated, he tipped them and bid them good day.

He once again sat at the end of the bed and pondered what to do now that he was sure he was under persistent and active surveillance. He wondered if he had caught them quick enough to prevent giving anything away that would put him or any of his sources in danger. *Why would anyone be in danger?* He thought to himself. After all, it was the CIA watching him; *they're on my team… right?* He shrugged as he stood up and began walking toward the lavatory and then stopped and worried about how the shrug would be interpreted by his new friends. He then remembered he needed to behave normally and continued walking into the bathroom. As he disrobed and stepped into the shower, he smirked slightly and thought *just pretend you're still in training rookie.*

July 2000

CHAPTER 51

MIGUEL FELIPE watched as Maria Guzman moved around her kitchen with grace, now letting her hair down as she was close to finishing up the meal. She was short in stature with raven black hair, beautiful greenish brown eyes, and had the epitome of a womanly figure. Not only was she easy on the eyes, she was an extremely talented cook; this combination made watching her prepare a meal absolutely mesmerizing. Once a week, Miguel would stop by for lunch. It was a ritual that started when Ruffy began questioning the AFOs decisions with regard to shipments. It was an insurance policy of sorts, that would guarantee that he continues his business as usual. Maria didn't mind, to her he was a work friend of her husband and someone that he presumably trusted. She enjoyed cooking, and this gave her a chance to try dishes out that Ruffy wasn't interested in. But today was different; Ruffy would actually be joining them for lunch as Miguel had something that he needed to discuss with him. It was an urgent matter and Miguel insisted that it be discussed at his home so that he wouldn't have to miss out on the wonderful meal he had become so accustom to.

As Ruffy made his way through the afternoon traffic, he wondered what could be so urgent that he needed to return home to discuss it. On one hand it made sense, Miguel didn't work any of the shipments, so he wouldn't see him during his normal work routine. But on the other hand, he could have just called him and given him any guidance that was coming down from the top. He tried not to overthink it and instead thought about what his wife might be making for lunch. He loved her cooking and his slight belly and love handles proved it. He adored his wife, and wondered how he had been so lucky to find and marry a woman so lovely. They were a good match for each other, he was a great provider and she was an equally talented homemaker. It was not lost on her how fortunate she was to be able to remain at home and devote her time to the family and home. Many of her friends had to take on jobs in the nearby town just to help their family make ends meet. They were truly blessed, and they counted those blessings each and every day.

As Ruffy pulled into the driveway, he noticed a large black SUV parked across the street. *I figured Miguel would be in something a little more luxurious* he thought to himself. As he exited the car, he picked up a fragrant waft of his wife's cooking. A combination of herbs, spices and meat, with the hint of the oil used to lightly crisp the arepas. As he entered the front door of his modest home, Miguel cordially greeted him. Maria removed one of the pans from the direct heat of the gas stove, to an unused burner so that she could welcome him without burning the meal.

"Hello my love." Maria said as she hugged and kissed him.

Ruffy hugged and kissed her back and shyly asked what was for lunch.

"Come on Ruffy" Miguel started. "Don't be all timid in your own castle, get in here and relax, let's eat!"

As he moved back to the dining table, Miguel turned his attention to Maria before again being seated. "Do you have any cervezas in that icebox?"

Maria brought them each a beer and returned to the kitchen to begin plating the food. She brought out the arepas, red beans, seasoned ground beef, chorizo, plantain, avocado and fried eggs.

"Wow" said Miguel, "Now this is how you eat right?" He said in a very jovial tone to Ruffy.

"Yes, I suppose." Ruffy replied with a hint of nervousness.

As they consumed their meal, Ruffy couldn't help but feel slightly perplexed by this visit. No business had been discussed yet, and it was nearing the time that he would normally be getting back to work. He sipped his beer and thought about how to broach the subject with Miguel, so that he could be on his way. As he checked his watch, he debated what route would be quickest at this time of day, *it shouldn't really be that bad,* he thought to himself.

"Do you have someplace you need be?" Miguel exclaimed as he watched Ruffy checking the time.

"Well, I would normally be back at work by now, I'm debating which route to take back to the office." Ruffy explained.

Miguel looked at his watch, picked up a piece of avocado, put it in his mouth, and began to chew it slowly. He picked up his beer and looked at the contents, holding it up to his face and turning the glass bottle slightly sideways so that the light would assist in revealing exactly how much he had left. He guzzled the rest of the bottle, set it back on the table, and looked over at Maria and asked her kindly for another. As Maria moved to the refrigerator, Miguel pushed back from the table and reached into his right front pocket. He pulled out a piece of paper and set it on the table between he and Ruffy. Maria returned with his beer, sat back down slowly, and began cautiously finishing her meal as she watched the awkward exchange.

"What is that?" Ruffy asked sincerely.

"Pick it up." Miguel responded in an almost joking tone as he moved his tongue over his teeth to remove a few food particles.

Ruffy picked up the paper and opened it. As he read the contents his heart began to speed up. He could feel his blood pressure rising as his artery walls tried to relax and meet the demands of the task his heart suddenly put on his life sustaining liquid; now being pushed at a frantic pace. His hands began to shake as his brain struggled to make sense of exactly what was happening, his face and neck began to turn red as his hypothalamus tried desperately to regulate his rising body temperature. As a bead of sweet began to take form on his forehead, Maria broke the silence.

"What is it my love?" She inquired.

Ruffy couldn't speak; his throat had become dry and he was for all intents and purposes, in a state of shock. The paper before him essentially spelled out the devastating horror that was likely to take place before the night was over.

"Tell her." Miguel said in a very calm and relaxed manner as he took another swig from his beer.

"I'll tell her." He said before Ruffy could gather his thoughts.

"It's a list Maria. A list of coordinates to runways dotted throughout the jungle. We, or should I say my associates rather, have been using your husbands' company to move drugs, money, women, and as of late, American contractors – not of their freewill mind you - to some of these locations to be moved around the country and beyond. Your husband has been heavily compensated for this additional workload and all we have asked in return is that he remain honest and loyal."

Miguel picked up his beer and before taking a drink, tipped it toward Maria as gratitude for getting him another, and then looked at Ruffy.

"I can't believe you didn't tell her. I would have thought you told her everything. I mean, you pretty much told everyone else. You left the paper in your unlocked desk drawer." Miguel said as he took another swig of beer. "Desk drawer!" He said again but this time to Maria as he changed pitch to stress how careless of an act it was.

Maria was a strong woman. She was never one to cry or attempt to move emotions that she thought she could handle onto her husband's shoulders, as she knew the pressures he was under to keep his business afloat. She sat up in her chair and nodded at her husband with a look of *we can get through this*.

"So now what." Maria asked Miguel. "What exactly does this mean? Ok, so he has something that he shouldn't, but you have taken his business and made it another extension of your criminal activities. You thought he was just supposed to sit back, watch and do nothing? We don't need your money; we don't want your money so just find another company to do business with. We haven't done anything wrong." Maria said firmly.

Miguel smiled coyly at Maria shaking his head slightly and wagging his finger at her in a way that suggested how naive she was and then turned his attention back to Ruffy. He pulled a pistol from the small of his back, and put it on the table in front of him. Maria began to slowly rock back and forth in her chair, as the angst of what was likely about to unfold now reached the portion of her brain that processed reality, specifically mortality. She looked at her husband, now with desperation, hoping and praying that there was something he could say to allow the situation to end peacefully. Miguel took another drink from his beer, before picking up the gun and pushing the slide back slowly for him to view whether a round was loaded into the chamber. He then grabbed the front of the pistol, rotated it so that the barrel was pointing at his own chest, and pushed it out gently to Ruffy for him to take it by the grip.

"Take it." Miguel said in a very cool manner while tilting his head down and to the right with his eyes closed suggesting his actions were genuine.

Ruffy took the pistol and held it just above the table with his wrist slightly limp, as if it was too heavy to hold up.

"Now, do what you know you have to do." Miguel said with a stern tone, never taking his eyes off of Ruffy.

Ruffy looked at Maria, who now looked confused and bewildered as her feminine emotions were beginning to get the best of her. She was breathing heavily, her bosom rising and falling heftily as she tried to comprehend what was happening in that moment. Ruffy, who now believed he had the upper hand, at least for a time, gained enough strength and courage to aim the gun at Miguel's head. As he pulled the trigger, Miguel picked up his beer again and sipped slowly while directing his attention at Maria.

'Click.'

Ruffy had purposefully pulled all of the slack out of that thin sliver of metal, only to audibly realize that there wasn't a bullet in the chamber. Maria, who could no longer hold in her emotions, began to weep silently into her hands while repeating *no* over and over again. Miguel took the gun from Ruffy's hands, set his beer back onto the table and walked over to the front door. He opened the door and motioned in the direction of the black SUV. Two men stepped out of the truck with two girls, Sonia age ten, and Carla age thirteen. They were Ruffy and Maria's daughters. As they walked into the house, Maria, upon seeing them, could no longer keep her composure and began to cry desperately while pleading with Miguel. Ruffy's eyes began to water as he extended his arms and hands out for his two girls who looked scared and confused. The men kept them from touching and moved them deeper into the home toward the kitchen.

"You know." Miguel began. "I'm not really here because of that little piece of paper. I'm here because of where you obtained that little piece of paper." Miguel paused briefly before continuing. "The men that I work for are very convinced that you have been conspiring with the Americans, the spies. Now, I am not sure how they have come to this conclusion, and it's not really for me to question. Honestly, I hate that I have to be here in this capacity, you all are good people. I just want everyone here to understand that this is nothing personal. It's a simple matter of failure to follow instructions, my bosses made a decision, and now, you must receive the consequences."

"I did this." Ruffy quickly said. "Do what you want to me, but please leave my family alone."

As Ruffy said the latter, Miguel mouthed the words with him; it was something that he had heard many times before. As he mocked Ruffy, he reached into his right back pocket and pulled out a bullet, opened the slide of the pistol, locked it to the rear and gave the appearance of placing the round into the chamber. He released the slide allowing it to slam forward, and handed the gun back to Ruffy, instructing him to take it in the same manner as before.

"I don't often do this…" Miguel said pausing, and now being very serious. "But I am going to give you a second chance to get this right."

June 2000

CHAPTER 52

ONCE BACK ON his private jet, Ramon thought about how the phone call he was about to make would unfold and take shape. He knew that this would not be a gratis transaction; there would be something that would be wanted in return. Perhaps not immediately, but at some point, in the future he would be called upon to either do, or provide something. And it would be *something* substantial. He had made acquaintances with this individual years ago at a White House banquet. At that time, all Ramon knew was that he was a plank holder in the CIA and had connections to just about everyone, and everything you could possibly want to dabble into. The problem with making a deal with a spook is that they never forget, and once you have put yourself on their radar, they make it a point to find out every little secret about you that they can exploit for use at a date of their choosing.

As he dialed the last remaining numbers, he glanced out of the window of his jet just as the landing gear was leaving the runway below. He enjoyed the privilege of private travel, avoiding the hassles and frustrations that came with commercial transportation. Even first-class passengers are subjected to delays, cancellations and overbooking. As he reached for his

Bloody Mary his call was answered.

"Well hello Ramon, can't say as I was expecting a phone call from you. What can I do for you?" The voice calmly asked.

"Hello, how did you know it was me?" Ramon asked inquisitively.

"Come on, we declassified caller I.D. years ago so that the population could enjoy that luxury. Nothing special about having your name stored." The man joked.

"I need a favor." Ramon started. "I have an acquaintance that would like to purchase a submarine. It would need to be operational and in a location that would allow him to take delivery of it without drawing too much attention. He is willing to pay whatever he needs to."

"That's a tall order Ramon, where are you now?"

"I'm south of the border headed to Martha's." Ramon answered.

"I'll give you a call before you touch down."

"Thank you." Ramon said almost relieved.

"Don't thank me, thank Uncle Sam." The man said jokingly.

Ramon sipped his drink and thought about what his fee would be for this transaction. He hadn't spoken to Mayo about it, but it wouldn't matter. The government could have no ties to any overtly illicit activities, so Mayo would never know the actual price of the vessel. He could skim profit off of the top of the sale and still make some sort of deal with Mayo regarding delivery for an additional payday. Considering the start, this was turning out to be a very productive day.

CHAPTER 53

AS THE FIRST SLIVER of sunlight breached the horizon, casting a soft glow over the runway, Darius's team, flanked by DEA agents, with the Commandos in the lead, departed the MSS. They slowly and methodically made their way to the long dirt strip that they now knew contained a rather large, twin-engine jet. They found it thoroughly concealed at one end of the runway near jungle canopy during infil. This made their primary objective of possibly destroying the runway a tricky, if not impossible proposition. They positioned themselves strategically around the aircraft. The air was thick with anticipation, every member of the team acutely aware of the stakes involved. They communicated through subtle gestures and quiet clicks on their radios, a silent symphony orchestrating a carefully planned breach.

The aircraft, a very commercial looking unmarked jet, sat ominously on the runway. Predicting that they would find an aircraft of this magnitude on their target runway was utterly impossible, but the fact that it was there meant these runways were serious business, and a crucial part of the cartel's operation. This was likely a critical node in a web that spanned continents, but nothing had prepared them for what they were about to uncover.

With precision that came from years of training, the team breached the aircraft. The entry was swift, the door giving way to a practiced but careful hurry after the lock was expertly bypassed. Inside, the cabin was deserted, an eerie silence greeting the team as they cleared the space. But it was what lay in the cargo hold that caught everyone off guard. A staggering amount of cash, neatly stacked in unmarked crates, millions of dollars abandoned with no guards, no accompanying paperwork, and no apparent destination.

The discovery was unprecedented. The team secured the perimeter, ensuring no late arrivals would disrupt the scene. As they reported their findings back to higher command, expecting orders for seizure and further investigation, the response on the other end of the line was chillingly calm and unexpected.

"Leave the aircraft undisturbed. Allow it to proceed to its intended destination. Do not interfere further."

The directive was unequivocal, leaving no room for questions or protest. The line went dead before any conversation could be had about the absurdity of this decision. The order suggested a level of foreknowledge and approval that was alarming. As the team withdrew, the realization dawned on them that this operation, and others conducted before it, had never been about intercepting a criminal enterprise. It was a charade, a performance staged for eyes and ears within layers of government to give the appearance that the U.S. was hard at work defeating powerful malicious organizations that threatened democracy; but this aircraft's journey had obviously already been sanctioned, money already allocated to a cause they were not privy to.

Disobeying part of the order, the team remained close enough to the airfield to observe the aircrafts departure. Hours passed before a small crew showed up and began to prep the aircraft. They removed the concealment from the fuselage and conducted a walk around of the aircraft. Not long after they finished, another vehicle arrived; they appeared to be the flight crew. It was shocking how normal they looked, if the team hadn't known any better, they'd think they were an American Airlines flight crew. Moments after preflight checks, the aircraft, with its illicitly gained cargo, departed the airfield, disappearing into the sky as if it had never been there. The incident, though undocumented in official records, would linger in the minds of those who witnessed it. The decision from command, the absence of guards, and the untouched millions—all pointed to a collusion that spanned across multiple government entities.

This episode, a stark deviation from the team's usual operations, confirmed the suspicions some had harbored for years: corruption had infiltrated every level of government, operating in the shadows, untouchable and omnipresent. Power seized through corruption and built strongly on a foundation of lies; mendacity. It was a sobering reminder that the fight against criminal enterprises was sometimes hamstrung by the very entities tasked with upholding justice.

As Darius and his team retreated, the weight of what they had been a part of settled in. The operation at dawn was not just a breach of an aircraft but a piercing glance into the abyss of corruption, revealing the depths to which those in power would sink to protect their interests. The realization that they were pawns in a larger game was disillusioning, but it also solidified a resolve to tread carefully in a world where allies and adversaries wore the same badges. Darius knew that Brayden would be crushed by this revelation; he just hoped he wouldn't choose this as the hill he died on.

The team spent the remaining months of their deployment gathering intelligence on Tiko's Gentlemen. They were a ruthless organization, with a plan to broaden cartel unification.

July 2000

CHAPTER 54

IN THE TENSE SILENCE that followed Miguel's offer, Ruffy's mind raced. His hands, still trembling, grasped the pistol with a newfound determination. He stared into Miguel's eyes, searching for any hint of deceit, any sign that this second chance was nothing but a cruel extension of his torment that may reverberate into his family. But Miguel's gaze was unwavering, almost encouraging.

Maria, through her tears, looked up at Ruffy with a mix of fear and hope. She had always known the man she married to be strong, resilient, and, above all, protective of his family. Now, more than ever, she needed him to embody those qualities. The presence of their daughters, Sonia and Carla, who stood silently, their eyes wide with confusion and fear, heightened the stakes immeasurably.

Ruffy's thoughts flashed to the many moments he had shared with his family, the quiet dinners, the laughter, the plans they had made for the future. All of that was now under threat because of choices he had made, choices that had led them to this precipice. He realized with a heart-wrenching clarity that his actions today would forever alter the course of their lives.

With a deep, steadying breath, Ruffy raised the pistol, his aim unwavering this time. But instead of pointing it at Miguel, he turned it towards his own head. The decision was instantaneous, born out of a desire not to play Miguel's game, not to succumb to needless bloodshed and violence directed at his innocent family as the solution. With a swift motion, he pulled the trigger, the loud report of the gun echoing through the room as the bullet instantly punctured his skin and shattered his skull simultaneously.

The room fell into a shocked silence. Maria gasped, her hands flying to her mouth, and her daughters screamed at the sudden noise, their cries piercing the heavy atmosphere.

Miguel picked up the pistol from where it had fallen next to Ruffy's lifeless body and placed it on the table, examining it with a curious eye. Without changing his glance, he addressed Ruffy's family. "I know you will never see this as a business transaction, but the fact that I have the latitude to leave you among the living will hopefully settle in over time; my family was not given this option."

Miguel stood up, grabbed the pistol and tucked it neatly behind his back, just into his belt. He turned to Maria; his expression somber but his tone matter of fact. "Your cooking is as wonderful as ever, señora. It's a shame this is the last time I will get to enjoy it."

With a nod to his men, he motioned for them to release Sonia and Carla, who immediately ran to their mother. Maria embraced them tightly with tears of both grief and relief mixing with those of fear.

As the door closed behind the men, the surviving family remained in a tight embrace, the silence around them a stark contrast to the chaos that had just unfolded. As Maria stared at Ruffy's corpse on the floor, she understood that violence could find them at any moment and that fear and dread would now be a way of life.

For Miguel, this was a bizarre atonement for his mistakes. His family had paid the ultimate price for his foley and he had resigned himself to never inflict that type of pain and suffering on anyone else, if he could help it. In his haste to complete the assignment; Miguel had completely missed the refrigerator magnet with an airplane picture and phone number, for Trenton Industries. He was too focused on the mission of premeditated murder.

Had Ruffy not made the decision he did, he and his men would be burning down a house containing four bodies.

August 2001

CHAPTER 55

"STOP THE CAR BRAYDEN." He could hear a great deal of interference on the line and it wasn't just a bad connection. He pulled the phone away from his ear and began looking at it with slight confusion before realizing it was the sound of the helicopter's turbine engine roaring in the background. He could now hear it in high fidelity surround sound, through the phone and above him as the bird slowly passed overhead and began to track the speed of the vehicle.

"Brayden, we need to talk now, it's important. You left the cabin before we could have a civilized conversation. There is nowhere for you to go."

He knew Steve was right. Escape was not possible. Even if all he had to contend with was the few vehicles he had in tow, he didn't have enough fuel for the chase to last much longer. He determined he would rather give up to Steve than gamble his fate with the men behind him.

"I will stop on one condition. We drive back to wherever you were holding me alone, you and me and no one else."

Steve agreed and watched as Brayden reluctantly brought the car to a stop.

The whole scene was like an ending to a California expressway high speed chase with police cars and helicopters, only Brayden's worries didn't include due process. He was in the Bad Lands and anything could happen to him at this point.

He watched as the helicopter came to a hover, stirring up dust and debris as it flared slightly before coming to rest in the middle of the road in front of him. The group of vehicles following him postured a few car lengths behind him, the occupants clearly unsure of what was about to transpire. Several men exited the trucks with high-powered rifles. Some remained slung over their shoulders and others began to slowly point them in his direction. Steve exited the aircraft that was still spinning at full speed ready to get aloft quickly, and ran over to the driver's side of the vehicle. Brayden climbed over the center console not wanting to risk exposure to a bullet by stepping out of the vehicle, and slid into the passenger seat. Steve entered the SUV and quickly glanced around before his eyes settled on the gas gage. "We *should* make it back to camp." He said before conducting a three-point turn and heading back in the direction Brayden had just fled from.

As they slowly crawled back through the extensive stretch of jungle he had just used as a drag strip, he was amazed at the distance he had covered and sobered up to the fact that he wouldn't have gotten away anyway. Brayden sat next to Steve in silence thinking about what questions to ask him. He was unsure whether he truly wanted to hear the answers to them, and pondered what possible explanation he could have in defense of his actions thus far. He was confused and leery of what Steve could conceivably be doing that would warrant or excuse the way he had been treating him. He decided the direct approach was best, no sense delaying the inevitable.

"Why haven't you killed me already." Brayden asked in a serious but non-judgmental tone.

"The only reason you're not dead Brayden is because of the confidence I have gained from the cartels. You have to know if you really think about it, that you haven't actually been treated that badly all things considered." Steve answered with a smug smile.

Steve was actually right. Brayden had received multiple stern beatings over the course of a few days, but it paled in comparison to what the drug lords were actually capable of inflicting. He still had all of his digits and extremities, and though his mind was a bit cloudy, he was certain that he was still walking among the living.

"You said that I didn't kill Javier but I know that I did. I studied his dossier for days before the mission and I know that the man I shot was the man in the photos I memorized. This was a sanctioned target; I refuse to believe that the agency got mixed up." Brayden said in a matter-of-fact way.

They were now approaching the "Y" in the road and from the blisteringly slow speed of travel Brayden almost thought they would make a hard right, but they continued straight.

"You shot Abdul Rahman Nour, a Yemeni Kindite, trusted friend and low-level operative for Osama Bin Laden. He was supposed to meet with Javier Rolando at the drug lab you conveniently showed up to, but Javier diverted at the last minute due to the unfortunate targeting of Abdul.

We chose the drug lab as a meet spot to give deniability of the true intention for the introductions. If spied upon, we could easily explain away the expansion of the trafficking operation and possible partnership with the Arabs. You know the deal Brayden, always cop to the lowest wrong you can in hopes of disguising the true nature."

Steve looked around for the first time since they started their discussion as if to ensure no one was eaves dropping on their conversation. In that moment it actually made Brayden feel uneasy, thinking about where they were and who controlled most of the area around them. If both he and Steve were remanded, there would be no one to dial back the torture, providing Steve was actually telling the truth.

Steve continued, "Javier is the top financier for the cartels and launders most if not all of the money that they acquire through drug trafficking into legal ventures. He was set to transfer an unknown amount of funds to Abdul to assist in the efforts to block the oil deal between Canada and the U.S. This would put Osama in good graces again with the Arabs and allow him to continue training his Afghan post Russia mujahedeen fighters. Javier was also going to give them access to the ratline they had built, allowing virtually unabated movement into and through the U.S.

In exchange Abdul was going to ensure that the cartels received a share of the booming poppy trade that was taking launch in Afghanistan. Javier was going to use his contact with Abdul to obtain a larger audience with the Middle East in an attempt to expand the ratline and shipping business. Now that Abdul is dead, we have no idea who his successor will be, we will essentially have to start over again. It will likely be impossible to get back into the good graces of the cartels and once again gain the trust needed to oversee high level deals."

It seemed that Steve had all the correct answers, but things just weren't adding up. He still hadn't revealed why he was actually there in the first place. Or why Brayden would have been given false information about Javier. And he obviously had to know where to find him; there is no way they could have oriented to him that quickly. Brayden sat up in his seat and looked at his hands as if giving them a preparatory command before asking his next question. Pending the words that exited Steve's mouth, he had accepted the fact that he would do his best to kill him right then and there.

"Both Javier and Abdul are bad guys, so why would I be told to retire one under the premise that he was the other? What exactly are you doing here? I mean, obviously you work for the cartels in some capacity. Are you part of the muscle arm for Trenton Industries? Are you an ex-patriot? Did you get lured in by the money and decide to…"

Steve cut Brayden off quickly and began to explain his position. He could feel the distrust in Brayden's voice and wanted to rapidly calm him down in the event they had to act quickly, and in unison.

"Stop." Steve began. "Listen Brayden, believe it or not we are still on the same side. I have been a deep cover operative within an arm of the National Clandestine Services now for close to three years. I began working with the cartels under the guise of a disgruntled ex-pat retired Special Forces operator. I started off designing training plans for the FARC and executing real world confidence targets and experience building missions against the Colombian Army. All of this was done to gain the trust needed to prepare the environment and gain the momentum needed to take on the most lethal group of individuals the U.S. has targeted to date.

I have been working for almost a year to gain the trust and confidence of the Binelli Cartel. They have been working tirelessly to elevate themselves from the business of exporting cocaine, to legitimizing their funding streams and strong-arming their way into the Colombian political sect. Right now, they have interests in several holding companies that fund operations all over the world, one of them being Trenton Industries. The fact that they use airstrips throughout the jungles to move people, product and money in and around Central and South America is nothing new to us. Our concern, as it pertains to their use of Trenton Industries, is how they are able to leverage CIA funded programs to move individual's trans continentally without so much as raising an eyebrow in Washington. Our mission has been compartmentalized, pulled out of the purview of the CIA and is being managed by a hand-picked group of individuals at the highest levels. The belief is that someone with access to high-level national security programs is leaking information, we just don't know who."

Steve hoped that he answered Brayden's question to his satisfaction. What he had not told him was that he was part of a small group of highly trained individuals whose mission was to find and report on possible back door CIA programs.

Steve was part of the Minute Men, the secretive action arm of the congressional oversight committee. They were formed after the Kennedy assassination as a means to keep tabs on what programs the CIA and other organizations had at any given moment, from the field. They would report these findings to the committee to help them keep checks and balances on the agency. After the president's death, rumors began to surface that the agency may have played an integral part in one of the largest conspiracies ever successfully pulled off on U.S. soil. Though unsubstantiated, they could not afford for something of that magnitude to happen again.

Trojan Scimitar, a plan to unwittingly use individuals that the agency had controlled at some point and released back into the wild, was pitched decades ago and denied by the congressional oversight committee. They viewed it as too risky; with no way to really track and control the individuals that were essentially operating under the laws that govern black side operations.

After the denial for discretionary funding by congress, a separate board was created within the ranks of the CIA that pooled resources in order to start up their own enterprises to fund that project and many others that would have no oversight. They could start and close select programs without answering to anyone because they fell under no U.S. Titles or authorizations therefore having no traceable monies tied to them. Many of these companies were started through criminal organizations that the agency had been tasked to infiltrate and defeat. At some point they began to believe they could control them. They had been providing sanction, security and safe passage to the cartels for years, in exchange for non-traceable money.

Steve and others like him had also been investigating a program called Missing Lynx, that had been initiated just a few years earlier, and was funded almost completely through Trenton Industries. Again, there was no oversight because the idea was never pitched to a governing body for a decision. The program allowed criminals seeking asylum and counter intelligence operatives from other countries protected traveling channels into the U.S. The problem with programs that have no oversight is the fact that at some point they usually end up being used maliciously, and this was no different. Various criminal and terrorist organizations began using the

U.S. sanctioned ratlines to get into and out of the country with no issues, and with no interference. It was, for the most part, secure travel with CIA guaranteed safe passage. The CIA also used it to get their personnel out of the country without it being tracked. It was put in place with good intentions, but the lack of thorough planning and precise backstops led to its bad execution.

Abdul was the only person with knowledge that could directly link the agency to the program. He had worked with an official from the CIA directly to expand the network into and around the Central Asian States. It was in the process of being activated when the Minute Men discovered its existence and worked a way to pull Abdul in. Had the meeting with Javier been a success, Abdul was to travel to Canada by way of the U.S., which is when he would have been held for questioning. Obviously, the agency found out about this and took steps to rectify, as they could not afford for this to happen.

As they pulled up to the entrance of the property, Brayden noticed large black SUVs lining the dirt strip that wound its way to the secluded cabin. All of them were identical and they all had very darkly tinted windows. Brayden looked over at Steve who at that moment looked just as confused as he.

"Well, I am guessing the cavalry has arrived, I knew it would happen at some point I just didn't think it would be that quick. Brayden, I want you to remember something before getting out of the vehicle." Steve paused, as he looked Brayden straight in face with conviction. "You were cut free from that helicopter for a reason. I'm on your side brother."

Steve put the SUV in park and exited slowly never diverting his attention away from the clearly Government Issued vehicles. Brayden, now in mental overload thinking about why anyone would want him killed, slid out of the passenger side and was reminded of the beatings he had received as his feet sharply contacted the ground and shuttered pain through his entire body. He reached back with his hands to brace his likely broken ribs when he brushed the pistol that he had taken from Steve in the initial struggle just before he fled the cabin. He pulled his tattered camouflaged top down over the pistol, to ensure it remained concealed in the small of his back and slowly walked to the front of the vehicle.

Brayden joined Steve on the driver's side of the SUV and they both stood staring at the non-descript vehicles waiting for someone to make a grand appearance. The cartel's armed men, presumably under Steve's control, began making their way up the drive, stopping just before the trail government vehicle.

The rear passenger door of the middle SUV opened and an older gentleman exited and stood in the opening. Steve could tell by the thickness of the door and its apparent heft that the vehicles were bullet proof. As the man limped slightly away from the vehicle and out of the cover of the door, Brayden finally realized who it was and shouted with a force that made him nearly double over in pain. "JAMES?"

"Hello Brayden."

James started as he began pointing vigorously in Steve's direction. He uttered no further introductions nor did he appear to care much about the severely battered and disheveled soldier standing before him that he once considered a pupil.

"This man is a traitor to our government. He is an ex-pat that has been down here aiding and abetting the enemy. You know this problem exists, and now you have seen it first-hand. He and the men that he works for are merciless killers." James said of Steve.

Brayden stared at James for what seemed like an eternity and suddenly began to wonder what he was even doing there.

"How did you know they had me?" Brayden asked, almost unable to speak because of the emotions running through him.

Steve pondered briefly on whether or not he should say something to Brayden, but thought it would be wise for the moment that he continue to let James speak.

"When I heard they might have you Brayden I pooled all the resources at my disposal to find you kid. We put up communications aircraft and diverted aerial surveillance platforms to search for you. We were able to pinpoint your last known location and we went from there. As it stands, I am nearing the end of my predator coverage."

James took a quick glance at his watch before continuing.

"You need to make a decision and quickly son. I want to get you out of this mess, and end this non-sense once and for all. I got you out of Costa Rica when you and your boys prematurely destroyed that submarine and I'm here to get you out now. We never leave a fallen comrade; you know that son."

Steve slowly stood and whispered to Brayden so that only he could hear it.

"If you go with him Brayden, he is going to kill you."

Brayden really wasn't completely convinced that the same thing wouldn't happen if he remained in the care of Steve. He reached behind him and wrapped his hand around the pistol he had tucked into his trouser waistband in the small of his back. He pulled it out and slowly brought it to his side, pausing briefly before he began bringing it up, all the while shaking it nervously in his right hand. Brayden was accustomed to dealing with firearms and knew the destruction they were capable of causing. His fretful movement was not due to the familiar feel of the composite plastic and metal object; it was because in that moment, for the first time in his life, he was seriously considering ending his own existence.

Suicide prevention was one of the top programs in the military. He had sat through the same briefings year after year about soldiers, sailors, marines and airman ending their lives for things that could have been dealt with if they had just held on a little bit longer. He had never understood how a single moment in time could be filled with such dark depths of churning emotional turmoil, that it could be quickly and seemingly rationalized and injected into their long-tormented souls, causing an unnaturally convincing narrative that such a permanent and irreversible act should be committed, until now.

He brought the pistol up to his head and paused, looking intently at James and then casting a distrusting glance over at Steve.

James backed away silently and watched almost with joy as Brayden was preparing to take his own life. The attempt at labeling Brayden a traitor and having him left for the wolves had not worked out as planned. But it now appeared that his last few days of angst had crushed his spirit leaving him physically and more importantly, mentally defeated.

James knew that with Brayden dead a very important piece of evidence died with him. And with Abdul Rahman Nour now dead, there was no one left that could prove anything. Brayden didn't know it but the documents that he had on his disk from Eduardo had more on it than John O'Brien had found. Hidden deep inside multiple layers were various programs that were being funded by the CIAs dummy corporations. The CIA couldn't risk the information being found at Langley during an audit, so they purposely hid it within the confines of one of their companies. They used the latest encryption algorithms and hiding techniques to bury their information from savvy prying eyes. They were under the assumption that no one would look in such a benign location, and even if they did, they wouldn't know what they were looking for. Sure, they may see the names of some political figures, but they would have no way of knowing that these were individuals that could be blackmailed into approving projects because of their unwitting investment in a deeply corrupt company. But more importantly, they underestimated Brayden's curiosity and the fact that he didn't follow the rules.

As Brayden stood there trying desperately to make sense of what was happening, replaying all the dialog that he could remember, confused and desperate with no apparent or clear-cut way out; a realization hit him so hard that he became instantly light headed, lowering the pistol back to his side and stumbling slightly as his heart began to beat so hard it felt like it would leap out of his chest. Brayden was remembering that he had never sent a report saying he destroyed a submarine while in Costa Rica. He knew for a fact none of his teammates would have said anything, Paul and his crew from the DEA gave their word; knowing the trouble they would have gotten into, to keep it silent until it surfaced. They all figured that somehow it would be leaked in the news or some other reporting venue by the Costa Rican government, but it never was. Miguel was the only person that had brought it up, and according to him, the cartels had no interest in involving government entities. To the contrary, they were trying to close ranks and identify leaks. Brayden started to get tunnel vision as he began to realize that he might have been set up. He began to sweat and now shake with anger at the thought that someone he respected and emulated was actually using him. He held the gun tightly to his side, shifting and settling his grip on the back strap and looked James directly in the eye.

"And how did you know about the submarine?" Brayden said with a stone-cold look and an exaggerated fluctuation in the pitch and tone of his voice as he rounded out the question.

"What?" James questioned as he chuckled slightly.

"Come on son, I got the reporting from Costa Rica, hell you had a diving injury and had to be recompressed on the ship after they picked you up. It didn't take long to figure out what you had been up to."

"You knew I was diving that day, but we never said we found anything, despite being the CIA you're not omnificent, you learn everything through reporting and I know for a fact that the submarine was never reported." Brayden fired back.

Brayden knew that even if CIA operatives had been watching them in Costa Rica, there was no way they would have known about the submarine and if James had successfully infiltrated a deep cover operative into the cartels, there would have been no need to launch a joint task force to figure out their ratlines. It was all starting to make sense.

"Just answer one question honestly." Brayden asked of James. "Why did you bring *me* into this mess? You knew what I was doing; yet you let me continue. You could have stopped me at any time? You had cartel members telling you what we were doing. You had agents following me and reporting my actions. You personally assigned me to an assassin that led me to, for all intents and purposes, your moneyman; and for what? So, you could take me out in this ridiculously over engineered manner? I don't get it!" Brayden was exacerbated. He had avoided closure on his relationship with Lisa for years, but this time he needed instant gratification; closure was coming now.

James shook his head and unbuttoned his jacket, slowly removed it, and threw it into the backseat of the SUV. "Boy it's hot down here ain't it?" He said with a drawl, attempting to make light of a bad situation. One in which he believed was still very much in his control. "Son" James started. "For some damn reason you believe that you have been holding all the cards. Well, you ain't never even seen the deck boy! You think you're playing some sort of video game, something that you can fail at and then respawn and try again. This is for keeps boy, ain't no winners and losers, only the living and the dead. I have been protecting our great nation and the American way of life for decades. Certainly, for longer than you have been on this earth. I have done things the right way, the way you are supposed to do them, and I have watched good people die because of it. Politicians are too worried about getting re-elected, or voting on a project that might make them look like they are abandoning diplomacy. They will never choose the course necessary to keep our nation safe." James began to angry as he continued. "You are an amateur son, an expendable puppet of my creation, but I need men like you in order to ensure the survival of our position as the world's greatest super power. Every damn thing you have done I predicted. Well hell," James giggled a little before continuing on. "I do have to admit I was surprised by the destructive nature that you have displayed. Bottom line kid, I own you; and like any great musician, I use my instruments until I can no longer dial in the right tune and then I discard em. It ain't personal I can assure you. You wouldn't even be in this predicament if you just followed damn orders and kept your nose outta shit that didn't concern you." After a brief pause, James rubbed his chin and continued. "I'll tell you what; today is your lucky day. You shoot that trader standing next to you and not only will you walk out of here alive, I will personally see to it that no criminal action is filed against you."

Brayden was tired, and at this point he had accepted that he was not going to ever see the sun set again. Talking to James was futile. He was a master manipulator and could spin any story he wanted once back safely in D.C. Brayden wondered how many operatives he had done this to in the past in order to protect his programs? I mean, if Steve hadn't been where he was at the time; Brayden likely wouldn't have even made it off the extraction point. From his vantage point, he was on borrowed time and had nothing to lose. He remembered a partial Martin Luther King quote; *there is nothing more dangerous than a man with nothing left to lose.*

"Why would any criminal action be taken against me if no one even knows that I'm here?" Brayden said with a straight face.

James now stared at Brayden with no expression as he watched him bring the pistol up to the ready and orient it toward him. Brayden, without hesitation, pulled the trigger and watched the tie resting on James's shirt flip up slightly as the round impacted his chest. James stumbled back indefinably just before he crumpled to the ground. Brayden's gaze drifted toward the well-dressed armed men in front of the motorcade James had arrived in just in, time to see them lifting their weapons to the ready in preparation to fire. Brayden, standing squarely in the middle of the battlefield between the CIA and cartel gunman, quickly dove face first, flat onto the ground into the only position he could. He shook and shuttered as stray rounds landed very near his body. The firefight lasted for seconds, but sounded like a training range with fully automatic weapons exchanging high intensity rhythmic volleys before stopping abruptly. Brayden slowly lifted his head out of the dirt and peered at James's lifeless body and the bodies of the men he had arrived with. He turned to look in Steve's direction and noticed he had been hit in the leg, but he was still conscious. Several of the cartels' men, that had been chasing him earlier, were dead or incapacitated. Brayden made his way to Steve and helped him apply the belt that he was already removing from around his waist, to his leg as a tourniquet. Steve grit his teeth and let out a low grunt as Brayden tightened the belt enough to control the bleeding. The helicopter that had been holding in the distance returned and evacuated the injured. The gunmen that were with Steve remained on the ground to await reinforcement; they would stay behind in order to clean up the scene. The Colombian Army wouldn't be arriving to these parts of the jungle; it was after all uncontested territory provided as a safe haven in a deal backed by the President of the United States.

The two men flew back to the Colombian Army base, on what Brayden now realized was a contracted aircraft, without saying a word. Brayden stared out of the window trying to comprehend everything that had taken place. He was an emotional wreck, though he would never admit that to anyone, and there were still so many questions that were unanswered. As he sat next to Steve, he actively stifled his impulses to begin interrogating the man that essentially saved his life.

Steve attempted to get his thoughts in order and come up with a logical way to present what he had uncovered to the committee. He knew that not everything he had done or allowed to happen had been completely ethical or legal for that matter, and he still didn't really think he had uncovered everything he needed to prove gross and egregious misconduct. Just as he was clearing his mind…

"I think I might have something you're probably going to need." Brayden said without turning away from the window.

September 2001

CHAPTER 56

BRAYDEN RECEIVED HIS debriefings, again having to sign statements about the confidentiality of the information that he had been exposed to. This time however, he was given a briefing that he had never received before. It was about the fabric of society and how the information he had could possibly be damaging to the *American way of life*. How it could shake voter confidence and possibly force some of the country's highest offices to explain their actions or the actions of subordinate agencies. Honest and law-abiding individuals holding various levels of office had invested in Trenton Industries and other companies like it. They were to be used as scapegoats and sacrificial lambs in the event that the true nature of the business was ever exposed. Of course, Brayden wasn't aware of how deep the corruption went and he really didn't care to know. His escapade was over, it seemed, and he had no desire at the moment to see how deep the rabbit hole went. He signed all of the required documents as quickly as possible in an attempt to get back to some semblance of a life.

After getting the disk to Steve, Brayden decided to return the picture of John and his family to Katie in person. He didn't really know John that well, but he thought it was the right thing to do. He had learned during one of his debriefings that John had died from an allergic reaction to a new drug he was taking for acid reflux. Brayden didn't really believe it, but he was not in the mood to once again become a target. He returned the picture and offered his condolences; it was really all he could do.

Steve vowed to keep in touch although he knew that he wouldn't. His job required him to live abroad most of the time, and with the secrecy of his comings and goings they would have limited conversations anyway. He could possibly see him in the field again one day; though he hoped next time it would be on better terms.

Brayden clicked on the television and sat behind his TV tray eating cold pizza from his delivery the night before. He was enjoying his time off, and thinking about where his next deployment would be. Colombia was off limits for now for his SFOD-A, but there was plenty of work to do in other places. As he flicked through the cable channels looking for a decent movie to watch, he received a phone call from his sister Lela.

"Are you watching the news?" She said without offering any type of greeting.

"Umm, no." Brayden replied confused at her lack of cordial welcome.

"Turn it on, doesn't matter which station. I have to call my friend in New York."

She hung up the phone abruptly.

Brayden sat confused for a minute before changing the channel to one of the big three news enterprises. As the talking heads began filling him in on what he had missed, almost hypnotically he set the remote down slowly and pushed away his TV tray. His heart became heavy with instant grief and he could feel his eyes filling up with unnecessary lubricant that would begin to fall away as tears at any moment. His body was almost frozen by the incredible scene that was now playing out in front of him live. He moved forward in his seat, getting right to the edge, intently focusing, not wanting to miss a single moment. As he watched the debris and smoke pour from the building, he realized that the reporting he was now barely hearing in the background through the fog of misery and destruction playing out in front of him, was attempting to educate the viewing audience to the unthinkable reality that what was actually falling from the building were the bodies of living souls choosing in that very instant to escape the burning inferno. Just as the extreme gravity of the situation was beginning to settle into his consciousness, he watched another Boeing 767 fly directly into the second tower of the World Trade Center.

ABOUT THE AUTHOR

Bryan is a distinguished veteran of both the 7th Special Forces Group (Airborne) and the 3rd Special Forces Group (Airborne), where he dedicated 25 years to serving his country with valor and distinction. Following his retirement from active duty, Bryan transitioned into the defense industry, where he continues to leverage the extensive knowledge and skills acquired throughout his military career.

His journey is one marked by a profound commitment to excellence, leadership, and innovation. Bryan's experiences on the front lines and behind the scenes have equipped him with a unique perspective on the complexities and challenges of military operations. This deep understanding of tactical and strategic dynamics, combined with a natural flair for storytelling, has culminated in his debut novel.

In this work of military fiction, Bryan expertly weaves together a tapestry of fictional characters, locations, and operations, all while grounding the narrative in real-world situations that reflect the authenticity of his experiences. His novel is not just a thrilling adventure but a tribute to the courage, resilience, and camaraderie of those who serve.

Beyond his professional and literary achievements, Bryan is a person of diverse interests and passions. His life outside the military and defense sectors is filled with pursuits that enrich his writing and reflect the depth of his character.

With his first novel, Bryan invites readers into a world where the lines between fiction and reality blur, offering a gripping, insightful, and deeply engaging experience. His work promises not only to entertain but to illuminate the valor and integrity of those who dedicate their lives to serving others.

BLACK TRIDENT

Made in United States
Orlando, FL
10 November 2024